EDEN
RISING

PRAISE FOR THE PROJECT EDEN THRILLERS

"Sick didn't just hook me. It hit me with a devastating uppercut on every primal level—as a parent, a father, and a human being."—**Blake Crouch**, best selling author of Run

"...a gem of an outbreak story that unfolds like a thriller movie and never lets up, all the way to the last page. Absolutely my favorite kind of story!"—**John Maberry**, *New York Times* bestselling author

"...not only grabs you by the throat, but by the heart and gut as well, and by the time you finish you feel as if you've just taken a runaway train through dangerous territory. Buy these books now. You won't regret it."—**Robert Browne**, best selling author of Trial Junkies

"You think Battles was badass before? He just cranked it up to 500 joules. CLEAR!"—**PopCultureNerd.com**

"Brett Battles at his best, a thriller that also chills, with a secret at its core that's almost too scary to be contained within the covers of a book."—**Tim Hallinan**, author of the Edgar-nominated The Queen of Patpong

ALSO BY BRETT BATTLES

THE JONATHAN QUINN THRILLERS

THE CLEANER
THE DECEIVED
SHADOW OF BETRAYAL (US)/THE UNWANTED (UK)
THE SILENCED
BECOMING QUINN
THE DESTROYED
THE COLLECTED
THE ENRAGED

THE LOGAN HARPER THRILLERS

LITTLE GIRL GONE
EVERY PRECIOUS THING

THE PROJECT EDEN THRILLERS

SICK
EXIT 9
PALE HORSE
ASHES
EDEN RISING

STANDALONES

THE PULL OF GRAVITY
NO RETURN

For Younger Readers

THE TROUBLE FAMILY CHRONICLES

HERE COMES MR. TROUBLE

EDEN RISING

Brett Battles

A PROJECT EDEN THRILLER

Book 5

EDEN RISING
Copyright © 2013 by Brett Battles
Cover art copyright © 2013 by Jeroen ten Berge

For more information about the author, please visit www.brettbattles.com.

What Came Before

THE EARTH WAS forever changed. Project Eden unleashed the KV-27a virus—known to all as the Sage Flu—and watched as the reaping of humanity began. It was part of the master plan, a necessary step toward a restart of the human race in which the Project would control the future.

Billions had already died, with the promise of more to come.

In a well-intentioned effort meant to save as many people as possible, the US government set up emergency camps for children and other survivors. Brandon Ash, after escaping the attack on the Resistance compound known as the Ranch, was picked up by military personnel and taken to one such camp in Colorado. It was not long, though, before the virus reached the camp. Brandon, with a few other children and one of the teachers, escaped the outbreak and found a cabin in the mountains to hide in.

Brandon's sister Josie and Chloe White left the Ranch to find Brandon. They traced him to the camp in Colorado, and arrived at the cabin as a Project Eden team attempted to capture the children. The kidnapping was averted, and Brandon was reunited with his family.

Martina Gable and Riley Weber descended out of the Sierra Nevada Mountains, where they left family members who had died, and returned to their hometown of Ridgecrest, California. There, they found several other friends still alive.

EDEN RISING

All had contracted the Sage Flu during the trial outbreak, which had apparently made them immune. Together now, they vow to survive.

Sanjay and Kusum led their group of survivors away from Mumbai, looking for someplace where they could all stay in safety, eventually finding an abandoned boarding school.

On Isabella Island, east of Costa Rica, the workers and guests of the island's resort were spared exposure to the flu during the virus's initial release. They knew, however, if they were going to continue surviving, they would need to keep anyone else from reaching their shores. Several times they had to turn away boats. They missed one, though—a small boat that drifted ashore with a victim of the virus lying dead inside. Dominic Ray, the resort's manager, unintentionally exposed himself to the body, and realized the only way to save everyone else was to swim out as far as he could away from the island. With the reluctant help of his friend Robert Adams, he sacrificed his life.

The Resistance, having failed to stop the pandemic and barely surviving the attack on its main headquarters, was forced to switch its efforts to do what it could to save those who were still breathing—a mission it knew would be more than difficult.

Then, on December 27th, Principal Director Perez of Project Eden gave the go-ahead, and all over the world, the televisions and radios that had days earlier fallen silent began broadcasting a false message over and over...

"My name is Gustavo Di Sarsina. I am the newly appointed secretary general of the United Nations. You are all aware that our planet has been undergoing a catastrophe beyond anything we have ever experienced. The deaths from the Sage Flu are...incalculable. Billions have already died, and many more continue to do so. Friends, family, loved ones. In the span of ten days, the human race has gone from our normal, everyday existence to a desperate race for survival. If you are hearing this, it means you are one of the lucky ones.

"The good news is, help is now available. A vaccine has been developed, and we are in the process of producing it in large enough quantities so that all those who have survived can receive it. To that end, we need to determine exactly how many of us are left and where everyone is located.

"The problem we now face is one of communication. Many of the world's telecom systems have begun to shut down, and we fear the same is starting to happen with power grids worldwide. In an effort to work around this problem, we have set up various means by which you can reach us—Internet, shortwave radio, and even a phone number those of you still with service can try. And if none of those are available to you, we are setting up dozens of what we are calling survival stations throughout the world. These might require a difficult trip, but they are an option. Those of you watching television will see the information scrolling across the bottom of the screen. If you're listening on a radio, I will give you the numbers and addresses at the end of this message.

"This is the most important part. Whatever you have been doing to survive, continue to do so. The virus is still out there and contractable. Until you have been vaccinated, you must avoid contact with it at all costs. If you need to travel to one of the survival stations, wear protective clothing and stop for no one.

"While we at the UN have also been hit, we are still here. Our only goal now is to save everyone we can.

As soon as the vaccine is ready, we will get it to you. After that, we will rise above the ashes of this horrible tragedy and ensure that this is not the end of the human race."

While the battle to keep the virus from being released had been lost, the war over who would survive had only just begun.

1

A LIGHT CRUNCH of gravel.

Footsteps, slow and steady, as if uncertain they should be there.

No surprise in their arrival, though. Matt Hamilton had been expecting to hear them since the moment he'd sneaked out of the Bunker and hiked to the ridge overlooking the Lodge. Time alone was not something he experienced much anymore.

He folded the piece of paper he was holding and slipped it into his jacket pocket.

"Matt?" Chloe's voice.

Again, not a surprise.

He waited until she was only a few feet behind him, and said, "It was always too big."

In the open meadow below was a pile of burnt rubble that had once been the Lodge. The massive building had not only been the Resistance's headquarters but also home to most of its members.

His home.

"I don't know," Chloe said, stopping next to him. "Seemed the right size to me. I liked that I could always find someplace to hide."

"It was good for that, wasn't it?"

Together they stared silently at the wreckage for a few seconds before Chloe turned to him. "I thought you'd like to know the others will be leaving soon."

"Is it time already?"

She nodded.

EDEN RISING

When Project Eden had attacked the Ranch on Implementation Day, less than a week earlier, the members of the Resistance had retreated into the Bunker deep below the Lodge, where they had ridden out the fight, and where they'd continued to live in the days since. But Matt knew the threat of another strike grew exponentially each additional day they remained there, and the next time they might not be as lucky. When he saw the weather projections showing a series of storms heading their way in the coming week, storms that would likely fill their valley with snow and trap them there for months, he knew he had no other choice but to order the evacuation to Ward Mountain, their base in Nevada. It wasn't as sophisticated as the Bunker, but it would be safer.

He hoped, at least.

Leaving the Ranch, though, was a complicated process. They may have lost the battle of keeping the Sage Flu outbreak from ever happening, but they were still in the fight to keep alive those who had survived. To that end, there could be no break in communications with those involved in the worldwide rescue operation the Resistance had initiated. If there were, it very likely would mean the additional deaths of survivors and the Resistance's field team members trying to help them.

An additional day was lost while trailers on the back of three semi trucks were converted into mobile communication hubs that could be manned throughout the trip. While this was going on, the other vehicles were packed with all the supplies and weapons they could carry.

But continuous communications wasn't the only problem with leaving.

There was Captain Ash, too.

The captain had been severely injured in an explosion during the early part of the outbreak. And while Dr. Gardiner was encouraged by Ash's recovery, he insisted the captain should not travel for at least several more days. It had finally been decided that a small group would stay behind until Dr. Gardiner gave his okay, or, more likely, until the weather forced their hand. Chloe had volunteered, of course, and

Brandon and Josie—the captain's children—refused to go anywhere without their father, so they had stayed, too. Matt had assigned an additional dozen trained men and women to act as escorts in case this second group ran into any problems.

He had always planned on staying with them, something his sister Rachel was not happy about. He kind of felt it was like being the captain of a ship, and thought it only proper to be the last one to leave. But when he received the message that was now tucked in his pocket, his reason for staying changed completely.

"Are you coming?" Chloe asked.

"I'll be right behind you," he said. "I promise."

"All right," Chloe said. "I'm going to go see if they need any more help."

Once the sound of her steps faded into the woods, he double-checked to make sure she was really gone, and then retrieved the piece of paper from his pocket.

At the top was the message as it had originally been received—a string of letters and numbers and symbols that were unreadable unless you had the key to the code, which Matt did. Below this, scrawled in his own handwriting, was the translation. The only thing consistent between the coded and decoded message was the first line:

To: MH

The translated portion then read:

Have been transferred to NB219 as part of new principal director Perez's support staff. He has decided that through the end of this phase of the operation, Las Cruces will serve as his base. I in no way believe this will remain true once we move to rebuilding phase. This is an opportunity, my friend. If you wish me to act, please give the order.

C8

It was indeed an opportunity. One that could mean

everything.

Matt had already sent a reply.

I will come to you.

December 31st

World Population
1,122,463,297

2

IT'S SNOWING AGAIN. So I guess that means the university's New Year's Eve party will probably be canceled.

That sounded a lot funnier in my head before I typed it down. I wonder how many people even realize that it is New Year's Eve. If anyone does, I doubt they care. I know I don't. What is today but one more day I'm alive? Perhaps the old calendar isn't even viable anymore. Maybe the day the virus hit should be day one of year one. Or would it be year zero?

What does it matter?

I'm not sleeping well. I keep thinking I'm hearing things in the building—someone coming up the stairs, breaking through the barrier I put up, stumbling into my dorm room. In my mind, whoever it is oozes sickness. But so far, if others have come into the building, none have made it this far up. Still, knowing this doesn't keep me from getting up six or seven times a night just to check.

EDEN RISING

By 5 a.m., I'm usually done, and pull myself out of bed. I'm careful with lights, though. I'm afraid of drawing anyone's attention, so when it's still dark outside, I never turn anything on in a room with a window. As I write this, I'm sitting on a pillow in the corridor, wrapped in a blanket, and using a desk lamp from one of my floormate's rooms that I brought out here with me.

I know at some point I'm going to have to leave. I don't have enough food to last more than a couple more weeks. What I really need to do is get to the survival station the UN has set up in Chicago. It's the closest one to me. When I get there, I can get vaccinated. Maybe that'll relax me enough to get a good night's sleep. Wouldn't that be a miracle?

The snow's the problem right now. First off, I don't want to leave during a storm, but the bigger problem is the roads. Those that I can see from my room are completely covered. No one's clearing them. I have to think it'll be the same problem on the highway. I mean, even if someone who isn't sick has a plow, why would they leave their home? So I either wait until the snow melts off the roads, or I hike out.

I can hear the television down in the common room. It's still playing the message from the UN secretary general. I've pretty much memorized it at this point. I have to say, his voice is comforting. There are TVs on in the other wings of the dorm. I can see them when I look out any of the windows, so I figure leaving mine on shouldn't draw undue attention. I've tried calling the numbers at the end of the message, but even though my phone shows I have a signal, I can't connect to anything.

I hope the snow stops soon. I hope we have a few

days of warm weather to melt it away.

I started to write that I hope I don't die here, but I deleted it because dying here of starvation or exposure has to be better than dying of the Sage Flu, right?

ISABELLA ISLAND, COSTA RICA
5:54 AM CST

THERE WAS THE Before and the After.

In the Before, when Robert had been the head bartender for the Isabella Island Resort, and routinely worked until three or four in the morning, the only time he would have seen the sunrise was after a particularly late night as he headed off to bed.

In the After, when Robert no longer poured the drinks, but was the de facto leader of the employees and guests who made up the group of survivors occupying the island, he seldom slept more than four hours a night, and found himself for the fourth day in a row on the beach staring at the horizon as the sun crested the sea.

Like he'd done every morning of the After, he allowed himself a few minutes to wish there was a way to go back to before Christmas Eve, to the time when the world as he knew it had yet to go insane. In this waking dream, the containers that had been secretly placed around the globe failed to open and spread their deadly cargo of Sage Flu, and his friend Dominic and all the others who had fallen victim to the pandemic would still be alive.

He had no idea how many were dead. Millions, surely. The horror he and the other Isabella survivors had seen on TV before the news channels stopped broadcasting made it clear the disease was not contained in only a handful of locations, but was everywhere. Worse, there had been no reports of recoveries.

Isolation is what had saved Robert and his people. Apparently the island had been too small to merit one of the deadly containers. Or, perhaps, it'd just been overlooked.

25

Whatever the case, it was a blessing, but it wasn't even close to a guarantee that those on the island would all remain safe from the flu. He'd been the first to realize it, to know their survival depended on not letting anyone from elsewhere on shore. It'd taken some convincing, but Dominic soon saw the logic in it, too.

This hard stance resulted in some tense encounters, but everyone on the island was still breathing and disease free. Everyone except Dominic. His death had been an act of self-sacrifice after he'd unintentionally come in contact with the disease from a body that had drifted ashore in a small boat.

Even if he couldn't resurrect everyone, Robert wished he could at least have his friend back. He would have even been willing to change places and be the one who died so that Dominic would still be here. Robert had no business calling the shots. He didn't have Dominic's patience. He was much better in the role of first lieutenant, not leader.

But Dominic was gone, and Robert was here.

"Good morning." The words were almost a whisper, as if the speaker feared talking any louder would wake the rest of the island.

Robert glanced over his shoulder. Estella, one of the resort guests, had walked up quietly behind him, a timid smile on her face. "Morning," he said.

He thought she was from Spain, but couldn't remember for sure. What he did recall was that she'd been on the island for only a day before everything went haywire, and was supposed to have been joined by a couple friends on Christmas Eve. They, of course, had never shown up.

She moved next to him, and looked out at the sea. "It's beautiful."

"Yeah," he said, though the truth was he was having a hard time seeing beauty in anything anymore.

"I guess this is why we all came here, yes?" She finished with a laugh, nervous, almost forced.

He smiled politely and nodded, but said nothing.

As she brushed a strand of hair off her face, Robert noticed her hand was shaking.

"Are you okay?" he asked.

"Yes. Of course. I am fine."

He smiled as if to say he was glad to hear it, but he knew none of them were fine. How could they be?

Estella looked out at the water again. "Have you been able to reach anyone yet?" He could tell she was trying to sound casual, but she wasn't pulling it off.

"Not yet," he said.

"But the message," she said. "I thought we would have reached them by now."

"We're still trying. I'm sure we'll get through to someone soon."

The message was from the UN and had been playing in a loop on TV for four days now. A day earlier, a list of several ways in which the organization could be contacted had been added at the end of the secretary general's speech. Robert had immediately used the resort's satellite phone to try calling the provided phone number. That's when he discovered that while the phone seemed to be working fine, it no longer had a signal. He then tried the two-way radio. Unfortunately, the resort's owners had invested in a transmitter only powerful enough to reach the Costa Rican mainland. Either Robert or Renee kept at it every few hours, but so far no one had answered them.

"Do you think...I mean, how many people?" Estella said.

"I don't know, but it didn't look—"

He stopped himself. There was an object in the sky just north of the newly risen sun. A dot. Probably a bird, he thought, but...

Estella followed his gaze. "What is it?"

"I'm not sure."

He narrowed his eyes to a squint to cut down on the sun's glare. The dot was growing larger.

It's gotta be a bird.

But even as the thought passed through his mind, he knew he was wrong. There was no flapping of wings, no subtle dips and rises of a bird riding the wind. The object was moving in a straight line, its speed constant.

Estella was the first to voice what they'd both realized. "A plane. It is a plane!"

The dot was no longer a dot, but a central tube with what could only be fixed wings sticking out on either side.

"It is a plane!" she said. "It is!" She started jumping up and down, waving her arms, and yelling as if her voice could reach across the sea to those aboard the aircraft.

It was her shouts that finally snapped Robert out of his trance. He turned from the water and ran toward the resort. If Estella knew he was gone, she made no indication. He could hear her continued attempts to get the plane's attention as he left the beach.

A few of the early risers were in the open-air bar as he crested the steps and jogged onto the deck.

"Is something wrong?" a man named Jussi from Finland asked.

"Is that someone yelling?" Monica, an American from the Midwest, asked.

Ignoring the questions and stares, Robert raced around the back of the bar to the room where the radio was. He found Renee inside. She had been the resort's assistant manager under Dominic, but had been more than happy to allow Robert to take charge after Dominic was gone.

"Are they transmitting?" he asked.

She looked over, confused. "Is who transmitting?"

"The plane."

"Plane? What plane?"

He hurriedly sat in the chair next to hers, and reached over to the radio's controls. As he started a frequency scan, he said, "There's a plane out there. In the east, heading toward the mainland."

"What kind of plane?" Her tone was cautious.

"I don't know. It was too far away to tell."

"Small? Big? What?"

"I don't know. Smaller than a commercial jet, bigger than a Cessna. Why?"

Instead of answering, she shook her head, and pushed his

hands from the radio. "Let me." She pulled the microphone in front of her, adjusted the broadcast frequency, and pushed the transmit button. "This is Isabella Island calling unidentified aircraft. Come in, please." She waited a moment and repeated the message.

The fourth try was the charm.

"Isabella Island, this is UN 132. Do you read me?"

"UN?" Renee said to Robert. "It's the UN."

For the first time since news of the pandemic broke, Robert felt the barest sense of hope.

"We read you, UN 132," Renee said, smiling. "We read you loud and clear."

"Isabella Island, good to hear your voice. Are you alone or are there others with you?"

"There are one hundred and twenty-nine of us here," Renee reported.

There was a slight pause, then, "Can you repeat that?"

Renee did.

"How many sick?"

"No one's sick."

"No outbreaks?"

"No," she said, sharing a look with Robert. They both knew that wasn't completely true. Dominic had caught the flu, but it had stopped with him.

"Are you sure?"

"Yes. Positive."

Robert leaned over and said into the mic. "We isolated ourselves as soon as we knew there was a problem. We haven't allowed anyone on the island since the outbreak occurred."

"That's great to hear," the voice said. "Do you have a landing strip?"

"No," Renee said. "The only way to reach us is by boat or seaplane."

"Hold for a moment, Isabella Island."

During the static that followed, neither Robert nor Renee said anything. They just stared at the radio as if worried the voice would not return.

A minute later, it did. "Isabella Island, are you still there?"

"We're here," Renee said.

"How is your food and water supply?"

"Good," she said. "Not an issue."

"Good to hear. We're out on a scouting mission right now, trying to locate survivors like yourself." A pause. "Our people will be bringing you enough vaccine for everyone there. But because of your isolated situation, it may be a few days while we tend to those in more precarious situations. Do you understand?"

Renee frowned and looked at Robert, clearly disappointed.

"Let me," Robert said.

She slid the mic over to him.

"We understand," he said. "Just knowing you're coming back is great news."

"Good news for us, too, finding you," the man said. "You just keep doing what you've been doing, and don't go to the mainland. You'll be fine. We'll be seeing you soon, Isabella Island. Take care, and stay safe. UN 132, out."

"You, too. Isabella Island, out."

That scant bit of hope Robert had been feeling morphed into full-on relief as he leaned back. They were going to be all right. They were all going to be vaccinated. The extreme stance they'd taken to keep others away had been justified. But most importantly, Dominic's sacrifice was not in vain.

"A few days?" Renee said, frowning.

He looked over at her, an eyebrow raised. After a moment, he started to smile, and then he began to laugh.

It was only a few more seconds before she was laughing, too.

**FIFTEEN THOUSAND FEET ABOVE THE CARIBBEAN SEA
NEAR ISABELLA ISLAND, COSTA RICA
6:23 AM CST**

"WE'LL BE SEEING you soon, Isabella Island. Take care, and stay safe. UN 132, out."

"You, too. Isabella Island, out."

The man operating the radio on the aircraft that was neither associated with the now nonexistent United Nations nor on a mission to help save survivors clicked the tab on his computer screen that ended the recording of the conversation. He attached the voice file to an e-mail, typed in the exact coordinates of the island, and sent the message.

Those on Isabella Island represented the largest single, unexposed group his team had come across so far. It would be interesting to learn what the higher-ups back at Project Eden headquarters decided to do—send actual vaccine or dose them with Sage Flu. But chances were the man and his colleagues would be busy elsewhere by then, having forgotten all about the island.

He activated the plane's internal comm system. "Back to our previous course," he told the pilot.

"Yes, sir."

The plane banked to the west, and within no time Isabella Island was behind them.

3

WHILE SOME OF the streetlights in Mumbai had stopped coming on at night, many still worked, providing Sanjay more than enough illumination to see Kusum peering down at him from the rooftop above.

She put a finger to her lip, reminding him to stay quiet. It was completely unnecessary. He knew the importance of silence as much as she did. She then extended her hands over the edge, showing five fingers on one and four on the other.

Nine men. That was a lot. Probably best if they made a wide arc around the building instead of passing so close to it. He started to mime the suggestion to her, but she quickly waved him off, and motioned for him to come up and join her.

He didn't want to waste the time it would take, but she had ducked out of sight before he could tell her no. With a sigh, he ducked inside and headed quietly up the stairs.

When the UN message had played over the radio, in the old headmaster's house at the boarding school that Sanjay, Kusum, and the others had turned into their temporary home, the initial shock everyone felt soon turned into excitement that there might still be order in the world. They had waited three days before the broadcast began including the location for the nearest survival station to them.

The delay hadn't worried them. Unlike pretty much everyone else who was still clinging to life, their particular band of survivors had already been inoculated against the

Sage Flu, thanks to the vaccine Sanjay had stolen.

When the survival station's address was finally revealed, the fact that it was located in Mumbai made sense. What didn't—to Sanjay, anyway—was that the address was the very same one belonging to the facility he'd stolen the vaccine from, the facility run by his former employers, Pishon Chem. They were the ones who had hired hundreds of local boys and men to spray Mumbai with what they had claimed was a malaria eradication solution but was really Sage Flu virus.

When Sanjay explained to the others the connection, the elation they'd all been feeling quickly dissolved.

"But does this mean the UN is spreading the disease?" Kusum's father had asked. "I cannot believe that."

None of them could.

"Maybe they are not the UN at all," Sanjay suggested. "Maybe they are just using the name to gain people's trust."

"If that is the case, then…" Kusum's mother didn't need to finish her thought.

If these were the same people who'd released the virus, then they could be luring in those who had escaped infection so they could finish the job they had started.

Some at the school thought they should keep their heads low and everything would blow over, while others—Sanjay and Kusum among them—thought if it were true, they needed to do what they could to warn the living.

The first step was finding out for sure.

Because Sanjay knew the Pishon Chem facility from when he had worked there, it was his job to find out what was going on. Kusum was not about to let him go alone, however. She and three others had accompanied him into the city, where they had set up camp in a small furniture factory a few kilometers from the survival station. Leaving the other three there, he and Kusum headed in for a closer look.

When Sanjay reached the top of the stairs, he carefully opened the roof door and slipped outside. Kusum was lying at the western edge. As he neared her, he lowered himself to his hands and knees and crawled forward, finally dropping to his chest and snaking his way up beside her.

"What is it?" he whispered.

"Look," she said. "But be careful."

He eased forward until he could see beyond the lip of the roof. Below and to the left, in the middle of the road that ran past their building, two police cars were parked front bumper to front bumper, perpendicular to what would have been the normal flow of traffic. There was just enough of a gap between the two front ends for one person to pass through.

He knew this couldn't have been what caught Kusum attention. They had seen the vehicles from the road. That was the reason Kusum had come up for a look in the first place.

He scanned the area around the cars. Standing nearby were three people wearing surgical masks—the same three they had seen when they'd spotted the vehicles—each with rifles slung over their shoulders.

"Behind the police cars," Kusum whispered impatiently.

Sanjay looked farther down the road. Parked almost a block away were three white vans. Painted in black on their sides were the letters UN. If there was no deception going on, the vans were probably used to transport new arrivals from the checkpoint to the survival station.

He pulled back until he was hidden from view again. "I do not understand what it is you want me to see."

"The men by the vans," Kusum said as if it should be obvious.

"What men?"

She scowled, and took a look herself. When she scooted away from the edge again, she looked more confused than upset. "They were there a moment ago."

"*Who* was there?"

"A whole group of soldiers. I counted at least forty."

"Forty? Why would they need so many soldiers?" he asked.

"Why would they need any?" she countered.

He thought for a moment. "I guess they could be worried that someone might try to steal the vaccine."

The scowl again, only a bit more playful this time. "You

mean like you did?"

He shrugged. "Perhaps."

"But the vaccine is not out *here*," she argued. "It is at the survival station. Would it not be better if that was where the soldiers were?"

"Maybe they have more there, too," he said, playing devil's advocate.

"Then I ask you the same question you asked me. Why do they need so many?"

They fell into silence, both thinking the same thing—this wasn't what the radio broadcast was saying it was.

"We are wasting time here," Sanjay finally said. "Come on."

They worked their way out of the building and back onto the street. They knew they had to be extra careful now. The soldiers Kusum had seen could be anywhere.

"This way," Sanjay said, starting off to his right.

He barely put a foot down before Kusum grabbed his arm. "You told me the Pishon Chem facility was closer to the ocean. That would be the *other* way."

"We will have a better chance of not being seen in this direction. At most, we will go a kilometer then cut through the middle of the city."

She thought about his plan for a second, then said, "Okay. That makes sense to me."

"I am glad to receive your blessing," he said with a dramatic bow.

She slapped him playfully on the arm. "It is only temporary."

LIVING AT THE remote boarding school for the last week, had, at times, created the illusion the world was still as it had been. But any trace of that false impression ended the moment they reentered Mumbai.

It had been a city of nearly twenty million, its streets never empty or silent.

Until now.

No running cars. No motorbikes. No pedestrians. No hawkers.

The only ones there were lifeless bodies of the homeless tucked in corners, lying against the side of a building, and stretched out in the gutters. Their stench wafted through the streets, increasing and decreasing in strength depending on the number of bodies and the direction of the breeze. Sanjay and Kusum had to cover their faces to breathe without gagging.

What made things even eerier were the lights. Not just the automatic street lamps, but the interior lights of stores and restaurants, and the illuminated signs mounted on their facades. It was as if all the establishments had opened for business, but no one had come, not even those who worked there.

On several occasions, Sanjay and Kusum came across vehicles that had crashed in the road, not unlike the accident Kusum had pulled the baby Nipa from as Kusum and her family fled the city. Most of these cars were empty—their occupants no doubt surviving at least long enough to get off the road—but a few were not.

"Go right," Sanjay said as they reached the next intersection.

They were only two kilometers from the Pishon Chem facility now, and while there were faster ways to get there, Sanjay felt it safer to stick to a more circuitous route along smaller streets and alleys.

As they turned, Kusum brushed a hand across her shoulder.

"What is it?" Sanjay asked.

"Nothing. I…" She took a deep breath. "I just feel like something is crawling all over my skin."

He knew what she meant. He felt it, too, an uncomfortable tingling all over his body. It didn't help that the narrow road they were now on only intensified the creepy factor. He would almost welcome some kind of monster roaring out of the shadows to chase them. At least that would give them something to focus on.

They were seven blocks from the facility when they heard feet clomping on asphalt. It sounded like at least a dozen people, jogging in unison down the road they were about to turn onto.

Sanjay threw his arm in front of Kusum. "Back, back," he whispered.

As they headed in the other direction, Sanjay began trying every door they passed, but all were locked. Then they came to one set back in an alcove. If nothing else, it might hide them from view.

"Here," he said, nudging Kusum off the sidewalk.

She reached the door first, and tried it. The handle stuck for a moment, then turned all the way and opened. Any elation, though, was squelched by the bell at the top of the frame that rang with the door's movement.

"Go," Sanjay said, pushing her.

The second they were inside, he grabbed the bell and moved it out of the way as he pushed the door closed.

He motioned to a rickety counter along the side. "Hide behind that."

As she ducked behind it, she gasped. Sanjay wanted to ask what was wrong, but his attention had been drawn back outside. The running feet were not passing through the intersection, but turning onto the road Sanjay and Kusum were on.

He hurried over to the counter, intending to duck down next to Kusum, but she had stopped very close to his end, and had left hardly any space.

"Move down," he whispered.

She shook her head. He looked around her to see what the problem was, and discovered why she had gasped. There was the body of a woman on the floor. She must have been one of the early ones to die, he thought, for her smell was nowhere near as strong as some of the others they'd come across.

"We can switch places," he said.

"No. I will be okay," Kusum told him.

Thoughts of the dead woman immediately vanished as

the sounds of the pounding feet slowed to a stop not ten meters outside the front of the store. Sanjay scrunched down as best he could.

A male voice. "It was down here. I'm sure of it. Something rang."

Another voice, also male. "It could have been anything."

"I still want to check. Everyone, spread out," the first voice said.

Sanjay pulled in tighter to Kusum.

Outside, they could hear those in the street splitting up and moving in different directions. One of them went up to the door of the clothing shop next door and tried the handle. Next, steps moving down the sidewalk and nearing their store.

The bell, Sanjay thought. He should have pulled it down. The moment the door opened, it would ring and they would know that had made the noise.

Not allowing himself to think about it a second time, he whipped out from behind the counter.

"What are you doing?" Kusum whispered.

"Stay there," he told her as he moved in a crouch back to the doorway.

Out the window on his right, he could see the shadow of a man, dressed in a soldier's uniform, heading toward the entrance. There was no time to grab the bell, so Sanjay twisted the lock closed, hoping it would hold, and dove behind a set of shelves.

Sure he'd been seen, he waited for the soldier to yell to the rest of his squad, but the only sound was that of the man walking into the alcove and grabbing the door.

A rattle of glass, and then nothing. Not even footsteps.

What was he doing? Peering inside?

Leave us alone, Sanjay thought as the silence grew. *Just go away.*

It took a few more seconds, but the soldier finally complied as he moved out of the alcove and back into the street.

Voices, stating they'd found nothing. Orders were barked, the men gathered, and then as one they jogged off down the street.

Once the sound of their steps had faded away, Kusum said, "Sanjay? Sanjay, are you all right?"

"I'm fine," he said, slowly rising to his feet. He looked out the window to make sure the street was truly empty before moving back over to the counter. "Come on. We need to keep going."

"You scared me to death," she said as she uncoiled from her crouch.

"I'm sorry. But I had to—"

"I know," she said, her face softening. "Thank you."

He was sorely tempted to pull her into his arms and kiss her, but that would have to wait. "Let see if there's a back way out."

The alley behind the store led to a warren of thrown-together shacks. Here the smell of death was even stronger than in the streets, as most had chosen to live their final hours in the place they had called home.

As difficult as it was to make their way through the slum, when Sanjay and Kusum exited the other side, they found themselves only two blocks from their destination. They hustled across a darkened part of the street, and up into a building Sanjay hoped would give them a view into the Pishon Chem compound. His plan, however, hadn't taken into consideration that the door to the roof at the top of the stairwell would be chained closed.

"Let's try one of the apartments," Kusum suggested. "The view should be nearly as good from there, yes?"

"I hope so."

They went down one landing and entered the top floor of the building. The apartments to the left were the ones they were interested in. There were fourteen doors on that side. One by one they began trying them. Number eight was unlocked.

Sanjay pulled the top of his shirt over his mouth and nose, sure that once he pushed the door open, they'd be greeted by the familiar putrid smell. When Kusum was ready, he gave the handle a shove.

"I don't think anyone is here," he said as he lowered his shirt. While the air inside was stuffy and stale, it was thankfully free of death.

Together they made a quick search of the apartment. Not only was it unoccupied, there was no sign that whoever had lived in the flat had made a run for safety. Everything was neat and in its place. It was as if the person had been out when the plague started and never come home.

With the place secure, Sanjay stepped over to the window of the main living area. Kusum followed right behind him. She had been right. The apartment was high enough to see over the buildings on the next street and into the compound.

The place was lit up with the same bright white floodlights that had been used when Sanjay and the others had worked there. What was different was the United Nations flag flying high above the administration building, and the white-helmeted, blue-uniformed soldiers stationed at various points in the compound.

The staging area Pishon Chem had used to distribute the spray tanks full of the virus had been clear of the former equipment and turned into two areas, each surrounded by double fences, separated by a gap large enough to drive a couple of trucks through side by side. Both areas contained a long building at the far end. While the zone on the left appeared empty, two people were standing outside the building in the zone on the right.

"Those look like prisons to me," Kusum said. "Are they locking people up?"

Sanjay traced the fences with his eyes until he found the gates. He couldn't tell from here if they were locked, but they were definitely closed. "I'm not sure what they are doing," he said.

He turned his attention to a group of men standing near the administration building. Unlike the others walking around outside the fenced areas, these men were not in uniform.

Studying them, he was drawn to the way one of the men was standing. It seemed familiar. Unfortunately, he was too far away to get a fix on the man's face so couldn't make the connection.

He scanned around, moving his gaze away from the compound to the street that ran just outside it.

After a moment, he said to Kusum, "Stay here. I will be back."

"Where do you think you are going?"

"I need to get a closer look."

"Then I am coming with you."

"No. You are staying here. If you are with me, it will be easier for us to be spotted."

"If you get into trouble, you may need my help," she countered.

"Kusum, I am not trying to argue with you. But I can make the trip faster and react quicker if I am alone. Please tell me you understand."

From her expression, he wasn't sure if she did, but she said, "If you are not back in fifteen minutes, I will come look for you."

"Make it twenty."

"Fifteen."

He blew out an exasperated breath. "Fine. Fifteen. But it does not start until I leave this building."

When it was finally agreed, he gave her that kiss he'd wanted to give her earlier, and headed out the door.

Back on the street, he threaded his way over to the rear of a structure directly across the road from the compound's administration building. Instead of trying to find a way in, he climbed a drainpipe affixed to the outer wall, all the way to the roof.

His new position was not as high as the apartment where he'd left Kusum, so he only had a partial view of the men he'd spotted. But he was close enough now that he could make out their faces.

He had hoped his doubts would be unfounded, that he'd find this was indeed a UN operation. But instead, Sanjay's fear turned out to be true.

The man with the familiar stance was Mr. Dettling, one

of the Pishon Chem managers Sanjay had worked with, and most decidedly *not* a member of the UN. Dettling's wasn't the only familiar face, either. Gathered with him were several other Pishon managers.

When he'd seen enough, he climbed off the building and returned to Kusum.

"Could you see anything?" she asked.

"They are not the UN," he told her.

She stared at him for a moment. "Are you sure?"

As concisely as possible, he described what he'd seen. "There is no question. They are the same people who had us distribute the flu."

"Why are they doing this, then? Why are they saying they are the UN?"

"Whatever the reason, it can't be good."

She glanced at the window. "The people inside those fences. Do you…do you think maybe they're ones who came here for help?"

He paused, then nodded. "I think very likely."

"What are they going to do to them?"

"That, I do not know."

Kusum put a hand on her husband's arm. "Sanjay. Are they going to kill them?"

He said nothing.

"If they are, we can't let that happen," she said.

"No, we can't."

4

A BITTER, COLD wind cut through the air, stinging Daniel Ash's cheeks as he gingerly climbed out the open hatch. Above, low gray clouds pushed in over the valley as if they couldn't fill the sky fast enough, the storm a lot closer than he had thought.

Josie Ash leaned down over the tunnel exit and grabbed her father's arm. "Let me help you."

"I'm fine, honey," he said, though that was far from the truth.

Ignoring his response, Josie guided him up the final rung of the ladder and onto solid ground. Once Ash was out of the way, Dr. Gardiner came up next, then Lily Franklin, and finally Chloe.

With the Bunker now empty, the hatch to the tunnel was shut and quickly covered by a few feet of dirt, some pine needles and branches, and a top layer of snow. When the job was done, it was almost impossible to tell anything was buried there.

"You all right?" Ash asked Matt. They'd been standing to the side, watching the others work—or at least Ash had been watching. Matt had been staring into the trees, lost in thought.

A few seconds passed before Matt pulled himself back and looked at Ash. "Sorry. Yeah, I'm fine. Just glad to be getting on the road."

Ash glanced up at the sky. "If you want my opinion, we're cutting it pretty tight. We could have gone yesterday."

The right corner of Matt's mouth ticked up. "Not according to the good doctor. Hell, he didn't even want to leave today. Said you needed more time."

"I'm good," Ash said. "Don't worry about me." The truth was, Ash was grateful for the extra night's rest. He nodded his chin in the direction of the hatch. "So are you going to destroy it?" Like the Lodge had been, the Bunker was wired for self-destruction.

"Not yet. I guess…I guess I'm hoping we'll be able to come back."

Ash could understand that. The Ranch had been Matt's home for a long time.

Matt rubbed his hands together. "No sense in waiting around here any longer," he said, then raised his voice. "All right, everyone, load 'em up."

They made their way over to the road, where four military-issue, light-armored Humvees they'd appropriated from Malmstrom Air Force Base in Great Falls stood waiting, engines idling.

"We're in number two," Chloe told Ash.

Ash trudged over and climbed into the back, finding his son Brandon inside. "How you doing, buddy?"

"I can sit on the floor if you need this seat," Brandon said, already starting to move.

"No, no. Stay. There's plenty for all of us."

"You sure?"

"I'm sure," Ash said, taking the seat across from his son.

Both Brandon and Josie had become ultra protective of him since the explosion that had nearly killed him. While a part of him was touched by their attention, he knew this wasn't the way things should be. He was the parent. He should worry about them, not the other way around. But the world was a different place now, forcing his kids to grow up way too quickly.

Josie and Lily entered through the far back, taking the jump seats there, while Chloe climbed into the driver's seat, and the doctor into the one beside her. Before Gardiner could close his door, Matt stuck his head in.

"All right there? Need anything?" Matt asked.

"All good," Ash replied.

"You need us to stop for any reason, have the doc or Chloe radio us."

"Sure."

Matt patted the outside of the truck with his hand. "Safe trip, everyone."

AMUND RINGNES ISLAND
12:04 PM CST

FOR THE FIRST time in over a week, Rich "Pax" Paxton could see clear sky. Given how far north the research station was, where he and his team had holed up, the sky was more twilight than the bright, sunny noon he preferred, but it was definitely clear.

They had come to the island searching for Bluebird, the headquarters of Project Eden, but had discovered it wasn't there. Which meant Bluebird had to be on Yanok Island, the island Captain Ash and his team had gone to investigate.

Pax had no idea what had happened since then. They had been unable to reach anyone on the radio, and the storm had damaged the facilities' satellite equipment, knocking out phone and Internet services.

The door to the observation room opened and Brian Darnell—*Dr.* Brian Darnell, as the man was fond of reminding Pax—entered. Darnell was the station's director, and would have undoubtedly put Pax and his team in a holding cell when they'd shown up at his door if the place had had one.

For the first two days, Pax's explanation for why they were there was greeted with skepticism at best. He didn't let up, however, and told them over and over about the plot by Project Eden, what was really in the shipping containers that had been spread around the world, and what would happen if the attempted genocide wasn't stopped.

Yes, Darnell and the other researchers at the facility had

heard about the containers, but the man wouldn't even consider that they could be part of something so heinous, and had not believed a word of Pax's story. So, with little choice, the two groups had settled into an uneasy coexistence while the storm continued to rage outside.

"Mr. Paxton," Darnell said.

"Doctor."

"I wanted to inform you that I sent my technicians out a little while ago to repair the satellite damage. I'm told that communications should be back up at any time."

"Glad to hear it," Pax said. He was desperate to find out if Ash had been able to stop Project Eden from implementing its horrifying plan.

"Perhaps you shouldn't be. Just so you know, my first call will be to the police. I'm confident the RCMP will send officers here to arrest you and take you in for questioning."

"If the Mounties are still around and want to arrest us, we'll be happy to go."

Darnell stared at him for several seconds. "Still sticking to your ridiculous story, I see."

Pax shrugged.

"I don't know what you're trying to do, or why you are really here, but—"

The walkie-talkie clipped to Darnell's belt chirped.

"Dr. Darnell to the communications room. Dr. Darnell to the communications room."

He detached the radio and pushed the talk button. "On my way." To Pax, he said, "I guess it's time."

"Mind if I join you?"

"I insist."

The station was a series of mobile home-sized structures, some positioned right next to each other, some set a little farther apart and connected to the others via fully enclosed and insulated passageways. The communications room was located in one such solo building at the south end of the base near a hill. The rise did double duty, playing home to the radio antennas near the summit, and providing shelter from the winds for the satellite dishes at its base—something it failed to do during the storm.

Two people, both station personnel, were in the room when Darnell and Pax arrived.

"So, are we up?" Darnell asked.

Frances Bourgeois, the head communications officer, glanced over from a desk covered with computer equipment and monitors. "Syncing with the satellite now. Give me a moment." She typed something on her keyboard before studying one of the monitors and then nodding. "There we go. Connection's strong. We're up and running."

Darnell made a point of looking at Pax as he said, "Excellent." He walked over to Frances's desk and picked up the headset sitting there. "We should check in first. Call the university."

Frances typed again. When she finished, Darnell stood at near attention as he focused on the call. After several seconds, he looked confused.

"All I'm getting is ringing," he said. "Are you sure you dialed that correctly?"

Frances checked the number. "I did, but I can try again."

"Do it."

His bewilderment only deepened the second time.

"It *is* New Year's Eve," James Faber, the other person present, said.

Darnell considered this for a second. "Of course." Looking back at Frances, he said, "Put me through to the RCMP in Ottawa."

This time as he listened, he looked stunned.

"What is it?" Frances asked.

Darnell licked his lips nervously as he shot a quick glance at Pax. "Put it on speaker," he said.

A second later, a voice streamed out of the speakers next to the monitor. "—home, and until services are restored, avoid all contact." The voice was female, her message clearly recorded. "Good luck, and may God be with you."

"What the hell is she talking about?" Faber asked.

Darnell held up a hand, silencing him.

There was a moment of dead air before the woman began

speaking again. "You have reached the Royal Canadian Mounted Police. Due to the Sage Flu crisis, there is no one able to take your call. If you are ill, remain where you are. Do not attempt to go to the hospital or any other medical facility. All facilities are currently closed to any new patients. You would do best to remain in bed, drink as much fluid as possible, and…"—she paused—"…pray. If you are unaffected at this time, stay in your home, and until services are restored, avoid all contact. Good luck, and may God be with you."

Pax closed his eyes, his chin falling to his chest. Captain Ash had failed. They had all failed. The very thing the Resistance had been formed to prevent had happened.

The woman's voice filled the room again. "You have reached the Royal—"

"That's enough," Darnell said.

Frances touched her keyboard and plunged the room into silence.

"You have Internet access now?" Pax asked her.

"We should."

As she started to type, Pax, Darnell, and Faber crowded around behind her. The first few websites she tried kicked back the message:

WEBSITE SERVER NOT RESPONDING

CNN.com, however, was working. Just below the standard banner at the top was a large, sunlit picture of Times Square. Pax figured it had been taken near midday. The buildings were decked out in holiday fare, and the electronic billboards displayed mainly Christmas ads and messages. Which made the fact that the streets and sidewalks were empty all the more eerie.

Across the picture in red, semi-transparent capital letters was the word PANDEMIC.

"Holy shit," Faber said.

Frances leaned toward the screen. "This hasn't been updated in over a week." She looked back at her boss. "How is that possible?"

"Check the CBC or PCN or Fox or MSNBC. All of them, if you have to."

She did, but the few that were still up displayed similar messages to CNN's.

For the first time since they'd been listening to the RCMP message, Darnell looked at Pax. "You were telling the truth."

"I was."

Silence.

"They're all dead? Everyone?"

"Not everyone," Pax said.

"But most?" Frances asked.

"If not yet, soon."

The room grew quiet.

Darnell finally broke the silence. "What happens now?"

Before Pax could answer, Faber, barely able to control his emotions, said, "What happens now? Now we're all going to die is what happens! Either we stay here and freeze to death, or go home and die from the flu." He looked at Pax. "Right?"

"That's one option," Pax said. "But there is another."

"What?" Faber asked. "Kill ourselves?"

"I mentioned it when I first told you what was going on."

All three looked at him, dumbfounded for a moment. Frances was the first to snap out of it. "Vaccine," she said. "You told us you had vaccine."

"Yes."

"Enough for everyone here?" she asked.

"More than enough."

Darnell grew wary. "I'm sure you want something for it."

"What does it matter what he wants?" Faber said. "There are more of us than them. We can just take it!"

"Unless you're all trained in combat like my men, I'd advise against trying that," Pax said.

"You surrendered your weapons the first day you were here," Faber said.

"Not all of them," Pax told him. "But we don't need to get to that point. You see, we don't want anything for the vaccine. We *would* like your help getting out of here, but you'll get inoculated either way."

"Bullshit," Faber said.

"Not bullshit. The vaccine is not for sale. It's for anyone who needs it."

"How do we even know it will work?" Darnell asked.

"You won't. Not until you're exposed, at least."

"I don't know if anyone here will want to take that chance."

"That's your choice," Pax said. "But I will say this. Without the vaccine you *will* catch the flu at some point."

"I want it," Frances said quickly.

After a brief hesitation, Faber said, "I'd like it, too."

NEAR FORT MEADE, MARYLAND
1:44 PM EASTERN STANDARD TIME (EST)

"WHOA, NOW THIS is cool," Bobby Lion said, his voice echoing down the hallway.

"Where are you?" Tamara Costello yelled.

"Down here."

She followed his voice to a large, black door that had been propped open. She stepped inside and immediately stopped.

She and Bobby had both seen plenty of high-tech rooms stuffed with equipment back when they'd both worked for the Prime Cable News network—PCN—she as a field reporter and Bobby as her cameraman. But this room blew away anyplace they had seen before.

It was two stories high, and at least a hundred feet wide in both directions. Taking up over half the floor space were rows of equipment racks mounted with computers and God only knew what else. Several long counters broken up into dozens of individual workstations filled the rest of the room. Perhaps the most impressive thing, however, was the gigantic digital screen that took up most of the wall the stations were facing.

"I take it this is it," she said.

Bobby grinned. "Oh, yeah. This has got to be it."

"So, can you get it to work?"

"Hope so. Need to poke around a bit."

"Don't let me keep you."

With a giddy smile, he all but skipped down the aisle leading past the workstations and disappeared into the equipment racks.

Tamara wished she could help him, but knew she'd only be in the way. She'd become more tech savvy over the last year, but the nitty-gritty of the electronics world fell outside her realm of expertise. She wouldn't have a clue about what was what here.

The room they had found was an NSA monitoring facility. Tamara had known several of them were in the DC area; that had always been the rumor in the news world. She and Bobby had first thought they'd find one at the main NSA facilities at Fort Meade. That didn't turn out to be the case. But the trip was not in vain, as they were able to dig up information that had led them to this building, a mere 1.2 miles away.

It still felt odd to be roaming around a place where they would have been shot for doing so less than two weeks earlier. Her reporter's mind couldn't help wondering about all the secrets they could uncover—not only at the NSA but the Defense Department, the State Department, hell, even the White House. Someday, perhaps, she'd do just that. If for no other reason than to satisfy her own curiosity.

But now they had other work to do.

So far, she knew her and Bobby's contributions to the Resistance's efforts had done little to help anything. They had spent months seeding videos on the Internet in an attempt to open people's eyes about what was coming, but more times than not, Project Eden had pulled the videos down nearly as fast as she and Bobby got them up. Their last attempt, what Matt Hamilton had referred to as their Worse Case video, had gone up when it became clear the virus was being released. Its objective was to help people survive, and it had actually remained up and viewable for several days. Tamara wanted to think it had helped a lot of people, but she knew that was probably not the case.

By that time, she and Bobby had moved to the safety of a beach house in North Carolina, both thinking they may be there for some time. But then the message from a man calling himself UN Secretary General Gustavo Di Sarsina took over the airwaves. The recorded message hadn't even been playing for an hour before Tamara's and Bobby's satellite phone rang, and Matt gave them the assignment that had brought them north to the DC area.

After about forty-five minutes, Bobby popped out from behind the racks and asked, "Any chance of finding something to eat? I'm starving."

"Are you going to be able to get it to work?"

"Not sure yet. But…I think so."

Tamara pushed up from the workstation she'd appropriated and said, "I'll go see what I can find."

In a break room on the second floor, she scored a couple of burritos from a freezer and zapped them in the microwave. Drinks were a couple sodas out of a machine, courtesy of some change she found in a guy named Fitzer's desk.

"Come and get it," she said as she reentered the hub. "I found some—" The words died in her mouth, all thoughts of food momentarily forgotten.

On the wall across the room, the giant monitor had come alive.

5

THE FIRST SIGN of discord occurred the same night the message from the UN had started playing over the radio. It began innocently enough. Martina Gable and the other eight survivors were gathered in the restaurant attached to the Carriage Inn—the hotel they'd decided to turn into their group home.

Everyone was excited, and though none of them—excluding, perhaps, Noreen—had truly thought they were the only ones left on the planet, hearing that others were alive was a huge relief. There were tears and laughter and smiles.

At some point, Valerie ducked into the kitchen and returned with two bottles of wine.

"I'm not sure we should be drinking this," Riley said. She was the youngest, but none of the other girls or Craig were of legal drinking age, either.

"Why not?" Valerie asked. "You think the cops are going to bust us?"

Several of the girls laughed.

"No," Riley said. "I mean…you know…" She frowned. "Never mind."

"Here," Amanda said, holding a bottle out to Riley. "It'll make you feel better."

"I don't want any, thank you."

"Come on. Just a little sip."

"I said no." Riley pushed out of her chair and stood up.

"Whoa," Valerie said. "Don't get all hurt. We friends here."

Martina put a hand on Riley's back. "Don't worry. You don't have to drink anything."

Riley hesitated a moment before retaking her chair.

"Martina," Amanda said, swinging the bottle in her direction.

Martina took it and raised it to her mouth. But instead of drinking, she merely let the liquid touch her lips, and then handed the bottle to Ruby.

It wasn't long before the volume in the room increased to the point they almost had to shout to be heard.

At some point, Martha slurred, "So do we leave tomorrow for this survival place, or what?"

"Idiot. They haven't broadcast the locations yet," Amanda said.

"Right, right. But when they do, we're going, right?"

She was looking at Martina, so Martina said, "When they do, we can figure it out then."

"Or we could figure it out now," Valerie said.

"Sure, if you want."

"Yeah," Valerie said. "I think we should take a vote now."

"What's there to vote on?" Craig asked. "Of course we're going to go." He looked at Martina. "Right?"

"Why you looking at her?" Valerie asked. "It's not her decision."

Martina donned a disarming smile. "I think we should save this for the morning, don't you? We're just having some fun tonight, that's—"

"Screw you, Gable," Valerie said. "I don't care what you think. You are *not* the boss here."

Smile still in place, Martina said, "Never said I was."

"You don't have to say it," Amanda threw in. "You just act like it."

It was amazing how old rivalries never died. Martina had been playing sports with or against Valerie and Amanda and most of the other girls since they were all kids. Some she got along with better than others. Valerie and Amanda had always proven more difficult. Martina had assumed their current situation had changed that. Apparently not.

To keep the peace, Martina excused herself to use the restroom, and had instead gone to bed. The next morning, there was no talk of the tension from the night before. Partly that was due to varying degrees of hangovers the others had, but mostly, Martina guessed, they just didn't remember.

When the location of the nearest survival station was finally broadcast—the parking lot of Dodger Stadium in Los Angeles starting on December 31st—the discussion of what to do had come up again. Fortunately, everyone was sober this time, but to avoid any problems, Martina let others lead the conversation.

When Martina had seen which way the vote was leaning, she had thrown in with everyone else, making the vote unanimous. They would caravan to Los Angeles the afternoon of New Year's Eve.

Until the evening before they were to leave, Martina had still thought she'd probably go with them. As she lay in her bed that night, she turned on her phone, hoping it would have a signal now and she could try to reach Ben.

At first, the same NO SERVICE message was at the top where it always was. But as she was about to turn off her phone, a single bar appeared. She stared at it, hoping for more, but that was all it gave her. And then her phone vibrated, letting her know she had voice mail.

The message on the screen indicated there were actually seven, all from Ben. The last had been sent earlier that day. She decided to listen to them in order received and brought up the earliest one.

But as it started to play, the reception bar was replaced by NO SERVICE, and a message appeared on her screen: VOICE MAIL UNAVAILABLE.

"No, please!" she said.

She waited, hoping the bar would come back, but it stayed on NO SERVICE. She turned off the phone and turned it on again, but that didn't change anything. Though she desperately wanted to hear his messages, she felt elated.

If she and the other members of her softball team who'd contracted the Sage Flu the previous spring were now immune, she'd assumed Ben would be, too. He'd gone through it with them, after all. But she'd had now way of knowing for sure. Until now.

Ben was alive.

When the afternoon of New Year's Eve came, Martina helped the others finish loading the cars, while leaving her own bag hidden behind the Carriage Inn's reception counter. Once they were done, they gathered in the parking lot.

"We need to keep in sight of each other in case anyone has car trouble," Valerie said. As had been happening more and more over the last several days, she was taking on the self-appointed role of leader. "Plus, we have no idea what kind of mess we might run into when we reach the city. Could be the roads are jammed up."

"Wait," Jilly said. "What would happen then? Would we have to walk?"

"Anything's possible at this point, but what won't help is whining about it, all right?"

She stared at Jilly, daring her to respond, but Jilly kept quiet.

"Good." Valerie shifted her gaze to the others. "Everyone has water? Something to eat?"

Nods and yeses.

"Then no time to waste, I guess."

As Valerie took a step toward her car, Martina said, "Hold on."

Valerie stopped and looked back, her eyes narrowing as if expecting a challenge. "What's wrong?"

"Nothing's wrong," Martina said. "I'm just...I'm not going with you."

"What?" both Noreen and Riley said.

The group instinctively moved toward Martina.

"What do you mean, you're not going?" Noreen asked.

"Just that," Martina said. "I'm not trying to stop you or anything, but—"

"You're going to stay here?" Riley asked.

"No." Martina paused. She hadn't really thought this part through. She had hoped saying she wouldn't be going would be enough. "I'll meet you guys there eventually, there's just something, um, I have to do."

"What could you possibly have to do?" Valerie asked.

Martina frowned. "Someone I need to look for."

A burst of laughter jumped from Valerie's throat. "Are you kidding me?" She looked out at the road and the desert beyond. "There's no one left to look for. Almost everyone's dead."

That may have been true, but all Martina said was, "I still need to try."

Valerie stared at her in disbelief. "Your funeral, I guess. Have fun." She started walking again.

"Can I go with you?" Riley asked Martina.

Martina cringed. Taking this kind of chance on her own was one thing, but putting others in danger? "I don't think it's a good idea."

"But my father, my…my sister. They might be out there somewhere." Riley's father and her twin sister Laurie had left the cabin where her family and Martina's family had been hiding from the flu before the others had died. Riley and Martina had searched for them when they returned to Ridgecrest, but had found no sign of them.

"If they're still alive, they would have heard the UN's message by now, and will probably head to the survival station, too," Amanda said.

"Well, if they do, then they'll be safe there," Riley said. "But if they didn't hear it…"

Martina couldn't miss the hope and pleading in the girl's voice. She knew if she were in Riley's position, she'd want to do the same thing. "All right."

Riley smiled. "Thank you."

"*But*," Martina quickly added. "They may not have even gone in the direction I'm heading, so don't get your hopes up."

"I won't," Riley said.

Martina looked at her friend for a moment, then said, "Grab your bag."

As Riley rushed to the cars, Noreen said, "I'm going with you, too."

"What?" Valerie said. "Are you crazy?"

Noreen, jaw set, said, "Martina's my best friend. I'm going with her."

Without waiting for a response, she turned after Riley.

"Anyone else want to get themselves killed?" Valerie asked, scanning the rest.

A shoe scuffed against the asphalt, and a hand shot up. "Me."

It was Craig.

"Oh, so, what? You going to be the big male protector?" Valerie asked.

Craig looked confused. "No. I just…no."

Martina knew why. Riley.

Valerie scoffed as she rolled her eyes. "Fine! Is that it? Anyone else?" When no one else spoke up, she said, "Then let's get the hell out of here."

Once everyone was loaded up, the driver's window of the lead car rolled down. "Last chance, Gable," Valerie said.

"Good luck," Martina told her. "We'll see you in L.A."

The look on Valerie's face as she rolled her window back up said she very much doubted that. One by one, the cars started pulling away. Most of the girls waved and shouted their good-byes.

"Think we'll ever see them again?" Noreen asked.

"I'm sure we will," Martina replied, trying to sound more confident than she felt.

They fell silent and watched the cars head north on China Lake Boulevard.

When the last of the vehicles fell out of sight, Craig said, "So, uh, who are we looking for?"

"A friend," Martina said.

"Ben, right?" Noreen asked. She turned to Craig. "His name's Ben."

Martina shouldn't have been surprised her best friend

58

knew. "Yeah. Ben."

"Is he your boyfriend or something?" Riley asked.

"Bingo," Noreen said.

"How do you know he might still be alive?" Craig asked.

"Because he left me a message on my phone."

"What?" Noreen said. "When? What did he say?"

"I only had a signal for a little bit. Not long enough to listen to them. But I do know the last one came yesterday."

"That's great," Noreen said, smiling. "Hey, that's great!"

"We should get going," Martina said. She picked up her pack and started walking toward the road.

"Wait. We're going to hike out of here?" Craig asked.

"Not the whole way."

When she'd thought she'd be going on this trek alone, she knew a car was more than she needed, and might even be a liability. Now, even with the extra companions, her opinion hadn't changed.

When they finally neared her intended destination, she pointed. "There."

In front of the building was a white sign with red letters outlined in black:

GLAZE'S MOTORCYCLES

SAN MATEO, CALIFORNIA
3:03 PM PST

BEN BOWERMAN WIPED the sweat from his brow. It had to be one of the hottest New Year's Eves ever recorded on the San Francisco Peninsula. Well, it would be, he figured, if anyone were still keeping records.

He knew the fact that he'd so far spent half the day digging into the ground probably influenced his opinion, but it still didn't take away from the fact that the day was warm, and that usually New Year's Eve was a time for jackets and scarves and sweaters.

He already had three of the graves completed, and the fourth almost done. They weren't the standard six feet deep—

59

more like four—but they would do just fine. After he removed the last bit of dirt from number four and evened out the bottom, he leaned against his shovel and looked out at the green rolling hills of the cemetery. In the past, a place like this was a peaceful home for the dead. Now, peaceful aside, it seemed like everywhere was home for the dead.

For days he had known he was going to have to come out here and do this. The only question had been, how many graves would he have to dig?

The pandemic took his father first.

Ben had been at his apartment in Santa Cruz two days before Christmas when his phone rang.

"Ben? Ben, please come home." It was his mother. He had never heard her sound more frightened.

"Are you all right? Is something wrong?"

"Yes, something's wrong. Haven't you been watching TV?

Of course he had. He'd been stuck on his couch riveted to the news coverage of the shipping containers that seemed to be spread around the world, belching out an as yet unknown substance.

"It's probably nothing," he said, trying to find words that might calm her down. "I'm sure it will all be over soon, and everything will be back to normal."

"Please, come home," she said. "I'd feel a lot better. The rest of us are here."

"Dad's not at work?"

"They closed his office today."

Those five little words did more to scare Ben than the hours of news he'd been watching.

"Please, Ben. Please."

"Okay. I'll be there in a couple hours."

"Thank you," she said, clearly relieved. "Oh, and Ben, if you see a drugstore open, can you pick up some cold medicine? Your father isn't feeling too well."

His dad had lasted until the day after Christmas. By then, his sisters Kathy and Karen had already come down ill, and his mother was starting to sniffle. Kathy held on the longest.

He kept hoping she'd pull out of it like he had in the spring. There was one day when she seemed to be doing better, but the next morning she was worse than before. Finally, just over twenty-four hours earlier, she had drifted off to join the rest of his family.

By then, he had no more tears left.

He had figured out pretty early that he was immune, had even sent out a silent thank you, but as his family continued to die, he began to wonder if being immune was actually worse. The only thing that kept him sane—the *only* thing—was thinking about Martina. If his previous exposure to Sage Flu made him immune, it would have been the same for her.

He had tried calling, but kept being immediately directed to her voice mail. Every time he'd left a message, but not once had she called back. Then, the same day Karen died, his cell phone stopped receiving a signal at all, so all he could do was focus on nursing Kathy.

He knelt down and checked his work. The bottom of the grave was nice and flat, the corners perfectly edged. It was important to him to be as precise as possible. It was the way his father, a US Navy vet, would have liked it.

The plots were near a tree on a west-facing slope, the very ground his parents had purchased several years ago for the day they would need it. He hadn't realized they'd taken the step until he found the information in their things.

Naturally, they had bought only two plots, so he was worried when he came out here that he'd have to double up, maybe his parents together in one, and his sisters in the other. But the spots on both sides of his parents' chosen resting places were vacant. Since it was unlikely anyone would claim the land, he did.

He had appropriated a Winnebago motor home from one of his parents' neighbors, and used it to transport his family to the cemetery. He started with his father first, half carrying, half dragging him across the lawn, then laying him as gently as possible into one of the center two graves. His mother came next, and then, flanking his parents, his sisters.

He'd considered finding coffins for each of them at first,

but one check of the available boxes inside the mortuary quickly dispelled that notion. They were far too heavy for him to move by himself, and would be even more so once they were filled. His parents and sisters would have to make do with the sheets he had wrapped them in.

Standing there in the shade of the tree, he wasn't sure what he should do next. To this point it had been almost a mechanical process—shroud the bodies, transport them, dig the graves, put the bodies in the holes. In fact, if it hadn't been like that, he may have never been able to finish. But now, with only the burying remaining, he felt he should do something more.

A prayer, maybe?

The only prayer he knew was the Lord's Prayer, and even with that one he was unsure about some of the wording. Still, it was better than nothing.

He moved to the foot of the graves and began.

"Our Father, who art in heaven, hallowed be thy name. Thy kingdom come, thy will be done, on Earth as it is in heaven. Give us this day our daily bread, and forgive..."

Is it "our trespasses"? That didn't seem right.

As he tried to recall the correct phrase, a memory came to him. His mother, young and vibrant, holding his hand in hers while carrying his sister—it must have been Kathy—as they entered a church.

When they were inside, she glanced down at him and said in a quiet voice, "Don't forget, Benjamin, no talking." She squeezed his hand and smiled.

It was a short memory, a minor detail of some forgotten day, but it was more than enough to knock him to his knees. He had thought he'd finished with the tears. He had thought his emotions had already played out.

He was wrong.

He rolled onto his back on the narrow strip of grass between his mother and father, the last time together as a family, the five of them in a row. How long he sobbed, he didn't know, but by the time he regained control again, the shadows had grown long.

It took all of his effort, but he finally forced himself to his feet and picked up the shovel.

Again, he felt the need to say something, but this time not even a prayer came to mind, so he stuck the blade into the pile of dirt and began filling the graves.

6

ASH AND THE others of the last contingent to leave the Ranch spent the entire day trying to stay ahead of the storm. Their luck ran out twenty-three miles north of Sheridan, Wyoming.

At first it was only a smattering of snow, the flakes hitting the road and melting almost immediately, but in no time, the intensity increased to a point the Humvees had to slow to a crawl.

"We'll stop in Sheridan and find shelter," Matt announced over the radio. "Looks like we're going to have to ride this out."

The final twenty miles took them nearly an hour and a half, so by the time they exited the I-90 onto Main Street, four inches of snow had already covered the asphalt.

"Pizza Hut!" Brandon said, looking out his window. He turned to his father. "You think the food there might still be good? Maybe we can make a pizza."

"Maybe," Ash said.

"Probably best not to get your hopes up," Josie told her brother.

"I know, but…it'd be great if we could."

Josie shook her head, but Ash could tell she was hoping her brother was right.

"There's a Super 8 motel up here on the left," Matt

radioed. "We'll pull in and check it out. The rest of you stay in your vehicles."

Chloe drove their Humvee into the lot and parked, leaving the motor running. Outside, snow swirled in the headlight beams as a brisk breeze rocked the truck. From their position, they could see a few lights on in the motel, but not much else.

"How are you feeling?" Dr. Gardiner asked Ash.

"Not as bad as I thought I'd feel," Ash said, truthfully.

"Any unusual pains or discomfort?"

"Nothing that wasn't there before we started."

That seemed to be the answer the doctor wanted to hear. "I can give you some pain pills before you go to sleep tonight."

"Keep them."

Gardiner studied him for a moment. "Are you sure? It'll help you sleep."

"I'll be fine," Ash said.

"Good," Gardiner said. "But no running around once we get out. I want you to find a bed and stay there."

"I'll make sure he does," Josie said before her father could speak.

Ash raised an eyebrow. "Oh, you will, will you?"

"I will," she said, meeting his stare.

The radio crackled.

"This is a bust," Matt said. "Most of the rooms are...occupied. I checked the phone book. There are several more motels we can try.

"How about that one?" Josie said, pointing across the street.

Through the storm, Ash could see a weakly lit yellow sign with a word that looked like "motel" at the bottom. "Tell him," he told her.

Chloe handed the microphone back to Josie. Tentatively, Josie pushed the talk button.

"Mr. Hamilton?"

"Who is this?"

"Josie."

"Josie? What is it?"

"There's a motel right across the street."

Silence for a moment. "I can't see anything from here," Matt said.

Ash took the mic from his daughter. "It's there, all right. We'll swing over and check it out."

"Okay. We'll meet you there in a minute."

The new place was called The Paradise Motel. It was one of those single-story structures like the Bates Motel from *Psycho*, hopefully minus the insane manager. Ash couldn't see all the way to the back, but there had to be at least a dozen rooms.

Chloe parked the truck near the front. "Doc, you want to join me for a look around?"

"What? Me?" Gardiner said, surprised.

"Unless you think it's all right for Ash to come along."

"No. Of course not. I'll, um—"

"I'll go with you," Lily said from the back.

"No, I'll do it," Brandon said.

"I don't think so," Ash said.

"Why not?"

Ash opened his mouth, but no response came to mind. Searching the motel would be nothing compared to the ordeal Brandon had gone through after Project Eden attacked the Ranch.

"It's okay," Gardiner said. "I can go."

"No offense, Dr. Gardiner, but I have more experience than you," Brandon said. He glanced toward Lily. "Than you, too."

As much as he hated to admit it, Ash knew his son was right.

"You can go," he said, "but only if you listen to everything Chloe tells you. She's in charge."

Brandon had the door open before his father had even finished. "Sure, sure. No problem."

BRANDON WAS TOO excited to feel the cold as he climbed

66

out of the truck. He thought for sure his dad would not back down, but he had.

"Over here," Chloe called from around the front of the truck.

As he jogged over, he said, "You want to start in the front and me in the back? Or the other way around?"

"Not so fast, hotshot. What I want is for you to stick close to me, okay?"

His smile dipped a little, but not much. "Sure. No problem."

They headed over to the covered walkway that ran down the length of the building. Approximately every twenty feet along was a door to a room, each with a window beside it. Most of the windows had curtains drawn across them, and those that didn't revealed rooms too dark to make anything out.

Chloe tried a few doors, but they were all locked.

"Office," she said, turning the other way. "They'll have keys there."

The office door was locked, too, but it took only a few shoves from Chloe's shoulder to pop the door free.

As she stepped inside, she pushed her hood back. "Son of a bitch, it's like a sauna in here." She shot a quick look at Brandon. "Don't tell your dad I said that."

"He says worse," Brandon said as he joined her. She was right. Someone had left the lobby heat on at a nice toasty temperature.

Along one wall was a ten-foot-long reception counter, and on the wall behind it, a cabinet consisting of several cubbyholes, each with a key inside. To the side of the cabinet was a closed door.

While Brandon checked under the reception desk for anything of interest, Chloe began pulling out the keys and setting them on the counter.

A noise from somewhere behind Brandon caused him to pause. "Was that you?" he asked.

"Was what me?"

"That noise."

She looked at him, waiting for more.

"It was kind of a, I don't know, whine?" he said.

"I didn't hear anything."

As she spoke, the whine that wasn't quite a whine returned for a moment.

"That," he said. "You heard it that time, right?"

She frowned. "No."

He looked around, and gestured at the closed door. "It came from over there, I think."

"You're sure?"

"I think so."

Chloe pulled out her pistol and crept over to the door. Placing her ear against the side, she listened.

"Anything?" Brandon asked.

"Get back," she whispered, motioning him to the other end of the counter.

As soon as he was out of the way, she eased the door open.

Another moan, this one long and high pitched and definitely coming from the other side of the door. No way Chloe missed it this time.

"What is that?" he asked.

"Shh!" Chloe said, and stepped through the doorway.

Unable to contain his curiosity, Brandon sneaked back along the counter until he had a decent view through the opening. The room on the other side looked like a living room. Perhaps it was where whoever owned the place lived.

As he stepped closer, he leaned across the threshold. Chloe was on the other side of the room, inching toward an open doorway. Quiet and smooth, she slipped her hand around the edge of the doorframe. Suddenly an interior light blazed on, bringing with it a renewed and louder moan. Brandon could see Chloe listen for a moment, and then move into the room, out of sight.

Silence. Then a screech, and a "Shit!" and a thump-thump-thump as several objects hit the ground.

Brandon took a step back. "Chloe, are you all—"

Movement coming out of the other room, low, close to

the floor. Chloe appeared a second later, glanced in Brandon's direction, and yelled, "Shut the door!"

He shot forward and grabbed the doorknob. As he started to pull it closed, he saw something skittering across the floor toward him—gray and fast.

He yanked the door the rest of the way, sealing Chloe and whatever that thing was inside, and held on tight to the knob.

On the other side, he could hear movement and a hiss, followed by something crashing to the ground. When the knob began to turn in his hand, he nearly jumped in surprise.

"Brandon! Let me out!" Chloe said.

The second he let go, the door jerked open and Chloe rushed out, immediately pulling the door closed again.

On the other side, more hisses and cries.

"What was that?" Brandon asked.

"A very hungry cat."

"You mean like a mountain lion?"

"I mean like a house cat. Probably been in there by itself for a week or more."

"So you ran away from a house cat?"

"What did you want me to do? Shoot it?"

"No, but—"

A whine from the other side, and then a scratch, as the tip of a paw appeared in the space beneath the door.

"Come on," Chloe said. "Let's check out the rooms."

"We're just going to leave him here?"

"If you want to get all scratched up, be my guest."

She started toward the front door, Brandon reluctantly following.

AS SOON AS the other Humvees arrived, Matt popped out of his vehicle and joined Ash in his.

"Was just talking to Rachel," Matt said. "She had someone check one of the NOAA satellites. Looks like we're going to miss the bulk of the storm. Doesn't mean we won't get pelted, though. They were able to confirm that it's still dipping south along the Rockies with no signs of stopping. Hoping it won't get quite as far as Colorado Springs, but if it does, we'll keep going south until we reach a clear road leading west."

"What's the news on survivors?" Ash asked.

"They've been able to pinpoint a couple dozen more groups." Matt paused, his face clouding with concern. "Many of them are reporting that they've been in contact with the UN, and are either expecting a delivery of vaccine at any time or are prepping to head to one of these survival stations the Project's been setting up. We're trying to get teams to as many of them as possible first, but there's no way we'll get them all."

"So we leave those we can't reach to die?" Ash asked.

"It doesn't make me happy, either," Matt said. "But we only have so many resources. The Project is going to get to a lot of these people. And who knows how many more survivors we haven't been able to contact will trickle into these places. Ash, I hate it as much as you, but we're not going to be able to save everyone."

"It's not acceptable," Ash said. "We have to do *something*."

"If you have a suggestion, I'm listening."

A door opened and Brandon stuck his head in.

"All clear," Brandon said. "Fifteen rooms."

Ash smiled at his son. "Good job, buddy."

Brandon smiled as he grabbed his backpack off the floor. "I claimed room number two for you, me, and Josie. That's near the front end," he said before heading back into the snow.

Ash stared after him, both proud and sad.

Matt reached over and patted Ash on the arm. "We can all use some rest," he said, and climbed out after Brandon. "We'll talk more in the morning."

"Sure," Ash said absently.

"Come on, Dad," Josie said. "I'll help you out."

PIZZA HUT TURNED out to be a bust. All the food was gone. Brandon was bummed, but not as much as he would have been in the past. It was the way things were, and like it or not, he was getting used to it. So, dinner was the usual selection of canned food that all tasted pretty much the same as far as Brandon was concerned.

He let his father and sister take the two beds, and stretched out on the floor using a few extra blankets from the maid's closet as his mattress. He could feel his eyes wanting to close, but he forced them to remain open as he waited until he heard deep, even breaths from the two beds. His dad knocked off first, but Josie wasn't far behind.

When he was sure they were out, Brandon picked up the small package he'd put aside and rose quietly to his feet. Slowly and silently, he donned his jacket and boots, eased the door open, and quickly slipped outside.

Through the still falling snow, he could see a light on in the cab of one of the Humvees, where the two men on watch would be, but he felt confident their attention was on the road, not the building, so he didn't think he'd be seen. He glanced toward the rear portion of the motel and saw light shining from only one of the windows. He was pretty sure it was Mr. Hamilton's room, and could picture the Resistance's leader hunched over a map as he tried to figure out the best route for the next day.

As light-footed as possible, he hurried to the busted office door, stepped inside, and crossed the small lobby. Pausing in front of the door to the back apartment, he opened the package he'd brought with him. It wasn't much, just a stack of cheese crackers he'd picked up at a convenience store during one of the caravan's stops earlier in the day. He pulled the wrapper all the way apart until it was a flat sheet and set it on the floor, spreading the crackers on top of it. He listened at the door. All was quiet on the other side.

"All right, cat," he said. "I've got something for you, but don't you come running out at me. You got that?"

Whether the cat got it or not, it made no response.

"I'm opening the door now," he said.

71

He turned the knob and inched the door open a crack. No cat, though it could have been hiding behind the door. He opened the door a little more, and scooted the cellophane wrapper into the room.

"There you go," he said. "I know it's not a lot, but it's got to be better than nothing."

As he eased the door closed, he thought he heard movement. Once the door was latched, he leaned in close, putting his ear against the wood.

Several scratches were followed by the distinct sound of a cracker breaking. Smiling, he stood up again and headed out, almost making it back to his room before the gunfire began.

7

PRINCIPAL DIRECTOR PEREZ watched as the ten monitors mounted on the wall across from his desk began filling with the faces of the next batch of Project Eden personnel. After the final screen came on, Claudia, the director's senior assistant, said, "The time is 8:10 p.m. Mountain Standard. Group fourteen's representatives are all present. Director Perez?"

Perez stared blankly at the camera for another few beats, before he asked the same question with which he began each of the previous thirteen conference calls. "We are now nine days past Implementation Day. Assessments?"

No one said anything, each looking as if he or she hoped someone else would reply.

This wasn't the first time he'd received the response, and he was well aware of the reason for the hesitation. Until the release of the KV-27a virus, the principal director of Project Eden had been someone else entirely. Perez's ascent into the position was a total surprise. He was not known in the traditional power circles of the project, and most had thought one of the senior Project members who had been passed over would be given the job. Perez was still an enigma, and he was happy to remain one.

"When I ask a question, I expect answers," he said.

The man in monitor number seven, Jumoke el-Masri, an

Egyptian by birth who was stationed at NB014 outside Rome, overseeing the Project's operations in the Mediterranean, cleared his throat and said, "I, of course, can only speak for my region. Our analysis shows a current penetration rate of 89.76%, topping out at a projected 98.12% in the next seven days. This will put us 1.71% short of the Project's goal. Closing that gap will take time, and will depend on how many of the current survivors we are able to reach. Best estimate, another month to month and a half should put us within a few hundredths of the 99.83% mark."

"We are seeing a similar result here," Ingrid Klausner, the woman in charge of Scandinavia and northwestern Russia, said from monitor number three. "Our percentages are a bit better than Mr. el-Masri's, but that has been helped, in part, by the military actions we've seen." In the wake of the outbreak, fighting had broken out along the borders between Russia and the former Soviet republics in the Baltic.

"Are you still seeing any fighting?" Perez asked. He'd read the reports and knew the answer, but he wanted to hear it from her.

"Only along a small stretch of the Russian-Estonian border. Last night, two of our aircraft sprayed the area with KV-27a. The last of the fighting should cease in the next twenty-four to thirty-six hours."

Others began chiming in. All were seeing the same results, give or take a few tenths of a percent—numbers that were within the expected range at this point of the operation. While it would have been nice to reach the Project's ultimate goal solely from the release of the virus on Implementation Day, to believe that would happen would have been grossly naïve. Hence the UN message to trick people into revealing their locations, and lure as many as possible to survival stations. A few lucky ones with desired qualities such as a needed skill set would be spared. The rest, while told they were receiving a vaccine, would actually be infected with a live version of the virus.

There were a couple trouble locations, also not surprises. One was the vast group of islands that stretched from eastern

Malaysia through Indonesia and Papua New Guinea, and finally up into the southern portion of the Philippines. It was a difficult area to cover, lots of people scattered on thousands of islands—logistically impossible to cover with the shipping containers that had delivered the bulk of the virus to the world.

The second problem zone was a similar group of islands, though fewer in number. These were located in the eastern Caribbean Sea, starting with the British Virgin Islands and moving southeast all the way to Trinidad and Tobago. Most of the islands had been exposed to the virus like the rest of the world, but a few had been missed, and were now home to large groups of survivors. These two geographically broad areas, as well as a few smaller pockets elsewhere, were in the process of being sprayed from the sky like the Russian war zone had been. It would take a little time to see results, but they would come.

"Mr. Muramoto," Perez said, zeroing in on monitor number nine. "The latest report I have indicates the survival station outside Seoul and the station in Shanghai have yet to open. Is this still the case?"

"Unfortunately, that is correct, sir. We have had—"

"I'm not interested in what you've had. I'm interested in how soon they will be operational."

"Of course." Muramoto glanced down, presumably looking at some notes. "Seoul should be open by four p.m. local time."

A little less than four hours.

"And Shanghai?"

More hesitation. "There have been some problems. Rioting and fires destroyed the facility we had planned on using. A backup was immediately identified, but it is taking longer than anticipated to get it into working order."

"How. Long."

"Another day. Maybe day and a half."

"So the location has not been broadcast yet?"

Muramoto licked his lips. "No."

"Broadcast it now."

"But some will arrive before they can go inside."

Perez leaned toward the camera. "And that's a problem? Station some of your people in the streets to meet whoever comes, and have them point people to surrounding buildings where they can camp until the station is ready. *Get the survivors there!* That is your priority now." He kept his gaze fixed on the camera. "That is the priority for *all* of you. Please tell me you understand that?"

"Yes, sir."

"Absolutely."

"Yes."

"Yes."

"Yes."

Perez let a few seconds pass, then said, "We are at a critical juncture in the plan. It is up to you to see that it goes smoothly. If you are not up to the task, you will be replaced." From the looks in their eyes, he didn't need to ask this time if they understood. "If there's nothing else…?" He waited, but no one said anything. "Very well. Back to work."

Claudia punched the button cutting off the monitors. She glanced at the clock on her computer screen and smiled. "You're getting better at this. Still have six minutes before group fifteen."

"What areas are in that one?"

She turned back to her screen, but didn't answer right away.

"Claudia?" he asked.

She looked up. "Sorry. We received a call from Sims a few minutes ago. If you'd like, I could get him on the line."

"Yes, do it."

Sims and his associates had become Perez's special projects team, handling the delicate matters the majority of Project Eden's membership didn't need to know about. Sims's latest task was one Perez had been putting off for over a week. It was a simple reconnaissance job, one he was sure would turn out to be a complete waste of time. Still, he couldn't afford to leave it unchecked, so he had finally sent out Sims.

Several seconds passed before the bottom center monitor filled with Sims's hard-edged face, surrounded by dancing snowflakes.

"Principal Director," Sims said.

"Report, Mr. Sims."

"Yes, sir. We arrived at the Montana location about two hours ago."

"Was there anyone left alive?"

"Sir, we didn't find anyone. Dead or alive."

That was definitely not what Perez had expected. "No one?"

The camera twisted away from Sims, but other than snow and darkness, Perez could make out nothing.

"The main building, the one that burned down during our attack, is that direction," Sims said. The camera swung a few degrees to the left. "The smaller building was over there."

"I'm familiar with the layout, Mr. Sims. I assume there is something new you're trying to tell me?"

"Sir, we made a thorough search of the wreckage. No one was in either building when they burned down."

"So they were already gone when you attacked? Didn't your team kill one of their men then?"

"Yes, sir. About a half mile from here. He was the only one seen that day. But, to answer your other question, I don't think they were gone." The camera swung in a one-eighty before tilting down. A pile of dirt and snow and pine needles sat next to a hole in the ground, and propped open in the hole was a hatch. "They had an underground facility. Pretty damn extensive, too. Lots of offices, storerooms, barracks." He paused. "It's also equipped with an indoor shooting range and medical facilities. Both high end."

Again, not what Perez expected. Perhaps he'd been underestimating the people who had been there. In his mind, they were no more than a gnat that posed no real threat to the Project. That was undoubtedly still true, but the sophistication of the facility Sims described was troubling. "And you found no one inside, either?"

The camera turned back to Sims's face. "No, sir."

"What about computers? Anything that might have information on it?"

"Unfortunately, the few computers left were thoroughly destroyed. If there were any other records, we didn't locate them." He looked away from the camera, scanning around. "I can tell you one thing, this place was *not* cheap."

"Any sign of where they went?"

"The snow didn't start falling until maybe an hour before we arrived. We found some indentations where tire tracks and boot prints had been, so I don't think they've been gone for long."

"They drove out?"

"I believe so. Yesterday at most."

A gnat could be annoying, but ultimately it couldn't hurt you. Chances were these people knew they were defeated, and were only trying to find someplace to stay safe as the dust settled.

"You think you can find them?" he asked.

Sims grimaced. "Possibly, but it won't be easy. Have to do it by instruments until the storm clears. If you'd like, we can give it a shot."

"All right. For a little while, but I don't want to waste too much effort on this, so if you feel like you're spinning your wheels, call it off."

"Yes, sir. We'll get right on it."

"Report in if you find anything," Perez said, then signaled Claudia that he was finished.

As she disconnected the call, she said, "Group fifteen is standing by."

Perez filled his glass with water from a pitcher, and took a sip. When he set the glass back down, he nodded and said, "Ready."

THE RANCH, MONTANA
8:18 PM MST

SIMS CLIMBED ABOARD the helicopter and pulled the door shut.

"Treetops," he said to the pilot. "Follow the road we

78

spotted earlier, out to the highway. The rest of you keep an eye out for tracks. Any questions?"

"No, sir," they said in unison.

A cloud of white swirled up around them as the rotors increased their speed and the aircraft lifted off the ground. When they rose to a point approximately twenty feet higher than the tallest tree, the pilot took them south and then east.

Whoever had built the road the helicopter was following had been very smart. Only the bare minimum of trees had been cleared to create the path. In many spots, the branches from both sides intertwined with each other for stretches of twenty, thirty—one time over one hundred—feet, making it impossible to see the road at all. The storm wasn't helping, either, as snow flew past them in waves of near solid sheets, momentarily obscuring the view.

When they finally reached the strip of open land where the road met highway, Sims keyed his mic and told the pilot, "Set us down near the intersection."

"Looks like it might be a little deep," the pilot replied.

"I've seen you land in worse."

"Doesn't mean I like it."

The pilot slowly lowered them over the road. By the time the skids came to rest, the top of the snow was only a few inches below the lip of the door.

"We won't be long," Sims said.

After exiting the aircraft, he and his men spread out to quickly cover more area.

"Sir!" Altman, one of Sims's men, yelled.

Sims twisted around, and spotted Altman fifty feet down the smaller road that led back into the woods. By the time he reached him, Altman had crouched down and was pointing at the ground.

"Tire tracks, sir," Altman said. "At least two sets."

Sims moved in low next to him. Running down the road were several wide depressions. They hadn't filled because of the partial tree cover.

"How old, do you think?" Sims asked.

Altman, Sims's best tracker, studied the marks. "Twelve

hours, give or take."

Twelve hours. Depending on what the weather had been when the vehicles came through, they could be as much as six or seven hundred miles away. They probably hadn't made it quite that far, but even three hundred would be a lot.

Altman rose to his feet, but stayed bent at the waist as he followed the tracks toward the highway. Sims walked right behind him. With each step the depressions became shallower and shallower, until Sims could no longer differentiate the tracks from the surrounding ground. Altman, though, was able to follow them nearly all the way to the intersection.

He finally stopped and straightened up. "It looks like they turned south."

"You're sure?" Sims asked.

"As sure as I can be."

South *did* make the most sense. A turn to the north would have meant heading into the meat of the storm.

"Don't think we're going to find anything else here," Sims said loudly enough for the other men to hear. "Everyone back on board."

Back in the warmth of the aircraft's cabin, he pulled up on his tablet a map of the state and studied it for a moment.

"South toward Butte," he told the pilot. "Your destination's the intersection of the I-90 and the I-15 a couple miles west of town. We'll see if we can pick up another sign of them there."

"Yes, sir," the pilot said.

8

CHLOE'S EYES SHOT open at the sound of the gunshot. She rolled off her bed and onto the floor, unsure where it was coming from. Once she realized none of the bullets were flying through her room, she scrambled across the floor and yanked on her boots.

"What the hell's going on?" Matt's voice boomed out of the radio in her jacket pocket.

As she grabbed the coat and pulled it on, Jared Lawrence, one of the men on watch, answered. "We've got at least two shooters. Think they're on the lot just south of us."

That would be the equipment rental place Chloe had seen next door. It was full of tractors and trucks and trailers parked around a large, central building.

"Do you have an exact position?" Matt asked.

"No, the snow's too—" Jared cut himself off as another burst of bullets sailed over the motel.

"Jesus," Matt said. "Everyone stay down. Jared, we need to silence those guns."

Chloe clicked the talk button. "I'm on it."

BRANDON DUCKED DOWN next to the motel wall. The gunfire sounded like it was coming from somewhere beyond the parking area. Worried that he might still be in the line of fire, he darted over to the cover of one of the Humvees, and then raised his head high enough to peer through the windows of the vehicle. All he could see were darkness and snow.

Over the radio inside the Humvee, he heard Matt's voice. "What the hell's going on?"

The answer confirmed what Brandon had already figured out.

He ducked back down as more gunfire rang out.

When it stopped, he could hear Matt say, "Everyone stay down. Jared, we need to silence those guns."

The response came almost immediately. "I'm on it." Not Lawrence's voice. Chloe's.

I'm on it? Was she going after the shooters alone? Even Brandon knew that wasn't a good idea.

He looked through the window again, this time searching the inside of the vehicle. Lying across the floor in the back were two M16 rifles. Careful and quiet, he opened the rear door and grabbed one. After checking that the mag was full, he eased the door closed. Because of his location, he was sure he'd have heard Chloe run by if she'd decided to approach the other property from the front, but there had been no footsteps in that direction, so she must've been heading around back.

He reached the rear of the motel only seconds before a shadowy form passed through the falling snow. He hesitated only long enough to convince himself it was indeed Chloe before he stepped off the walkway and disappeared into the storm.

"GET ON THE floor!"

Josie's eyelids fluttered open as she pulled herself out of a deep sleep.

"Josie! Down!" her father yelled.

Before she could move, she heard the smack-smack-smack of several items hitting the roof of the motel.

Bullets.

As she started to roll off her bed, she saw her father struggling to detangle himself from his covers. She stepped across the gap that divided their beds and yanked off the blanket.

"Don't worry about me!" her dad yelled. "Get down!"

Ignoring him, she grabbed his hand and helped him scoot off the mattress onto the floor.

"Are you okay?" Josie asked once they were lying side by side. "Did you get hit?"

"I'm fine," her dad said. He raised his head and looked toward the area beyond the beds. "Brandon, are you all right?"

No response.

"Brandon?" Josie asked. "Are you okay?"

Still no answer.

"Brandon!" her father yelled.

He started to push himself up, but Josie put a hand on his arm.

"I'll check," she said.

As she crawled to the end of the beds, she prayed she wouldn't find her brother lying in a pool of blood. No blood, but no Brandon, either. Only the blankets he'd been using for a mattress.

"Brandon, where are you?" she asked.

She moved out from between the beds so she could check the rest of the room.

"Is he there?" her dad asked.

"No. He's not in the room."

"What about the bathroom?" her father asked.

The bathroom. Why hadn't she thought of that? *He's probably hiding in the tub.*

Getting to her feet but staying low, she sprinted across the room.

"Brandon?" she said as she reached the open door.

He wasn't there, either.

"Did you find him?" her dad asked.

"No, Dad, he's not here."

More bullets flew over the building. Josie dropped to the carpet with a scream.

"Are you hit? Josie, are you okay?"

"I'm okay. It just startled me, that's all."

"Come back over here."

When she reached him, she said, "Where could he have gone?"

"He'll be fine," her father said. "Brandon knows how to take care of himself."

That may have been true, but Josie sensed her father was as worried as she was.

CHLOE WORKED HER way west, onto the property directly behind the motel, before turning south. Her plan was to circle around to the other side of the equipment lot, and come at the shooters from behind. With the dark and the snow, they would likely not know she was there until too late.

As she moved parallel to the back of the equipment-business property, she was able to use the sounds of the shots to determine that the gunmen were on the roof of the big building at the center of the lot. She was also pretty sure there were only two shooters, or maybe one person firing two different rifles. Didn't mean there wouldn't be others around, however.

She reached the far side of the property, and moved down the chain-link fence until she was approximately halfway back to the main street. Up and over she went, her landing cushioned by a waist-high drift of snow.

The building was about a hundred feet wide, street side to back, and a hundred and fifty from Chloe's end to the side closest to the motel. Two floodlights were mounted on poles out front, lighting up the parking area. One was positioned wide enough to spill a bit of light on the south side, where she approached the building.

The roof peaked at the center, with the low end hanging off the side she'd approached. About thirty feet back from the front was a utility room built against the wall, maybe four feet square. All she needed to do was get on top of that, and she could easily reach the eaves and pull herself all the way up.

A noise behind her, faint, but sounding very much like something falling into the snow.

84

She whirled around, her rifle instantly off her shoulder, pointing into the storm. But whatever had made the noise was out of her limited range of visibility.

Sticking to the tracks she'd already made, she retraced her route back to the fence. Her fear was that the shooters up top had a friend down here, but she made it all the way to the drift she'd landed in without seeing anything.

It was probably something blowing out of a tree, she guessed.

Several more shots rang out.

She whipped back around, focused once more on her mission, and hurried back to the building.

BRANDON LAY IN a deep hole in the snow, holding his breath.

Following Chloe had been a simple matter of stepping in her boot prints. When he had reached the fence where she'd climbed over, he scaled the chain-link as quietly as possible. What he didn't anticipate was slipping off the top rail and falling into the deep patch of snow on the other side.

At first he was too stunned to move, then he heard Chloe heading his way and realized his fall had made enough noise to alert her. While he knew he should probably stand up and let her know he was there, a part of him worried she'd shoot him if he did. Another part, a more vocal one, was concerned she'd send him back to the motel. That was the last thing he wanted to happen. He wasn't a kid anymore. He was a soldier like the others, like his dad. His place was here whether she wanted him around or not.

The sound of her boots stopped only a few feet away. If she came any closer, she would see him for sure.

Two rifle shots boomed from the roof of the building. As the echo subsided, Brandon realized Chloe had moved away. That's when he finally allowed himself to breathe again. As soon as he felt sure she wouldn't be able to see him, he rose and started to follow her again.

THE UTILITY SHED was easily scaled. When she stood on top, the eaves of the main roof came all the way down to her chest, making it even easier than she'd anticipated to pull herself all the way up.

As gunfire erupted again, she used the noise as a mask, and sprinted up the roof toward the peak. Five feet short of the top, she lowered herself to her belly and slithered the rest of the way up.

As she'd suspected, there were only two shooters. They were set up about two thirds of the way down from the peak, each sitting upright, with the barrels of their rifles resting on large sacks of grain. Both were bundled up tight in dark winter gear, the only difference between them was that the one on the left was smaller than the one on the right.

A man and a woman?

Didn't really matter. What did were the guns they were using to shoot at Chloe's friends.

Both of them had their eyes to scopes mounted on their weapons, looking toward the motel. She hadn't expected that. If they had scopes, that meant they could have zeroed in and hit pretty much anything. Instead, their shots, at least when she had still been inside, had flown harmlessly over the top of the motel.

No time to figure out the why, though. Climbing to her feet, she raised her rifle and started walking down the other side. The first sign that one of the shooters knew something was wrong was a tilt of the smaller one's head, as if she or he were trying to listen for something.

Chloe, only fifteen feet behind them now, took another step forward.

This time the small one twisted all the way around. "Rick!" A girl's voice.

Her companion grunted and pulled back from his scope.

"Rick!"

"What?"

The girl nodded toward Chloe, and her friend turned to see what was up.

"Oh, shit!" he said, grabbing for his gun.

"Don't," Chloe commanded, her voice calm and even.

Rick didn't seem to hear her. He wrapped his hands around the stock of the rifle and started to lift it off the milk crates.

"Drop it," Chloe said. "I *will* shoot you."

"Rick, put it down," the girl said.

"Don't tell me what to do!" Rick said.

"Please, Rick! Please!" The girl turned to Chloe. "Please don't shoot him. We weren't trying to hurt anyone. We were just trying to scare you off."

"Put the rifle down," Chloe said.

She could see Rick's chest rise and fall with a deep breath.

"Rick, put it down!" the girl said again.

A tense second later, Rick swore under his breath and dropped the gun.

"Now stand up. Both of you," Chloe said.

The girl complied right away, while Rick took a moment to do the same.

Now that Chloe was able to get a better look at them, she saw her suspicions were right. They were both kids, the big one probably a teenager, but the girl no older than Brandon.

"We're sorry, ma'am," the girl said. "You're the first new people we've seen in a while. We were afraid you were going to make us sick. We don't want to be sick."

"Shut up, Ginny," Rick said.

Chloe jerked in surprise. "What did you call her?"

Rick didn't answer her.

"What did you call her?" Chloe repeated.

"Ginny," the girl said. "That's my name."

Something clawed at Chloe from the dark space in her mind, the space that had contained the memories taken from her by the Project Eden assholes years before, and it was as if the rest of the world suddenly disappeared.

Ginny. But not *Ginny*.

And a girl. But not this girl.

"Rick! Don't!"

The shout snapped Chloe out of her trance just in time to

see a rifle magazine flying through the air toward her. She ducked to her left, and the metal casing flew past her shoulder, almost clipping her ear.

But the near miss came with a cost.

Chloe slipped, her foot shooting into the air, and she landed hard on her hip against the sloped roof. The impact loosened a wide section of snow that began sliding downward, taking her with it.

"Chloe!"

She twisted her head and spotted Brandon standing at the peak of the roof.

How the hell had he—

But the thought went unfinished as she flew off the edge, and arced through the air toward the ground.

THE BIG ONE, the one the other had called Rick, dove for his gun as Chloe sailed off the building.

Though Brandon wanted to scramble down so he could help her, he knew he had to deal with the problem at hand first. He aimed his rifle and pulled the trigger without warning.

The bullet smashed into the side of Rick's weapon, knocking it away and taking at least one of the kid's fingers with it.

"Son of a bitch!" Rick yelled.

He grabbed his hand and looked as if he might charge up the slope at Brandon.

Brandon, the gun still tight to his shoulder, said, "Stay right there or the next one goes through your head."

"Rick, listen to him. Please!" Ginny pleaded.

Rick was only able to glare at Brandon for a second before pain forced him down onto his knees. Ginny immediately crouched next to him.

"Are you okay? Let me see," she said. "Oh, God."

"You'd better wrap that up," Brandon said.

Ginny looked at him, stunned, before nodding and setting to work.

BRETT BATTLES

Without taking his eyes off the two shooters, Brandon yelled as loudly as he could, "Mr. Hamilton! It's Brandon! I've got the shooters! But I think Chloe's hurt!"

It took only a few minutes for the others to get there. They found Chloe unconscious in the snow just a few feet from the scoop end of a tractor. Dr. Gardiner made a quick assessment and had four of the men carry her back to the motel. He then examined Rick's finger, and accompanied the boy and Ginny—with two other men acting as guards—back to the Paradise.

When Brandon entered the motel parking lot, Josie raced over and threw her arms around him. His father followed, but at a much slower pace.

"What were you thinking?" she said. "You had us scared to death."

"Did Chloe ask you to go with her?" his father asked, clearly concerned.

"No," Brandon said. "She didn't know I was there, not until she fell, anyway. I...I followed her."

"You followed her?" his father said. "Why would you do that?"

Brandon looked at his dad, wondering why it was even a question. "Because family always has each other's back. You told me that. Chloe was going alone." He paused. "She's family." He looked past his father at the other members of the Resistance. "We're all family now, aren't we?"

His father stared at him for a long moment before reaching out and pulling Brandon into a hug. "We are," he said. "You did good. Just...next time let me know first."

9

THEY HADN'T TRAVELED nearly as far as Martina would have liked, but she was to blame for that.

After taking possession of three Honda Shadow motorcycles, and a Kawasaki Ninja for Craig, they'd spent nearly an hour making sure Noreen and Riley—neither of whom had ever driven a bike before—were comfortable enough with their rides before heading out.

When they finally hit the road, they raced through Inyokern and up the slope to Highway 14. Heading south, they had one last look at the valley. As always, brown was everywhere—the hills, the brush, the buildings. Even the trees people had nurtured to life looked tan from the highway.

Martina couldn't help but wonder how long it would be before she might return. She would, of course. At the very least, she had to bring her family down from the mountains, and bury them in the place they always called home.

For a little while, after the valley fell away, Martina could almost pretend the world was as it had been. Highway 14 had been at its busiest on weekends in the winter when skiers from L.A. sped north to the slopes of Mammoth Mountain, another three hours past Ridgecrest. But most other times, traffic was few and far between, so being the only ones on the road was not unusual.

They made it a few miles past Red Rock Canyon before

the illusion vanished. A set of abandoned buildings sat to the left of the highway, the remnants of someone's long-ago attempt to farm the desert. For several years, Martina had thought of the structures merely as markers to and from home. She could never remember seeing anyone walking around them, or any vehicles parked nearby.

That wasn't the case now, though. Close to a dozen motor homes were there, each parked neatly next to its neighbor. There was an area in front of the vehicles where several camping chairs had been set up. The majority were empty, but a few were occupied.

At first, Martina thought maybe she'd come across more survivors. She'd slowed down and angled over to the side of the road closest to the gathering. But as she neared, she could see that the people sitting would never be leaving their chairs again.

Why were they all there? Had they come to die together?

She added those to the list of questions whose answers she'd never know.

The town of Mojave came into view a few miles before Martina and her friends actually reached it—gas stations and convenient stores and fast food restaurants lining the east side, a handful of railroad tracks lining the west. If there had been a way to go around it, she would have gladly taken it. But there had been no such path.

She stopped at the turn into town and let the others pull up beside her.

"You guys doing all right?" she asked.

"Yeah, I think I'm getting the hang of it," Riley said.

"Don't get too confident," Martina warned. "Noreen?"

"I'm fine," her friend said, though it was clear she was still a bit nervous.

"Anyone need to stretch their legs?" she asked.

"Can we just keep going?" Noreen asked.

"I like that idea," Craig said. He looked left down Mojave's main drag. "This place kind of gives me the creeps."

"Me, too," Riley said.

Me, three, Martina thought. "All right. As long as you guys don't need a break."

They made the turn and headed through town. Deserted streets, near empty parking lots, and no obvious bodies to be seen. Like back in Ridgecrest, apparently most people had chosen to die at home.

After they drove over the bridge at the south edge of Mojave, Martina allowed herself to breathe normally again. If she was this tense going through a small town, what would it be like to pass through someplace larger?

My God, what about Los Angeles?

Her friends should have been getting close to Dodger Stadium at that point. If her reaction was any indication, they must be nervous wrecks.

As Martina's group came around the east side of Mount Mojave, the highway transitioned into a four-lane divided freeway. This allowed them to pass by the town of Rosemead without actually driving through it. In the distance, she could see the buildings of the Lancaster/Palmdale area. Over three hundred thousand people had lived there. How many of them were still alive? Were any?

Thankfully, she didn't have to find out.

A few miles south of Rosemead, Martina exited the freeway onto Highway 138. This shot them due west, bypassing both Lancaster and Palmdale, and taking them all the way to the famous Grapevine portion of the I-5 in the mountains north of Los Angeles.

When they finally reached the interstate, Martina pulled over on the transition road, and retrieved her jacket from her bag on the back of the bike. Her friends eagerly did the same. Unlike the warm day back in the desert, it was considerably cooler here.

"A little something to eat might be nice," Craig said as he climbed back onto his seat.

"And I gotta pee," Noreen added.

Martina checked the old map she'd picked up back in Ridgecrest. "Gorman's just a few miles to the north. We should be able to find someplace there we can take a break."

"Sounds good to me," Craig said.

"Yeah, whatever," Noreen said, looking like she was going to burst. "Let's hurry."

The someplace turned out to be a Carl's Jr. burger joint on the north side of the freeway. It was thankfully free of the dead, and with little effort, they were able to get the heat turned on.

They sat silently for a while, already weary from their journey as they ate some of the food they'd brought with them.

Riley spoke first. "So where do we go from here?"

"Up the Five," Craig said. "That's the way we always go to the Bay Area. Dad always says…" He paused, the hint of discomfort. "Always said it was the fastest way there."

Martina didn't respond right away. The problem was, there were two main routes up the coast. Craig was right. The I-5 was the fastest, but the 101 freeway over on the coast went there, too. And while the latter route *did* take longer, it was the route Ben preferred. He called the I-5 the Mind Number and refused to use it. What if he were heading down to find her? Just because he hadn't yet didn't mean he wouldn't do it at some point. The last thing she wanted was to miss him because she and the others took the wrong road.

The I-5 or the 101?

Their break stretched to an hour and a half as she tried to decide which way they should go. By then, it was growing dark, and the brisk air from earlier had turned frigid. Though she still didn't have an answer to her quandary, she knew the last thing they should do was travel in the dark.

Next door to the Carl's Jr. was an Econo Lodge motel. They selected two rooms with an adjoining door—one for the girls and one for Craig. Craig found a DVD player and several movies in the main office, attached the device to his TV, and asked the others to join him. Noreen passed, and was soon fast asleep. Martina declined, too, though her mind was too occupied to shut down just yet. So Riley went to Craig's room alone. Which, Martina thought, was how Riley and Craig had probably wanted it to work out.

EDEN RISING

At least someone isn't alone.

Martina lay in her bed for nearly an hour, staring at the ceiling as the weapon fire and dialogue of what sounded like *Aliens* seeped through the partially closed dividing doors. Her mind was filled with memories—her family fleeing to the mountains; a trip with Ben to the aquarium in Monterey; tossing a football with her brother in the backyard; a cough from the back room of the cabin; her mother's eyes, rheumy and unfocused; her father dead.

All of them dead.

She pushed herself angrily out of bed, pulled on her shoes, and grabbed her jacket. As she passed the adjoining doors, she peeked into the other room. Riley and Craig were propped up on the bed, riveted by the movie, their arms around each other.

Quietly, Martina opened the main door and slipped outside.

The cold air made her cheeks feel as if they were freezing in place. Each exhalation created a cloud of vapor three times the size of her head. But the cold didn't bother her at the moment. It was nice actually, a distraction.

She wandered down the road toward the freeway entrance. There was a Chevron gas station just ahead, and to her right a small strip mall that consisted of a jewelry store, an antique shop, and a combination mini-market and liquor store.

She almost kept walking, but something in the half-lit liquor store window caught her attention. Framing the top and sides were strings of silver and red garland, and sprayed on the glass in a frosted white:

MERRY CHRISTMAS

Christmas had been a week ago, a day that had gone uncelebrated as the world began to die. In fact, it had been almost *exactly* a week ago, which meant today…

She checked her watch. It was fourteen minutes until midnight. There was still time.

She hurried across the street to the liquor store and pulled on the door, but it was locked.

"Crap!"

She looked around. Typical cement blocks marked the ends of the nearby parking stalls. The blocks were old, and a few were cracked and broken. She grabbed a loose chunk of cement and slammed it through the glass window.

She looked at her watch again. Eleven minutes. No time to waste.

She ducked through the opening and searched the store for the rack she wanted. It took a few minutes, but she finally found it. Two bottles would probably be enough, but she grabbed three just in case, and stuffed them into a bag she found behind the counter. In another aisle, she snatched up a bag of plastic cups and headed back outside.

It was exactly 11:59 when she threw open the door to her room and flipped on the lights.

"Hey, everyone!" she yelled. "In here."

She set her bags on top of the dresser and started unloading the bottles.

"What's going on?" Noreen asked, only half awake.

"Get up," Martina told her without looking back. "We don't have much time."

Suddenly alert, Noreen said, "Is something happening? Do we need to leave?"

Martina ignored her and ripped open the plastic holding the cups.

"What's with all the noise?" Riley asked, walking into the room holding hands with Craig.

"Over here," Martina said.

She ripped the foil wrapper off the top of the bottle, removed the metal safety cap, and popped the cork.

"Is that champagne?" Craig asked.

Martina smiled, and poured four even cupfuls.

"Come on!" She forced a cup into each of their hands.

"I don't know," Riley said.

"You just need to take a sip," Martina said. She looked at her watch. "Okay, here we go. Ten, nine, eight, seven, six…"

"What are you doing?" Noreen asked as Martina counted.

"Five, four, three, two, one." Martina raised her glass. "Happy New Year."

Noreen was the first to laugh, then Riley followed, and finally Craig joined in.

"Happy New Year," they said.

They all drank.

"Hey, this is pretty good," Noreen said. "Can I have some more?"

"Sure," Martina said. "It's New Year's."

Another round of the wine was shared.

"I thought you were going to tell us we needed to run," Noreen said.

"Why would we need to do that?" Craig asked.

"I don't know. Could be anything."

Martina knew exactly what her friend was thinking. "Don't say it."

"Don't say what?" Riley asked.

"I swear, Noreen, if you say it…"

"I didn't," Noreen said.

"Didn't say what?" Riley pressed.

"Didn't say zom—"

"Noreen!" Martina said. "What did I just tell you?"

"Zombies?" Craig asked.

Noreen shrugged. "Maybe."

Riley rolled her eyes. "Oh, great. Now I have that in my head."

Martina looked at her. "Your fault. You kept asking."

They laughed and joked about it for a while and had some more champagne.

When the conversation lost some of its steam, Craig said, "I'm not really sure we should actually be celebrating New Year's. I mean, what's there to celebrate?"

"The most important thing of all," Martina said. "We're alive."

The others contemplated her response.

After several seconds, Craig raised his cup. "To being alive."

The others raised theirs. "To being alive."

January 1st

Year 1

World Population
1,000,207,113

10

SANJAY PEERED OUT the third-floor window at the alley. It was still empty.

Where was she?

It shouldn't have taken Kusum more than four hours at most to make the round trip, but five had already passed. He cursed himself for about the thousandth time. He should have been the one to go, not because he thought she was incapable, but at least he would know what was going on. Instead, he could only sit there as his anxiety spiraled out of control. But the decision had apparently not been his to make.

"You went for the close-up look of the survival station," Kusum had said. "That means it is my turn."

"Why do we need to take turns?"

She looked at him, clearly thinking it was a stupid question.

"Maybe we should both go," he suggested, hoping for at least a partial victory.

"Someone needs to stay here and keep an eye on what is going on," she said. "*You* are familiar with both the buildings and the people—"

"Not all the people," he interjected.

"Many of them. You will stay. I will go."

He was beginning to see the pitfalls of falling in love with a woman who was smarter and potentially more competent than he was. "If you take too long, I will come look for you," he said.

"You will not," she said. "If I do not return by sundown, you will go to the camp, but you will not come looking for me. Do you understand?"

"Sundown? Impossible. I cannot wait that long."

"Sanjay," she said, her voice mellowing in the way it did when she tried to point out the obvious. "There are many people counting on us now. If something happens to both of us, they will have no chance."

"I will not let anything happen to you."

"I know. And I love you for that. But do not come looking for me."

What else could he do but agree? Of course, that didn't mean he had to stick by the bargain. He looked down the alley again. Nothing.

Dammit. *Where are they?*

Kusum had gone to the furniture factory to fetch the three others who had come with her and Sanjay into the city. Given the situation at the Pishon Chem compound, it seemed a good idea because their help might be needed.

Patience, the voice of Kusum said in his head.

He moved across the room to the window on the other side. His hideout was an apartment in a building two blocks from the compound. Though the Pishon Chem facility was visible from the window where Sanjay was perched, he could see only the very tops of the Pishon Chem buildings and a small portion of the fence that surrounded the property.

He was supposed to be closer, had been closer, in fact, until just an hour ago when he'd returned to this meeting point, expecting to find Kusum and the others waiting for him. Seeing they weren't there, he didn't even consider going back to his former position.

On the roof of one of the compound buildings, he spotted one man in a UN uniform patrolling the top. It was disturbing to him how hard they were trying to sell the United Nations angle. Most survivors would arrive at the facility in a state of shock. If the soldiers were wearing jeans and T-shirts, and only had the letters UN hand painted on the sides of their helmets, people would believe them.

The sound of something scraping the ground floated through the window on the other side of the room. Sanjay quietly ran over and looked outside. The alleyway was no longer devoid of movement. At the far end was a man approaching along one of the walls, his movement odd, off-balanced.

It was another few seconds before he moved into a shaft of light.

Not just any man. It was Prabal, one of the people Kusum had gone to fetch.

He was limping, his right leg swinging carefully forward with each step. And running down the side of his face, a wash of blood.

WHILE IT HAD been disturbing enough moving through the seemingly empty city with Sanjay, Kusum found it downright terrifying doing so on her own as she made her way back to the camp.

The quiet was the worst part. Here she was in Mumbai, one of the largest and busiest cities in the world, yet there wasn't the sound of a motor, the cry of a child, the laugh of an adult. There was no music, either, something that been such an integrated part of the background noise that she noticed the lack of it now more than she'd ever noticed its presence.

Sticking to smaller streets and pathways, she was easily able to avoid the soldiers, seeing only a single group of three near the site of an old market. She hoped the same would be true when she and the others headed back to Sanjay.

The camp was set up in the courtyard of a small factory that had made and repaired furniture. Semi-organized piles of chair legs and tabletops and bed frames took up much of the courtyard space, but there was still plenty of room for Kusum's and Sanjay's friends to spread out. The best feature of the place was that it allowed them to hide from view if anyone passed by on one of the surrounding streets, while still having open air above them. If they needed shelter, there was plenty of that inside.

Kusum entered through a back door that led into a basement, where she took the stairs up into the main workshop. Along the interior wall was a large door that could be opened onto the courtyard, but whoever had left the business last had shut it and locked it in place—a hopeful act that he or she would return. She exited through the smaller door on the right and stepped into the outdoor space.

"Stop." The voice was low, the tone commanding.

"It is only me," Kusum said.

"Kusum?"

"Yes."

Darshana stepped from the shadows behind a stack of wooden planks, in her hand an iron rod. After she could see it was indeed Kusum, she lowered her weapon.

"Sorry, I did not realize it was you," she said.

"Never be sorry for this," Kusum said. "I could have been anyone. I would have been surprised if you had not greeted me like this."

Darshana tried to maintain a neutral expression, but Kusum thought she saw a flash of pride cross her friend's face. Though they were about the same age, Darshana and the rest of their survival group considered Kusum and Sanjay to be their leaders, and looked up to them more than Kusum thought they should.

"The others?" Kusum asked.

"Sleeping."

"We must get them up. I need you all to come with me."

"This way."

Darshana led Kusum around the piles of wood and metal to the open area where Prabal and Arjun were stretched out on thin blankets.

"Wake up," Darshana said, shaking first Arjun's shoulder then Prabal's. "Come on. Wake up. We need to go."

Prabal rolled onto his back with a groan. "What?" he asked, his eyes struggling to open.

"Kusum is here. She needs us to go with her."

Arjun raised himself on an elbow. "Kusum?" He looked

around as if he didn't quite understand, and then his gaze fell on Kusum. "Oh. Oh, Kusum." He sat all the way up. "I am sorry. I am…um…still…"

"It's okay," Kusum said. "Please get up and gather your things."

Arjun immediately began rolling up his blanket.

"What's going on?" Prabal asked, slowly sitting up.

"I need you all to come with me," Kusum said. "We found something and we might need your help."

"What did you find?"

Darshana shoved Prabal in the back. "You don't need to ask what. If Kusum needs us to go with her, we go."

"Of course, we go," Prabal said. "I was just wondering what we were going to. It was only a question."

"It is a stupid question," Darshana said. "We will find out when we get there."

As Prabal rose to his feet, he said, "It is *not* a stupid question. It is simply a question. Who are you to—"

"Please," Kusum said. "There is no need for this. Nothing is a secret here. We are going to a place close to the so-called UN survival station."

Prabal shot a see-it-wasn't-stupid look at Darshana.

"So-called?" Arjun said. "So it is not what they are saying?"

Kusum shook her head. "It does not look like it. Many of the people there are the same ones who were in charge of distributing the disease throughout the city."

"Are you serious?"

"It is even worse than that," she said.

"How worse?" Prabal asked.

"Survivors are coming in and being locked in holding areas."

"You have seen this?" Arjun asked.

"Yes. Not too long before I left, a group of four women arrived. Thirty minutes later they were led to one of the holding areas."

"What is going to happen to them?" Prabal asked.

"No way to know for sure, but I cannot imagine it is

good." She let this sink in for a moment, then said, "We need to go. There may be nothing we can do, but if there is, we need to be in a position where we can help them."

Darshana, clearly not needing to hear more, started repacking her bag. Within seconds, Arjun and Prabal were doing the same.

As they headed through the building, Kusum said, "Keep conversations to a minimum. There are soldiers patrolling the city. They will be dressed in UN uniforms, but I do not think they are really from the UN. We need to consider them dangerous."

"Perhaps we should leave all of this alone and go back to the school," Prabal suggested.

"If you want to return to the school, you can," Kusum said. She looked at the others. "Any of you can. But Sanjay and I will not leave these people in danger if there is a chance we can stop it."

"Do not worry," Darshana said, shooting a look at Prabal. "We are all coming with you."

"I was not saying I would not come," Prabal said. "It was merely a suggestion."

"Maybe you should keep your suggestion in your head," Darshana said.

"If anyone else has something to suggest, say it now," Kusum told them. "Once we go, you need to be quiet."

When no one spoke up, she led them out of the factory onto the street. From there, she kept to the same route she'd used on her trip to the camp.

She could tell the silent city was having its effect on the others. The looks on their faces were often wide eyed and shocked, as if this couldn't really be Mumbai but perhaps a replica or a movie set they had somehow wandered onto.

Their path took them through a dense residential section that had once been teaming with life, each place they passed no longer a home but a tomb.

"Please tell me we don't have to walk through something like that again," Prabal said, after they came out the other side.

Darshana twisted around and shushed him.

"No more like that," Kusum whispered. "But we are getting close now, so we need to be extra careful."

She led them down the street, keeping them tight to the buildings.

The roar of the motor seemed to come out of nowhere— one moment silence, the next a car engine revving to life only two blocks away. Kusum jammed to a stop, and pressed up against the shop they were passing. The others followed suit. Down the street, headlights popped on, pointing in their direction.

She glanced back the way they'd come. The businesses lining the street were smashed together, in a continuous wall with no breaks between them for at least a hundred meters. No way she and the others could make it down and around the end without being seen. Most of the entrances to the stores were flush with the wall, providing no place to hide.

Swinging her gaze back around, she focused on the cars parked at the curb only a few feet away.

"Down," she said, pointing at the ground near the vehicles.

As they ducked behind the cars, she was sure it was too late. The car with the headlights was already heading in their direction. She could almost feel the light touch her skin.

"Listen," she said quickly, and gave them an address. "That is the building we are supposed to meet Sanjay in. Third-floor apartment, number sixteen. Say it back to me." They each did. "If we have to split up, go there."

From the increasing growl of the vehicle's engine, she knew it was almost abreast of them. For a second, she thought maybe their luck would hold and the car would drive by, but a squeal of brakes and a drop in RPMs told her the problem was not going away so easily.

A clomp, clomp, clomp of feet hitting the road, but no sound of doors opening. *Strange.*

"Please come out," a male voice said. "We know you're there. We are here to help you, not hurt you."

Kusum looked back at her three friends and mouthed,

"When I say run, run."

They stared back at her, all three looking as scared as anyone Kusum had ever seen.

"It will be okay," she whispered.

"Come out now, please. If you are ill, we can treat you. If you are not ill, we can vaccinate you so that you will stay that way. We're here to help."

Kusum could see a question forming in Prabal's eyes, that perhaps whoever was out there was not as evil as Kusum and Sanjay thought they were.

"Stay down," she whispered, emphasizing her words by patting her hand against the air.

When she felt confident they would do as she said, she stood up.

"I'm here," she said.

Three armed soldiers stood in front of a roofless Jeep, the barrels of their rifles pointed at the ground.

"There were others with you," the nearest soldier said. From the sound of his voice, she knew he was the same one who'd called out a moment before.

"No. Only me."

"I saw others." He started walking toward her.

Kusum moved around the car and onto the street. "I'm the only one here."

She could see hesitation in his eyes, and knew he wasn't sure if he'd really seen anyone else.

"It would be a mistake to lie," he said. "We're only here to help."

Trying to sound both desperate and relieved, she said, "You are the first people—I mean, living people—I have seen in three days. Tell me, do you really have a vaccine for the flu?"

"Yes. It's back at the survival station."

"I did not think it was possible."

"If you'll come with us, we'll take you there," he said.

The last thing she wanted to do was get into the Jeep with them, but she didn't see how she had a choice. She was sure if she said no, they would force her to come anyway, and they'd probably search around the car to make sure she hadn't been lying. The only way to save Darshana, Arjun, and Prabal was to sacrifice herself.

She donned a relieved smile, and parted her lips to say, "Yes, thank you," but the words never left her mouth.

PRABAL KNEW HE was probably about to die. The men standing in the street were surely armed, and if what Kusum said was true, then the men would consider it no big deal to kill four more people after they'd already murdered millions, maybe even billions.

"Stay down," Kusum whispered.

Stay down? Of course, he was going to stay down. Standing up would be suicide, would be—

—exactly what Kusum was doing.

No! For a second he wasn't sure if he'd only thought it or said it out loud. He knew Kusum whispered something more, but he didn't hear what it was. In fact, he was having a hard time hearing anything other than the blood rushing past his ears.

Kusum, not content to make herself merely a stationary target, moved around the front of the parked car and out into the street where the men were. Again Prabal wanted to shout, "No!" as the voices of Kusum and the man who'd called out to them mixed together into an incoherent drone in Prabal's head.

You have to get out of here. You have to get out of here.

He tried to concentrate, to hear what was going on, but the warning booming through his mind was too loud.

You have to get out of here!

A hand clamped down on his shoulder. He jerked, thinking one of the men had sneaked up behind him, but it was Darshana. She was holding a finger to her lips, her face tense.

What did she mean? He wasn't making any noise. He'd be the last to make any noise.

You have to get out of here!

107

The voice was right. No matter how quiet he kept, the soldiers—they had to be soldiers, right?—were going to find him.

You have to get out of here! You have to get away!

Yes, away.

Now!

He ripped Darshana's hand from his shoulder, jumped to his feet, and began to run.

"Hey! You! Stop!"

Prabal didn't hear that, either, but it wasn't the blood in his ears that was masking the shouted words. It was the sound of his own scream.

THE YELL SURPRISED Kusum as much as the soldiers. Instinctively, she glanced over her shoulder.

Prabal was racing down the sidewalk away from them. Why he hadn't stayed hidden, she didn't know, but at the moment the answer was unimportant.

"Run!" she shouted. "Run!"

As soon as she saw Arjun and Darshana jump to their feet and take off, Kusum whipped around and started to run in the opposite direction.

"Stop them!" the main soldier yelled to his colleagues, pointing after Darshana, Arjun, and Prabal. Instead of going with them, though, he headed after Kusum.

Putting her head down, she sprinted to the next intersection and turned left, away from the survival station site.

"Where are you going?" the soldier yelled, still behind her. "We're here to help!"

If they had really been there to help, Kusum was sure that instead of chasing her and her friends, they would have remained by their Jeep, dumbfounded that anyone would flee their assistance.

The soldier must have realized the same thing, because he gave up the argument after another try, and focused his efforts on cutting the distance between them. Though Kusum was young, in good shape, and a better-than-average runner, she knew if she couldn't shake him quickly, his better stamina would win out.

The slums were the answer. All she had to do was race into the maze of cobbled-together homes and she could lose her pursuer. Unless her sense of direction was completely off, it would be to her left.

As she took the next corner, she heard the man's voice again, but it wasn't loud enough for her to make out his words.

Forget about him. Just run!

PRABAL DIDN'T REALIZE he'd been screaming until he turned onto the empty block and heard his own voice. He cut off the sound so abruptly that he swallowed spit down the wrong tube, and fell into a coughing fit until he was finally able to breathe halfway normally again.

The spasm had slowed his pace and caused him to momentarily forget why he was running at all—a reality that came rushing back in a flash as Arjun suddenly sped past.

"Keep going!" Arjun said. "They are right behind us."

Prabal took off after his friend.

"Darshana…Kusum…where are they?" he asked between breaths.

"Do not know," Arjun said. "Thought Darshana was behind me."

Prabal checked over his shoulder. No Darshana, but the two soldiers were a ways back, running after them.

"We have to hurry," he said. "They are only—"

Prabal's foot plunged into a basketball-sized pothole, his shin slamming into the side of the ripped asphalt, spilling him to the ground. While his chest and shoulder took the brunt of the impact, his forehead knocked against the pavement, opening a cut above his right eye.

Hands grabbed him under his arms and tried to pull him up.

"We have to keep going," Arjun said.

On his feet again, Prabal took a step and nearly fell back to the ground, the ankle that had gone into the hole howling in pain. Seeing his condition, Arjun tucked himself under Prabal's arm and swung his own around his friend's shoulder.

"As fast as you can," he said.

With Arjun's assistance, Prabal hobbled forward, but they both knew there was no way they would outdistance the soldiers now.

Arjun looked around, then said, "Over here."

He helped Prabal into an alley just wide enough for a car to pass through. About twenty feet in was a pile of rubbish—bags and loose trash and who knew what else.

"Hide in there," Arjun said, nodding at the waste.

"What?"

"Just hide. I will lead them away, then come back for you after I lose them."

The idea of crawling into the trash disgusted Prabal, but he didn't see how he had any other choice.

Arjun half carried him to the pile. "You can do it yourself, yes?"

"I think so."

"Good. Stay quiet. I will be back."

Before Prabal could say anything, Arjun took off down the alley.

Knowing he had very little time, Prabal dropped painfully to the ground and pulled several big pieces of trash on top of him. When he heard the soldiers' footsteps right around the corner, he stopped moving, hoping he was covered enough.

A particularly strong wave of pain rushed up his leg as the soldiers entered the alley. He gritted his teeth and squeezed his eyes shut to fight off the sensation. As the throbbing subsided, he realized that while he could still hear the men's running footsteps, they were already past the rubbish pile, fading away.

They hadn't seen him.

He was safe.

He wouldn't be taken away.

He wouldn't be killed.

He wanted to fling the debris off then and there, but what if the soldiers came back this way? Best, he thought, to stay as he was until Arjun returned, no matter how unpleasant the smell.

Between bouts of stinging pain, he listened as best he could for any approaching noise. For the longest time there was nothing, and then somewhere down the alley he heard something scratch or, maybe, tap the ground. He'd almost convinced himself it was just the breeze when he realized it was getting close.

Scratch-scratch-scratch. Pause. Scratch. Pause. Scratch-scratch-scratch.

Very close, actually.

When the odd sound was only a couple meters away, he realized what it must be.

He shoved the garbage away and jumped to his feet. His ankle screamed in pain, but he was too freaked out to pay any attention to it.

The scratching retreated several meters, but not far enough away that he couldn't see he'd been right.

Rats. Two big, ugly ones.

A shiver ran up his spine. If he hadn't moved, he was sure they would have tried to make a meal of him.

"Get away," he whispered through clenched teeth as he took a threatening step toward them.

The rats backed off another half meter, but apparently saw no reason to go into a full retreat.

Prabal took a breath and looked around. Where the hell was Arjun? More than enough time had passed for him to lose the soldier and return.

Had something happened to him? Had he been caught? Or maybe killed?

Prabal looked both ways down the alley, as if expecting soldiers to round each corner and close in on him like a vise. But except for the rats, he was still alone.

They'll be back, he thought with sudden certainty. *I can't stay here.*

Without a map, it would be hard to find the address Kusum had made them all memorize, but he knew it was close to the new UN compound—or, rather, *fake* UN compound. He wasn't excited about going in that direction, but his only other choice was to head out of town and try to find his way back to the boarding school.

Though Prabal could be an ass sometimes, he could, on occasion, pull himself together and do the right thing. It was why he'd volunteered to come on the mission in the first place. Sanjay would need to know what happened, and Prabal might be the only one left who could tell him.

He repeated the address once more, and then limped toward the end of the alley.

AFTER SANJAY HELPED Prabal up to the third-floor apartment, he listened to the man's story. As concerned as he had been before Prabal showed up, it was nothing compared to now.

"You do not know what happened to the others?" Sanjay asked.

"No."

"Not even if any of them were taken?"

"I am sorry. I wish I knew, but I do not."

"How long ago did this happen?"

"I am not sure. I must have lain in that alley for at least thirty minutes waiting for Arjun to return before I left. As you could see, I cannot walk very fast. I do know it was still very dark when I started."

Outside the sky had lightened with the imminent sunrise.

"One hour? Two hours?" Sanjay asked.

"I do not know."

It was clear Sanjay wouldn't get anything else of use. "All right. I want you to stay here in case someone else shows up," he said. "Can I trust you to do that?"

"Of course, but where are you going?"

"Where do you think?"

11

I WOKE UP two hours ago to a freezing room. My first thought was that maybe I had inadvertently brushed against the thermostat and turned the heat off. I wrapped myself in my blanket and walked over to check. The slider was set at 72° where I always leave it.

I stepped out into the hallway, thinking I could warm up there, but the hallway was just as frigid. It seemed the heating problem wasn't limited to my room. My first thought was that something had happened to the heater, and I would have to go down to the basement and try to fix it. Never mind that I don't know the first thing about heating systems or, well, pretty much anything mechanical. We all have our things, I guess. That's not one of mine.

I was so focused on the heater itself that I almost didn't realize the cause of the problem was right there in front of me. For safety purposes, a few of the hall's lights are always on. I have a feeling it's probably some kind of OSHA rule for dorms, or maybe apartment buildings—those kinds of places. You can't have residents tripping around in the dark. Only now, my hallway was exactly that. Dark.

I reentered my room, and saw that the digital clock on my desk had gone blank. Already fearing what I knew was going to happen, I flipped the switch for the room light. Nothing.

My floor had lost power.

Hoping that was the limit of the outage, I hurried down to the common room, and looked out at the dorm wings across from me.

Every day since I'd found out what was going on, I could see the flicker of televisions in many of the common rooms. For the first time, all the rooms were dark.

In the interest of telling the full story (though I don't know who I'm telling it to, will anyone ever read this?), I lost it there for a little bit. I guess at some point I sat down on the floor, because when I finally got ahold of myself, that's where I was, leaning against the window, my face cold and wet with tears.

I finally walked back to my room. I had this insane notion that if I just crawled into bed and shut my eyes and forced myself to sleep, when I woke again everything would be as it was. Not pre-plague; I couldn't hope for that much. But like yesterday and the day before that, when I was still alone but the power was on.

By the time I reached my door, though, I knew I couldn't afford to ignore the reality of my situation. The first thing I did was dress as warmly as I could. (Layers are your friend! That's what Mom always said.) I ate two cans of cold ravioli one of the other girls on my floor had left behind when she'd gone home for Christmas. Not the best breakfast in the world, but without the microwave to heat up some oatmeal, I couldn't be too choosy.

When I finished, I sat down at my desk and opened this journal. My thoughts have turned to what I should do now. The one thing I know for sure is that I can't stay here. This place is already unbearable enough. Another twenty-four hours of no heat and I'll probably be dead of exposure.

The easy answer (using the word easy *very loosely) would be for me to find a house nearby that, hopefully, still has power or, better yet, a generator. At the very least, one with a fireplace and a supply of wood that will last awhile. Here in Madison, that is/was pretty much a prerequisite for home ownership.*

The harder answer is Chicago.

I can't help thinking about the UN survival station there, and that if I don't start heading for it soon, I'm liable to be snowed in here until spring—if I survive that long. The problem is, the trip to Chicago could be just as dangerous. I could still freeze to death or run out of food or, I don't know, get attacked by a pack of dogs? (I've seen a few passing by the buildings.) But the prize at the end is so much better than the prize of staying here would be.

What's also tipping things in Chicago's favor is

that yesterday's storm passed through sometime during the night, and this morning the skies are blue and the wind is pretty much nonexistent. If I am *going to go, today would be a good one to start.*

It's a 150-mile trip. In a car, less than three hours. But without the roads being plowed, that's not really an option. So that means walking. I have no idea how long it would take. Days? A week? A month? Best probably not to have any goal in mind. Just walk what I can, rest when I need to, and get there when I get there.

I guess my mind's made up, isn't it? Better to die alone searching for others, than to die alone where no others may ever come again.

Work to do now. More later.

SHERIDAN, WYOMING
6:19 AM MST

BRANDON WOKE TO the sound of someone walking by the door to his family's motel room. He sat up and looked around. Both his father and Josie were still asleep. Given the last evening's excitement, he knew he should be, too, but he was done sleeping.

After changing into the cleanest clothes he had, he found a pad of paper in the drawer of the nightstand and jotted down a quick note:

> I'm right outside.
> Brandon

He left it on the nightstand, tiptoed to the door, and let himself out.

Though it was still dark, he could easily make out the clouds hanging over the town. The good thing was the storm seemed to have tapered off, only a few scattered flakes still falling. In fact, it had dissipated enough that he could now easily see the building on the lot next door, where all the action had been.

Hours earlier, when he'd scrambled to the top after Chloe, he hadn't even thought about its size, but this morning it looked huge. Pre-plague, Brandon probably wouldn't have climbed it in the dark, with a rifle, no less. Post-plague, Brandon would not hesitate to do it again, or whatever it took to protect his family and friends, even if it meant shooting someone else.

Rick, it turned out, was Ginny's cousin.

"My dad and Rick's dad were brothers," Ginny had told them once they were all back at the motel. Matt was the one doing the questioning, while several others—including Brandon, Josie, and their father—looked on. Rick was in another room having his missing finger treated by Lily while Dr. Gardiner finished with Chloe. "They owned Thorton's Equipment together."

"What happened to your parents?" Matt asked.

Ginny bit her lip, fighting back tears. "Mom and Dad, they...they died quick, day after Christmas." She paused for a second. "Uncle Jerry held on for a couple more days. He's the one who gave us the rifles. Told us to protect everything."

Brandon couldn't help but ask, "From what?"

"Looters," she replied. "Bad people. People who would make us sick."

"Did you ever have any looters?" Matt asked.

She shook her head. "We saw a few people walk by, a couple cars, but that was it. No one even tried to come through the gate."

"When was the last time you saw someone?"

"Before you?"

"Yeah."

She thought for a moment. "Three days ago...no, four now."

"So when you heard us..." Matt left the sentence unfinished.

"Rick thought you were type of people Uncle Jerry warned us about. He thought that if we shot in your direction for a while, we could scare you off. I wasn't so sure who you were. I was just..." Her tears started to flow. "We were only...I'm sorry."

Matt put a hand on her shoulder. "Hey, it's all right. I understand. We all do. You were doing what you thought you had to."

She looked like she wanted to believe him but was having a hard time. Brandon knew he should do something, but didn't know what. Josie didn't seem to have the same problem. She walked over to Ginny and put her arms around the girl.

I should have done that, Brandon thought at the time.

And now, as he remembered what Ginny had told them before they'd all finally gone to sleep, he had the same thought again. He wasn't sure why, but somewhere in the middle of her story, he had started to feel protective of her. Maybe it was because she was about the same age he was, or maybe it was because she'd done the same thing he would have done if their roles had been reversed.

He entered the motel lobby and walked over to the door behind the counter. Carefully, he opened it a few inches. There was just enough light for him to see the cellophane wrapper he'd shoved in the room the night before. While a few crumbs had been left behind, all the crackers were gone.

The cat whined.

Brandon nearly snapped the door shut in surprise. The animal was much closer than he expected, not more than a few feet behind the door. He reached into his pocket and found he still had a couple sticks of the string cheese he'd been snacking on during the drive yesterday. He peeled back the wrapper on one, but instead of tossing it inside as he first intended, he held the stick out so that it protruded beyond the edge of the door.

The cat made a sound that was part whine, part meow. Quiet for a moment, then the sound again, much closer.

"Come and get it," Brandon said. "All yours."

A low, audible whine, as if the cat really wanted the cheese, but couldn't bring itself to close the remaining distance.

"It's right here. All for you. Come on, kitty."

A silent standoff.

Finally, a nose topped by long tan fur peeked around the door. A sniff was all it took for the head to follow. The cat looked at the cheese, and then at Brandon. Another meow.

Are you going to give that to me, or what? That's what it sounded like to Brandon.

"Sure," he set the cheese stick on the floor and let go.

The cat looked at it again before taking two hesitant steps forward. It lowered its mouth, and nibbled at the end of the stick before it seemed to remember Brandon was there. It clamped down on the cheese and dragged it away from the door, out of sight.

Brandon pulled out the second stick, but before he could open it, he heard Josie's voice. It wasn't quite a yell, but it was plenty loud enough for him to hear his name. He pulled the apartment door closed so that whatever heat was still in there would remain, and headed for the door. When he stepped out onto the pathway, he saw Josie looking in the other direction.

"Brandon, where are you?" she said.

"Right here."

She twirled around. "Why did you take so long to answer me?"

"Because I just heard you."

"Where were you?"

"Why is that important?" While there was really no reason not to tell her, he didn't like the tone of her voice.

"I'm...because...never mind. Dad wanted me to get you."

"You could have said that first."

The door near the far end opened, and Matt stepped out. "You two done waking everyone up?" he asked.

"Oh, sorry," Brandon said.

"Sorry," Josie chimed in. "I was looking for my brother."

"It's all right," Matt said, laughing. "It's time we all got up anyway. Do me a favor and spread the word—meeting in my room in fifteen minutes."

BUTTE, MONTANA
6:54 AM MST

WHEN SIMS AND his team reached the junction of the I-90 and I-15 outside Butte the night before, there was no reason to set down. If any tracks had been left showing the direction the others had taken, the storm had completely obliterated them.

He ordered the pilot to continue on to Butte, where they found shelter for the night in a large house near the outskirts of town. They removed the bodies inside—a task that was nearly second nature at this point—and fell asleep on mattresses arranged around the fireplace.

Upon waking in the morning, Sims checked outside to get a sense of the weather. It was still snowing, maybe a tad less than the night before, but not by much.

"Dammit," he said under his breath.

It would be hours at the earliest before they could get underway again, and if the storm kept up like this, they might not be able to leave at all.

He pulled out his phone, knowing it was time to update the principal director.

12

RACHEL HAMILTON LEANED against the wall of the communications room, exhausted. Unlike the comm room in the Bunker back in Montana, the one at the Resistance's alternate headquarters, hidden in the Humboldt-Toiyabe National Forest, was a confined space where only three people could fit comfortably. At the moment, five were present.

If Rachel hadn't been the one in charge during her brother's absence, she would have slipped out into the comparatively fresh air of the narrow corridor. But since that was not currently an option, she ignored as best she could her growing sense of claustrophobia by focusing on the terminal Leon Owen was manning.

"There," Leon said, pressing the left side of his headphones closer to his ear. With his other hand, he tapped one of the arrow keys on his keyboard several times. "Got it. Much clearer now." He flicked another button, and suddenly static burst from a set of speakers on his desk.

Rachel leaned forward but it all sounded like white noise to her.

"There it is again," Leon said.

The other three nodded.

"Yeah," Crystal agreed. "Sounds like coordinates."

"Or a phone number," Dennis suggested.

Rachel frowned. "I don't hear a damn thing."

"It's very faint," Crystal said. "It took me a few seconds to pick it out."

Rachel smirked. "What you're really saying is that I'm old and my hearing sucks."

"You're not old," Paul said.

"Thanks for that."

The other four focused once more on the speaker, and Leon began jotting something down on the pad of paper by his keyboard. When he finished, they all looked at what he'd written.

Rachel tapped Dennis on the back. "May I see?"

"Oh, sorry," he said, and moved to the side.

Written on the top sheet was a twelve-digit number.

"Correct me if I'm wrong, but you need two sets of numbers for coordinates," she said.

"No, you're right," Leon replied. "This is the only one they've been repeating. I'm sure of it."

"So was Dennis right, then?" Rachel said. "Is it a phone number?"

Leon brought up a list of country codes. The number he'd written down started with 881, but the only codes on the list that began with 88 were 880 for Bangladesh and 886 for Taiwan.

"No 881," he said.

"Maybe you wrote it down wrong," Paul suggested.

Leon looked at him, annoyed. "Neither zero nor six sounds anything like one."

"Yeah, but there's a lot of interference," Dennis countered.

"Be my guest, then." Leon brought up the phone application on his screen and held out his headset.

"I'm just trying to look at all the angles," Dennis told him without taking it from him.

"We should at least try, don't you think?" Rachel said. "Leon, give it a go."

Leon didn't exactly scoff as he put the headset back on, but he came close. He dialed the number using the 880

Bangladesh prefix. It took only a couple of seconds before a series of tones came out of the speakers. These were followed by a message informing them in heavily accented English that no such number existed.

He tried 886 next. This time there was a delay of several seconds, but the number turned out to be another dead end.

Crystal's terminal began emitting a soft *bong-bong-bong*. She checked her screen. "It's Matt," she said as she donned her headset and clicked the ACCEPT button. "Hey, Matt. It's Crystal...she's right here. Hold on."

She gave her headset to Rachel.

"Are you back on the road?" Rachel asked her brother when the headset was in place.

"Not yet," Matt replied. His voice sounded as tired as hers must have sounded to him. "Had a little incident last night."

"What kind of incident?"

He gave her a quick rundown of what had happened.

When he finished, she asked, "Is Chloe going to be all right?"

"Just a few bruised ribs and a sprained wrist. Physically, she'll be fine."

"Physically?"

He hesitated a moment before replying. "Something happened to her while she was up there. I don't know how, but I think she's starting to remember."

Rachel almost asked, "Remember what?" when she realized what he meant. "You've told me yourself that's not possible."

"We don't know that for sure."

My God, Rachel thought.

She caught sight of Leon and the others. They all had their eyes on her, no doubt trying to figure out what Matt had said. "Hold on," she said into the mic, then put her hand over it. "Can you guys give me the room for a moment?"

Crystal looked at her terminal, obviously not comfortable with the thought of being away from it.

"If a message comes in, I'll come get you," Rachel

assured her.

"Okay," Crystal said. "Sure."

"No problem," Dennis said.

Leon stood up. "If you need us, we'll be right outside."

"Thanks," Rachel said. "Shut the door on the way out."

Leon looked disappointed, but he nodded and followed the others out.

Once alone, she said, "So what has she remembered?"

"Nothing definite. It's, well, the girl we found last night—she's about Brandon's age. Her name's Ginny. I think that might have triggered something."

Though Ginny was not Jeannie, the name was very close, and if the girl was Brandon's age...

Oh, Lord.

"What did she actually say?" Rachel asked.

"Nothing, really. It's more that she knows there's something there to remember." He paused. "I'm sure it's going to be fine. I'll keep a closer eye on her."

"My God, Matt. If she remembers, and starts to ask questions—"

"We'll deal with that if that happens."

"You need to keep me informed."

"I will, but like I said, it's going to be all right," he said. "Tell me where we are with the interventions."

She gave herself a moment to lock away her concerns about Chloe, and then said, "We've identified seven more groups overnight. And have told them we'll bring them vaccine, so most have agreed to stay where they are for at least another twenty-four hours."

"Can we get people to all of them in that time?"

"We think so. It'll be tight. One of the groups is in Nova Scotia. They're really itching to get over to the survival station in Montreal. I have a plane that can get to them after a stop in Pennsylvania, but I'm concerned the Nova Scotia group won't stick around." She paused. "Matt, people are really buying into the whole UN angle. A couple times we've even had to pretend we're with the UN, too. I don't like lying like that. Could be a problem for us later."

124

"If that's what it takes, then it's a problem we can live with," Matt said. "Have you heard anything from Tamara and Bobby?"

"She checked in yesterday," Rachel said.

"And?"

"They found the NSA monitoring facility."

"Thank God. Can they pull it off there?"

"Tamara says Bobby thinks so. He's got some of the equipment running, but he's having problems with the uplinks."

"He's got to get it working, and it needs to happen *now*."

"I know how important it is. They know how important. They're doing everything they can."

"I realize that, but it's….Listen, tell them the minute they're ready to go, they shouldn't wait for the okay from us. Just do it."

"All right. I'll tell them," she said. "How long until you get here?"

"The storm has really messed things up. We were able to tap into a NOAA satellite a little while ago. We're not getting hit too hard here anymore, but it's still pounding the Rockies and continuing to head south. I'm thinking we're going to need to dip down into New Mexico to get across, and it'll probably still be pretty slow going even then. If we can get to Nevada in three days, it'll be a miracle."

Rachel frowned. "Don't lie to me, Matt. I know what you're thinking."

"What are you talking about?"

"New Mexico?"

"Don't know if you've looked at any satellite images, but that storm's pretty bad."

"I know the storm is bad, but you'd be heading for New Mexico anyway, wouldn't you? That's why you want Tamara and Bobby to hurry up. You need their distraction."

In the silence that followed, she knew he was regretting showing her the message from C8.

"Matt, it's *too* dangerous. You don't have a large enough team. Besides, we haven't done the necessary recon."

"I've been there before," he said.

"A long time ago."

"And nothing will have changed since then," he said.

"Except that they won't be welcoming you at the door."

"You never know," he said, trying to make a joke.

"If you have to go through New Mexico, you damn well better stay to the north. Albuquerque straight into Arizona. Las Cruces is off limits."

"You've seen the message, Rachel. He's there. NB219. Cut off the head and the body dies."

"Bullshit. It didn't work at Bluebird. Why would it work now?"

"*Because* of what happened at Bluebird. They're already weakened. If they lose their second leader in a few weeks, it will rip them apart."

"Can you even imagine how much security he'll have in place?" she argued.

"Less than you think. In his mind, who's going to come after him?"

"Us."

"He doesn't even know who we are."

"He knows exactly who *you* are," she countered.

"That's not what I meant, and you know it. And as far as anyone at Project Eden is concerned, I'm buried in the past. Rachel, don't you see it? This could very well be the only chance we will *ever* get. They've pulled off their eradication plan; there's nothing we can do about that. What we can do is stop them from being the ones who benefit from it. Someone is going to have to lead the human race into this new age, but I'll burn in hell before I let it be any of them. Right now, they're still decentralized. It won't be long before this new principal director and his puppet directorate are buried beneath layers and layers of protection. We have to take advantage of this situation and you know it."

As much as she wanted to argue that point, she couldn't.

"Have you told the others?" she asked.

"Not yet."

"They might not be happy you kept it from them."

"I'll deal with it."

She rubbed a hand across her forehead, her eyes closed. "If you do this, you can't fail," she whispered.

"I have no intention of failing."

"That's not the same thing."

"I won't fail. Better?"

It wasn't.

WHILE THEY WAITED in the hallway that connected the comm room with the rest of the base, Leon, Crystal, Dennis, and Paul couldn't help but speculate on what Rachel and Matt were talking about. But any attempt to find out came to an abrupt halt the moment the door flew open, and Rachel, her face strained, strode out.

"How's Chloe?" Leon asked.

Rachel looked at them as if she hadn't expected them to be there. "Chloe? Um, she fell off a roof, but she'll be okay."

"How did that happen?" Dennis asked.

Rachel started walking away again, but went only a few feet before she turned back. "Have we heard from Tamara and Bobby this morning? Have they made any progress?"

The others all looked at Paul. He was the one who'd last spoken to the former PCN reporter and her cameraman.

"No contact yet today," Paul said.

"I need to talk to them as soon as possible."

"Uh, sure. I'll see what I can do."

Rachel walked off without another word.

"Now I really want to know what's going on," Leon whispered to Crystal as they filed back into the room.

Returning to their respective desks, they got back to work. For Leon, that meant trying to tease out what the series of numbers he'd written down from the radio message meant. Not coordinates. Not a phone number. A web address?

Though the Internet had become spotty, with many websites unreachable as servers began to malfunction, other sites still worked exactly as they had been designed to do. He typed the number into his browser and hit ENTER.

WEB ADDRESS UNKNOWN

Not a web address, then. At least not one that worked anymore.

Taking the shotgun approach next, he pasted the number in the box of a still functioning search engine, and clicked. He was presented with a long list of links, but none were direct hits.

He was running out of ideas fast, and was tempted to consider it a dead end. But someone out there had broadcast it, someone who was still alive. He had to exhaust every possibility.

That's when he realized he had never dialed the exact number he'd written it down, but only tried alternate country codes. Given that there was no 881, he was sure he'd experience the same failure as earlier, but in the interest of being thorough, he had to make the attempt.

He punched the numbers into his phone app.

No series of tones. No *call failed* message.

A ring.

He slapped Crystal on the arm.

"Hey! Watch it!" she said.

He turned on the external speakers just in time to catch the third ring.

"Who are you calling?" she asked.

"The number," he said, holding up the piece of paper.

"But it didn't work."

"I didn't try it exactly like—"

"*Hailo?*" A man's voice, tentative and surprised.

"Hello?" Leon said. "Can you hear me?"

"Yes. Can."

The person on the other end sounded older, with an accent Leon couldn't place yet.

"Were you broadcasting your phone number on the radio?"

"Yes! Yes! Radio. Number. Thank you, call."

"You're welcome. My name is Leon. Who are you?"

"Wait. Wait."

There was movement over the line, and then nothing.

"Hello?" Leon said. "Hello?"

"Are you still connected?" Crystal asked.

According to the computer, he was. He tapped the button that would record the call, something he should have done right away, and said to Crystal, "Go get Rachel back here. She'll want to hear this."

Crystal clearly didn't want to leave.

"She can't have gone far," Leon said. "Go and come right back. You won't miss much."

She rose with reluctance and headed out the door.

"Hello?" Leon said into his mic.

Still nothing from the other end. He double-checked to make sure his mute function wasn't on, and that the line was truly still connected, and everything was as it should be.

The sound started out so soft he wasn't sure he heard anything, but as it grew louder and louder, he realized he was hearing steps.

"Hello?" a new voice said. A woman this time, younger.

"Hello. My name is Leon. Who am I speaking to?"

"I am Jabala." She sounded excited. "So good to hear you."

"Good to hear you, too, Jabala. Where are you?"

"The St. William Boarding School."

"Where exactly is that?"

"I am sorry. I do not know the name of the town."

"Well, where is it near?"

"Oh, um, it is a few hours away from Mumbai."

"Mumbai? Mumbai, *India*?"

"Yes. India. Where are you? Are you close? Are there others with you?"

He pulled up the list of country codes again. India was 91, not 881. "No, no. I'm in, uh, the US. And not alone."

"I am so happy to hear that."

"How many are with you?"

"There are thirty-two of us now."

He pulled up the protocol sheet for first contact so he

wouldn't miss anything. The first question always made him pause. "Uh, how many of you are, um, sick?"

"Sick? You mean with the flu?"

"Yes."

"No one. How many of you are sick?"

He knew from experience gained over the last several days that some survivor groups had at least a few people starting to show signs of the disease, so he was relieved to hear Jabala's people were untouched. Still, she could have been hiding the truth. "We're okay here, too." Wanting to probe a bit further, he asked, "You've been able to avoid contact with anyone ill?"

"For the most part, yes. But we are safe. We have been vaccinated."

Leon could feel his chest contract. Vaccinated? Was this St. William Boarding School one of Project Eden's survival stations?

"Where exactly are you?" he asked.

"What do you mean? I have already told you."

"Tell me, Jabala, when did you receive the vaccine from the UN?" In his mind, he was already starting to write them off as future Sage Flu victims.

"The UN?" she said. "We did not receive the vaccine from the UN."

That stopped him for a moment. "Then who gave it to you?"

"My sister's husband, Sanjay. He stole it for us."

Leon's tension eased a bit. This Sanjay had probably gotten his hands on some kind of home remedy, or perhaps some antibiotics from a hospital. Neither would be effective against the virus, but they also wouldn't be as deadly as Project Eden's "vaccine."

"Maybe I should speak to Sanjay," he said.

"He is not here now."

"Okay, maybe I can talk to him later, but you need to listen to me very carefully. The people who are claiming to be from the UN are lying. They are not here to help anyone." Behind him, he heard Crystal enter the room. He glanced back and was surprised to see she was alone. "You need to stay away from them. In fact, you should stay away from Mumbai completely. It's not safe."

"We already know this," Jabala said.

Again, her response caught him off guard. "What do you mean, you already know?"

"Sanjay. He told us the same thing. It is why he and Kusum went to the city. To find out for sure."

"He and...Kusum are in the city?"

"Yes."

"That's very dangerous. They could get—"

"They are very careful. They know what they are doing."

Maybe, maybe not, but there wasn't much Leon could do to help them at the moment. "What made Sanjay think they were lying?"

"The UN people are using the same location as the company that spread the disease through our city," she began.

When she finished telling him about Pishon Chem and the "miracle mosquito spray" Sanjay and others had been hired to douse the city with, Leon realized that maybe the vaccine Jabala's brother-in-law had given everyone was the real thing after all.

"I definitely need to talk to Sanjay as soon as he comes back."

"I could send someone to bring him back."

"No!" he said quickly. "You shouldn't send anyone else to the city. It's too dangerous. The most important thing you can do right now is to stay alive, and that means you and your people should stay where you are. Do you understand?"

"Of course. Staying alive is what we are doing already."

"We're happy to count you among our new friends, Jabala. We can definitely help each other." Leon gave her a number that would connect her directly to the comm center. "Call that number anytime you want to talk to us. Someone will always be here to answer. And I'll definitely check back with you later."

"Okay. Thank you, Leon. It is good to have you as a new friend, too. Good-bye."

"Good-bye, Jabala."

Leon disconnected the call. After staring at his keyboard for a second, he looked over at Crystal, eyes wide.

"What?" she asked.

STATE OF MAHARASHTRA, INDIA
9:51 PM IST

JEEVAL WHIMPERED, WANTING to be lifted up, as Jabala set down the satellite phone.

"You are fine where you are," Jabala said. She wasn't as fond of the dog as her sister was, but while Kusum was away, Jeeval had become her responsibility.

"Well?" Naresh asked. He had been the one who'd figured out how to work the shortwave radio, and had taken to broadcasting a few times a day the number of the satellite phone Sanjay had found in a building the next town over.

"The man said the same thing Sanjay told us, that the UN is not the UN," she said.

"Sanjay did not tell us that. He said *maybe* not."

"Well, the man on the phone did not say maybe, so I think Sanjay's instincts were correct."

"Based on a conversation with someone you have never met," Naresh pointed out.

"I feel that he spoke the truth. You do not believe him?"

"I could not hear what he said, but if this is what he told you..." Naresh paused, and shrugged. "I believe him, too."

"Then why did you fight me?"

"I did not fight you. I merely pointed out something that needed to be taken into consideration."

Grunting in annoyance, Jabala looked away.

While she had been concerned when Kusum, Sanjay, and the others had left, she was extremely worried now. What if they ran into trouble with these people claiming to be with the UN? What if they needed help?

What if they needed help right now?

Ap, ap, ap, Jeeval barked, pawing at Jabala's leg.

"Jeeval, not now!"

She pushed the dog away harder than she meant to,

132

sending Jeeval tumbling backward into Naresh's chair. Jeeval yelped as she scrambled back to her feet.

Jabala immediately knelt down and stroked the dog's head. "I am sorry. Are you okay?"

A whimper, followed by *ap, ap.*

She picked up the dog. "Good dog," she said. With her free hand, she picked up the satellite phone and looked at Naresh. "How does this work?"

"A signal comes down, and—"

"No. That is not what I meant. Does this have to stay in one place, or can it move around like a mobile phone?"

"Of course it can move around. Do you see any wires?"

"Why are you being difficult? Does it have other equipment that needs to travel with it, or is this it?"

"What other equipment would it need?"

She bit back her frustration. "I will assume that the answer is no."

"Well, it does have a charger," he said. "The battery does not last forever."

"And where is that?"

13

"MY DAD WAS right," Rick said, his eyes narrowed to slits. "All you want to do is take what's ours."

The teenager was sitting on the bed of the motel room he and Ginny had been put in after the previous evening's events. Matt was surprised they hadn't tried to get away. Of course, if they had, they would have found one of Matt's men stationed outside.

"All we want to do," Matt said, "is get out of town. But the only way that's going to happen is if we clear the roads."

"So you're going to just take one of our snowplows." It was amazing how little the kid's lips moved as he spoke.

"*Two* of your plows," Matt corrected him. "And one of your cargo trucks to haul gas in."

Rick's uninjured hand unconsciously rolled into a fist. "They don't belong to you."

"That's why I'm asking."

"And if I say no?"

"That would be disappointing."

"You'll still take them, won't you?"

Matt stared at him, his expression neutral. "Rick, do you realize what's going on?"

"I know you're going to steal our stuff."

"I mean, the bigger picture?"

Rick glared at Matt for a moment before looking over at his cousin by the window.

"I asked a question," Matt said.

"Lot of crazy things going on."

"That's one way to put it." Matt adjusted his position on the end of the bed. "The human race is dying. There's not a lot of people left. If we're all going to survive, we're going to need to work together. So, yes, we will take those vehicles, but they will still technically be yours because the two of you are coming with us."

"Like hell we are," Rick said.

Matt leaned back. "So you'd rather stay here? What happens when you run out of food? Or don't have anything left to burn to stay warm? Maybe you make it through this winter, but what about the next? Any prepackaged food you'll find will have gone bad by then. You'll have to spend your entire summer growing food for when things get cold again. Do you know how to farm? Do you know how to store food so it will last the winter? Do you really want to bet your cousin's life on that?"

"We can take care of ourselves!"

"Can you?" Matt looked down at Rick's bandaged hand. "You're lucky we have medical personnel with us to take care of that. What happens when you're out in the field, using a piece of equipment you've never used before, and you slice open your leg? Or what if you get sick? I'm not talking Sage Flu. Out here, by yourself, pretty much anything could kill you."

Silence.

"Rick," Ginny said. "I think we should go with them."

"Shut up," Rick told her.

"I don't want to die," she went on. "He's right. We will if we stay."

"I said, be quiet!"

She took a couple steps toward the bed. "What if no one else comes by? This might be our only chance to get away."

"We'll be *fine* on our own!"

Ginny bit her lip, clearly not agreeing with him, but Matt could see the will to argue with her cousin—someone she'd been putting all her faith in up to this point—draining away.

"You won't be fine," Matt said. "Ginny knows it, and you do, too." He stood up. "But I'll tell you what. If you want to stay, you can stay."

"What about our vehicles?" Rick asked.

"Two plows, one cargo truck go with us. But we'll pay for them."

"With what?" Mick scoffed.

"I'll leave you a high-powered field radio. Maybe someday you'll want to try to reach someone."

"Doesn't seem like a very fair trade."

"You're right. It isn't. I could probably find a dozen plows within a mile of here, and twice as many cargo trucks. A good, working radio? That's what's hard to find. It's worth more than all your vehicles combined."

Though a sneer was still on Rick's face, there was also uncertainty in his eyes.

Matt held out his hand. "So, do we have a deal?"

"For something you'd take anyway?"

"I'd rather do it this way, man to man."

Rick looked at the proffered hand, and finally took it. "All right. It's a deal."

"Good." As Matt released his grip, he turned to Ginny. "If you have anything you want to bring along, you should go get it now. We'll be leaving soon."

"Whoa!" Rick said, jumping up. "Ginny's staying with me."

"You think so?" Matt asked. "Ginny?"

She looked from her cousin to Matt and back. "We'll die if we stay here," she said, her voice not much more than a whisper. "Rick, please."

"We've done fine so far," Rick said.

"For a *week*," Matt pointed out.

"We have to go with them," Ginny said.

Rick stood motionless for a moment. "Okay," he finally said. "That's fine. Go with them. I'm staying."

"What?" Ginny said. "No!"

"You want to go, you go. But I am staying." He turned to Matt. "When do I get my radio?"

BRANDON WAS MISSING yet again. They'd been packing up their things in their room when he said he had to check on something, and left. Josie ended up having to load not only her and her father's bags, but her brother's, too, into their Humvee.

When she returned to the room and he was still not there, that was it. Enough.

"Brandon!" she yelled as she stepped back out onto the walkway. "Brandon, where are you?'

Around her, the others moved in and out of the rooms as they prepared to leave. She asked a few if they had seen her brother, but no one had. She was about to start a room-by-room search when Brandon came out of the door to the motel office. In his arms was a blanket that appeared to be full of something.

She marched toward him. "What have you been doing? It's almost time to—" She stopped in the middle of the sidewalk and stared at him. "What happened?"

Across the right side of his jaw were two thin lines of blood. Scratches.

"What?" he asked.

She pointed at his face. "That."

He touched the wounds and looked at the blood on his fingertips. "Oh, uh, yeah. Nothing."

"Nothing? That's not nothing. Did you fall?"

"No. It's nothing. I'm o—"

The blanket he was holding began to twist as if something were squirming inside.

Josie took a quick step backward. "What have you got in there?"

Looking defeated, Brandon said, "I couldn't just leave him there." He peeled a portion of the blanket back, and revealed the head of a tan, very scared-looking cat.

"Where did you find him?" Josie said, moving in for a closer look.

"Chloe and I found him yesterday when we searched the motel," he said. "Please don't tell Dad."

"You think he's not going to notice?"

"I mean, don't tell him until after we get started. It'll be too late then."

Josie moved her hand cautiously over the cat's head. Its eyes followed the movement, but when she began stroking the area between its ears, it seemed to relax some.

"Fine," she said. "I won't say anything. But if he gets mad, I don't get in trouble for this."

Brandon smiled. "No, of course not. It's all my fault."

She petted the cat a few more times. "Does it have a name?"

"I don't know what it used to be called, but I was thinking Lucky would be good."

She smiled. "No kidding."

WHILE THE SNOWPLOWS were checked out and the cargo truck loaded up with canisters of gas, Matt had one of his men take a spare radio into the room Rick was in and show the kid how to use it. When everything was set, the whole group gathered in the motel parking area.

"You can still come with us," Matt said to Rick.

"I'm fine here," the teen answered quickly, as if he'd been rehearsing the response for an hour.

Despite Rick's words, Matt could tell the kid was terrified. "All right. You change your mind in the next four or five hours, give us a call on your radio, and we'll send someone back to get you."

Rick took a step back. "You'd better get going."

"Rick, come with us," Ginny said. "Please."

Her cousin shook his head. "No reason for you to stay here any longer. Go on. Get out of here."

He turned, walked back to his room, and shut the door.

Josie put an arm around Ginny. "Come on. You can ride with us."

Tears rolling down her cheeks, the girl let herself be led away. Soon the only ones standing outside were Matt and Hiller, one of his men.

Matt pulled a zippered case out of his pocket and handed it to Hiller. "Hopefully you won't have to wait long, but if it goes more than a couple of hours, use this."

"Yes, sir."

"There's vaccine in there, too. For after," Matt told him. "Be careful."

As Hiller hurried off, Matt walked over to his Humvee and climbed into the front passenger seat. They had quite a convoy now. Ahead of him were the two plows, and behind, the rest of the troop transporters and the cargo truck.

He grabbed the radio mic and clicked the talk button. "Let's move."

RICK PACED BACK and forth through the garage area of Thorton's Equipment Rental Center. In one of the bays was a pickup truck that had been in mid-repair when everyone started dying, and in another, a tractor with a busted axle. Tools and oil jugs and parts were scattered everywhere, all reminders that Rick was alone now, and that the only one who could finish fixing any of the vehicles or could put everything away was him.

You screwed up big time, he told himself.

What the hell had he been thinking? Stay here? Alone? That was suicide. But even if the others had still been out front, pride and the words his father had said not long before dying would have prevented him from taking the offer.

"You're in charge now," his old man had told him. "You need to take care of things."

He'd already messed that up, hadn't he? Ginny was gone. She was family. He was supposed to take care of her. He wanted to be pissed off at her for defying him, but did he honestly think she would have been safer here with him?

No. Not even close.

He'd always thought being a grown-up would be so easy. No one to answer to. All the decisions his own. And yet here he was, with the freedom he'd been hoping for, and he just wanted to go back home, curl up under his covers, and stay there forever.

He wanted to be a kid again

He wanted things back to normal.

At some point he realized he'd been crying, but he couldn't stop. Back and forth he paced, his mind in turmoil as the minutes turned to hours.

"All right, that's enough. You're making me dizzy, kid."

Rick thought the words were only in his head until the man stepped out from behind the damaged tractor. Even as the man walked over to him, he couldn't quite process what he was seeing. The man was alone, but...

"Hey!" Rick said, trying to jerk away as the man stuck a needle into his arm.

But the guy grabbed him with his other hand and held him in place. "Sorry about that. Was really hoping you'd decide to follow my friends on your own. Could have avoided this."

"What?" Rick was suddenly dizzy, and while he heard the man's words, he couldn't quite understand their meaning.

"It's all right. Here, let me help you down," the man said.

Before Rick realized it, he was sitting on the concrete floor.

"What are you doing?" Rick asked, the words feeling heavy in his mouth.

The man had another needle in his hand and was moving it toward Rick's arm.

"You don't want to get sick, do you?"

The prick of the needle stung less than the one a moment before. Still, Rick wanted to brush it away. He tried to raise a hand, but apparently it was content to stay in his lap.

"Sorry for all this," the man said. "But we couldn't let you die out here."

Rick closed his eyes and put a hand to his forehead as the world began to sway.

"Just relax," the man told him. "Here."

Rick was moving backward, slow and steady. When he opened his eyes again, he was staring up at the ceiling.

"Let it take you," the man said.

140

Take me? Rick thought. *Take me where?*

"Close your eyes."

As if acting on their own, his lids slid shut, and everything went black.

"Sleep."

Once more, the power of suggestion worked its magic.

HILLER CHOSE THE best of the last three remaining snowplows on the lot, loaded the kid into the passenger seat, and headed south. Between them was the portable radio Matt had never intended to leave behind.

When they reached the interstate, Hiller turned on the radio, checked to make sure it was set to the right frequency, and picked up the mic.

"Retrieval to M1," he said. "Retrieval to M1."

Matt's voice jumped out of the speaker only seconds later. "This is M1. Go, Retrieval."

"En route. Had to go active."

"That's too bad. Glad you're on the way, though. Wait for you at checkpoint three."

"Copy. Checkpoint three."

TWO HUNDRED MILES to the west, on board the Project Eden helicopter that was now flying in a parallel southward direction, the copilot, charged with monitoring radio transmissions, picked up the faintest of voices, hearing words like "is" and "route" and "bad" and "three." The static was so bad, though, he couldn't tell if it was one voice or two.

As he tried to fine-tune his reception, the transmission ceased. He hunted around, hoping to pick it up again, but there was nothing.

Since he had no idea what was being said, and no way of knowing which direction it came from, he decided not to disclose the information to Sims and the others. If he did, he was sure his boss would order them to search for the source, a task that would only succeed in keeping them through the storm.

Better to keep heading south. In a few more hours, they'd be in the relative warmth of New Mexico.

14

MARTINA KNEW IT was a bad idea before she tried it. But she also knew, if they were ever going to get on the road again, the first step would be to open her eyes.

Thankfully, she had had the sense to close the curtains before toppling into bed after their New Year's Eve celebration. If not, she'd have been permanently blinded by the sunlight.

Dear God, her head hurt.

How much had she had to drink? Three glasses of champagne? Or was it four? Could her head hurt that much from only four glasses? She had no idea. She hardly ever drank, and quite possibly never would again.

Maybe it had been more than four. She had a fuzzy memory of someone—Noreen, she thought—suggesting they walk back to the liquor store for another bottle when they ran out, but she had no recollection of actually doing so.

What was it her college roommate Crissy told her? "For every glass of alcohol, drink a glass of water. That's the secret."

Well, Martina had drunk absolutely no water the night before. That was one thing she did remember. Though it would be hours too late, she could probably use some now.

She flopped her legs off the bed and sat up. Immediately, she froze as her stomach did a complete somersault, threatening to disgorge everything it held.

"Please don't, please don't, please don't, please don't," she said under her breath.

When the tumult in her abdomen eased, she tried slowly rising to her feet. The trip to the bathroom was made in a series of step-pauses that probably would have looked hilarious if she had not been the one doing it. There had been a glass on the sink the evening before but it wasn't there now, so she cupped her hands and fed water straight from the tap into her mouth.

The first couple gulps went down with relief, but the third was a mistake. She barely lifted the lid off the toilet before the water and the rest of her stomach contents made a quick, loud exit.

When she was through, she felt better. Even her headache had eased. Though she was apprehensive, she knew she should drink some more. This time she stopped at the two gulps and was relieved when they seemed to stay down.

Thinking a shower would help even more, she stripped off her clothes and climbed in. She was pleased to find the motel's water heater still worked. Standing head bent under the warm stream, she let the water pound into her neck and shoulders for several minutes before washing herself. When she finally climbed out, she actually felt, if not exactly normal, 65 to 70 percent there. She toweled off, carried her dirty clothes into the other room, pulled out something clean from her bag, and got dressed.

Though she knew she'd been making a lot of noise, both Noreen and Riley were lying exactly as they had been when Martina had gone into the bathroom. She tiptoed to the door adjoining the two rooms and peeked inside. Craig was still out, too.

Well, this was going to be fun. "Happy New Year, everyone," she said in as loud a voice as her head would allow her. "Time to get up!"

"THE ROSE PARADE," Noreen said.

All four of them were sitting around the same table at

Carl's Jr. they had used the night before. Martina had found some frozen sausages and hamburger buns in the back, and had been able to get enough of the kitchen gear working to warm everything up.

At first, no one wanted to touch the food, but after the initial bites were taken, everyone devoured his or her portions and asked for more.

"What about it?" Riley asked.

"I missed it. It's always over by now."

Martina eyed her friend wearily. "Noreen, I'm fairly certain there was no parade this year."

For a moment Noreen said nothing, lost in melancholy. "I know that. It's just kind of a tradition. Mom and I would always get up early on New Year's Day and watch."

"It's just a boring parade," Craig said. "You're not missing anything."

Martina and Riley turned on him, glaring.

"What?" he asked.

"Were you born an idiot?" Martina asked.

"It's okay," Noreen said. "He's right. It is boring. *Was* boring. The last couple of years Mom had to force me to get up with her." Her gaze drifted out the window. "I really wish she'd had to do that today."

Martina thought her friend would start crying, but Noreen's eyes remained dry.

"Let's finish up," Martina said. "We're closing in on noon. I'd hoped we'd be on the road for a couple hours by now, at least."

"Have you decided which way we're going?" Riley asked.

Martina nodded. "To the coast, I think. If Ben heads south, that's the way he'd come."

SANTA CRUZ, CALIFORNIA
10:10 AM PST

BEN SPENT ONE last night in the house he'd grown up in. Maybe he'd come back. Maybe he'd never see the place again. He wasn't sure which he preferred. He just knew at that

145

moment the place held nothing but memories of death and loss.

South was where he wanted to go. South to the desert, to Martina.

What happened after he found her, they could figure out together.

He loaded up his Jeep with supplies and clothes and camping gear. As he walked through the house for the last time, he considered grabbing photo albums and mementos, but, in the end, the only thing he took was a framed family picture of the five of them. It had been taken at a neighbor's barbecue. Nothing fancy, just his mom and dad on one side of a wooden picnic table, and he and his sisters on the other. A quick "look at the camera and smile" kind of thing, but his mother had always loved the shot, had said more than once it was her favorite.

Climbing into his Jeep, he tucked the photo under the front seat and started the engine. He had to force himself not to look at the house again. If he did, he knew he would probably be sitting there all day. So he kept his eyes forward, shifted into gear, and pulled into the street.

Even though it had been days since he'd seen anyone else moving around, it was still surprising to be the only one driving down the freeway. Here and there he'd pass abandoned cars, most pulled over to the side, but a few left in the middle of lanes.

A straight drive to Ridgecrest would be, at most, an eight-hour trip, but he wasn't going straight there. He needed to make a stop at his place in Santa Cruz.

As he moved out of the city and into the hills, he turned on his radio. Like always, it automatically synced with the phone in his pocket, and began playing the song it had left off with last. In this case, Green Day's "American Idiot." He dialed up the volume and blasted it. It was something he would have never done in the past, but who would care now?

Thirty minutes later, as he entered the city of Santa Cruz, the Arctic Monkeys gave way to Adele singing "Someone Like You." The song was too maudlin for his current mindset, so he reached toward the radio, intending to skip to the next track.

His finger had barely touched the button when something darted into the upcoming intersection.

"Oh, crap!"

He slammed on the brakes, the tires squealing and the Jeep shimmying from the sudden deceleration. For half a second, he thought the back end was going to swing around and he'd flip over, but he was able to keep control and bring the vehicle to a stop.

Ten feet.

That was all that separated his front bumper from the large, brown horse that had run in front of him. Instead of continuing on its way, the animal stopped in the middle of the road, looking at him much like he was looking at it, as if neither could believe the sight of the other.

A bray, not from the horse in front of him, but from back the way horse had come. A moment later a second horse and then a third ran into view, both nearly as big as the first. Behind them a fourth jogged out, this one clearly younger, half the size of the others. Dark gray halters were strapped around each of their heads and noses. The second horse had a dangling rope that looked like it had been cut so it wouldn't drag on the ground.

The three joined the first on the street, and as a group they continued on.

Ben sat there, parked in the middle of the road, watching in near disbelief until they passed out of sight. Had their owner, knowing he or she was about to die, used a last bit of strength to let them go?

Ben suddenly realized there must be other horses trapped in stables and corrals, unable to get free and forage for themselves. Not just horses—goats and cattle and sheep. Dogs and cats, too, locked in backyards and houses. He had thought about nothing but his family and Martina since the outbreak had begun, hadn't considered what had happened to all the animals that relied on humans to survive.

He looked around and saw several houses down the road

the horses had come from. Were there animals in them? Should he check?

It was a Pandora's box, he realized. Check one and he'd have to check the next and the next and the next. He made a pack with himself. Any home he came close to in the course of doing something else, he would open a door, or, if it was locked, bust out a window. If there was anything inside, it could then come out if it wanted to.

As the adrenaline that had coursed through him began to subside, he started to laugh.

A horse. He was the only driver on the road and he'd nearly run into a horse. That was not something that happened every day.

THE APARTMENT BEN rented was a small, one-bedroom place over the garage of a house about a mile from the university. His landlords, the Tanners, were a newly retired couple who had treated Ben like one of their family, often inviting him down for dinner.

As he pulled into the driveway, he wondered if they had survived. Probably not, but at least their bodies wouldn't be inside the house. They had gone to their daughter's place in Los Angeles for the holidays before all this had begun.

Instead of parking in his usual spot, he drove all the way up to the garage and pulled around the side where the stairs leading up to his place were located. The moment he shut off the engine, he was enveloped once more in the near silence that had taken over his world. The sound of leaves rustling in the trees, the squawk of a distant bird, but that was it.

He headed up the stairs, anxious to get back on the road. The main room of the apartment served as living room, dining room, and kitchen. A small bathroom was directly opposite the front door, and taking up the back half of the available space to the right was the bedroom.

He headed to the latter and went straight to his dresser. The item he'd come for was tucked in the bottom drawer. He moved a pile of sweaters to the side and pulled out the box.

Palm-sized and only an inch thick, it was wrapped in red Christmas paper, with a white bow on top that was bigger than the box.

Martina's Christmas present—a pair of small but brilliant diamond earrings. They had cost him more than he had intended on spending, but they were perfect.

It was ridiculous, really, coming back here for this. He could have stopped at a hundred places on his way to Ridgecrest, and picked out something ten times as nice for free now. But he had chosen this, had *paid* for it himself. To him, that meant something more.

After he slipped the box into his jacket pocket, he grabbed his favorite sweater, a couple T-shirts, and his UC Santa Cruz hoodie before heading back outside. He stuffed everything into the duffel that had the most room, and was about to climb back into the driver's seat when he remembered the promise he'd made not fifteen minutes earlier.

He looked down the driveway. The Tanners didn't have any pets, so he didn't need to worry about their place, but he knew some of the neighbors did.

Three houses in either direction and the ones directly across the street, that's it, he told himself.

The people right next door had one of those small dogs, a Yorkie or something like that. It was a yappy thing that had kept Ben awake more than once. He went there first. The front door was locked, so he let himself into the backyard and tried the sliding glass back door. It was also locked. He found a gardening trowel and used the butt of the handle to smash the window.

He didn't bother calling the dog. If it was there, it would find its way outside. Returning the way he'd come, he almost shut the gate before realizing that would be almost as confining as leaving the animal in the house, so he propped it open and moved on to the next place.

Over and over he repeated this procedure. He found some doors unlocked, but most of the places required a window to be broken. Limiting his range to only three houses on either side proved to be impossible, however. His conscience wouldn't let him stop until he reached the end of the block.

He finished up and headed back toward his apartment, not really sure how much good he'd done. Not once had he seen a pet wanting to get out. Still, he was glad he'd made the effort.

He had just turned onto his driveway when he heard something in the distance that sounded like a voice. He twisted around and looked down the street. No one there.

He was probably hearing things. A few times back in San Mateo, as he cared for his dying sister, he'd thought he'd heard voices, too, but every time he'd investigated, he'd found nothing.

Wishful thinking then, and wishful thinking now.

He turned back toward his Jeep and started walking again.

"Help!"

That was no wishful thinking.

He turned in a circle, trying to figure out where the voice had come from.

"Please! Help!"

To the right. A woman's voice.

Ben raced up the driveway to his Jeep, jumped in, and backed it out to the street. At the first intersection, he turned right in the general direction toward the voice. Then he threw the engine into neutral and popped up on his seat.

Cupping a hand around his mouth, he yelled, "Where are you?"

"Oh, my God! Can you hear me? Please, get me out of here!"

The voice was closer than he expected, again to his right somewhere.

"I don't know where you are!" he shouted. "Keep yelling!"

"I'm over here! Please help me! Get me out of here!"

Ben drove slowly forward, zeroing in on her voice.

"Are you there? Hello? Don't leave me here!"

As he came abreast of a tired-looking Cape Cod place, he rolled to a stop.

"Am I close?" he yelled.

"Here! I'm right here!"

Her voice was coming from between the Cape Cod and a ranch-style house on the other side of it. He killed the engine and jumped out of the Jeep. As he ran across the front yard, he yelled, "I'm coming!"

"Oh, thank God! Thank God!"

He nearly slipped on the grass as he skidded around the corner. About fifteen feet back, a tall wooden fence stretched between the two houses.

"Which house?" he asked.

"What do you mean, which house? This one! Please help me!"

Her voice was coming from behind the Cape Cod. The gate was locked, so he pulled himself over the top, and dropped onto a concrete patio on the other side. She wasn't in the side yard, so he moved around the corner and came to an abrupt halt. She wasn't in the backyard, either. What the hell?

"Where did you go?"

"I didn't go anywhere. I'm right here."

The voice seemed to have come from almost directly behind him. He whirled around.

Low on the back of the house was a basement window, broken and barred on the outside. Looking out of it was the woman. She had a dirt-stained face and a head of tangled brown hair, and looked to be in her mid-twenties.

"Oh, thank God, thank God, thank God," she said, spotting him. "Please, help me."

"Are you trapped down there?"

"Yes! Yes! I can't open the door."

Ben looked around for an outside entrance to the basement, but didn't see any. He would have to go into the house. "Hold on. I'll be right down."

He needed to smash a window to unlock the back door, but he didn't think the woman would mind. The smell of death hit him the moment he stepped inside. He clapped a

151

hand over his mouth and nose, and had to blink a few times as his eyes watered up. After his vision cleared, he scanned the interior.

To the right was a kitchen, and to the left, a space that would've probably been considered a family room. The only furniture, though, was an old couch and a wooden coffee table. Both the furniture and the rooms looked dated but well maintained.

No basement door, though.

He moved into a hallway. The smell was stronger here, and seemed to be coming from the left, so he went right. He didn't have to go far before finding himself in a living room where the spartan décor continued—in this case, two chairs, another coffee table, and a magazine basket, the latter filled but neat. Again, no entrance to the basement.

Tightening his grip on his face, he returned to the hallway and began opening doors. The first two led to a bathroom and an understocked linen closet. When he opened the third door, he found a room that, unlike the rest of house so far, was fully furnished—a bed, a nightstand, a dresser, a desk, and a full bookcase. The walls were covered with pictures and posters, most of which featured an early-twenties Justin Timberlake. It was obvious this had been a teenage girl's room.

He moved on. Only one door was left, the one hiding whoever had died. Ben pulled it open, already sure it wouldn't be the door to the basement, but he had to check. Sure enough, it led into a second bedroom.

This one, apparently, had been the master. A simple dresser sat against one wall, and a queen-sized bed against the other. The body of a middle-aged man was on the bed, half covered by a blanket. In a rare break from the cleanliness Ben had seen throughout the house, used tissues were scattered on the carpet.

Ben blinked to keep his eyes clear as they watered up again, and scanned the room, looking for a basement door he knew wouldn't be there. The only things he saw were three pictures hanging on the wall, family portraits of a man, a woman, and a girl. In the oldest one, the girl was maybe twelve or thirteen, and in the most recent, probably almost out of high school. The man was definitely the guy in the bed.

"Hey! What's going on?" The floor muted the woman's voice, making her hard to understand.

Ben hurried out of the bedroom and yelled, "I can't find the basement door!"

"It's just off the kitchen!"

"I didn't see it."

"Come on! Get me out of here!"

The only thing just off the kitchen was a laundry room consisting of a washer, a dryer, and a closet half filled with neatly arranged cleaning supplies.

He started to close the closet.

"Did you find it?" the woman yelled.

Instead of being muted by the floorboards this time, her voice seemed to be coming through the closet. He ran his hand across the back and found a latch. As he pulled it up, the whole back wall moved out of the way. Someone had gone to great lengths to hide the door.

"Found it!" he shouted as he headed down the steps.

At the bottom, he was confronted with another door, this one metal. He tried the knob, but it was locked.

"Open it," the woman said from the other side.

"It's locked from this side. You can't open it from there?"

"Do you think I'd still be down here if I could?"

"Well, I can't kick it down. It's too strong." He turned for the stairs. "Maybe I can find a crowbar or something. I'll be right back."

"No, don't leave me!"

"I'll just be a minute." As he headed up, he wondered how long she'd been there. A couple hours? A day? Two?

Reentering the laundry room, he knew there was an easier solution than hunting for something he could break down the door with. There had to be keys somewhere. The problem was, the most likely place they'd be was with the dead man.

Overcoming his reluctance, he went back into the bedroom. The search was mercifully quick. In the top drawer of the dresser, he found a set of keys sitting next to a wallet, and was back at the basement door in no time.

Half a dozen keys were on the ring. The one that worked was the fourth he tried. As he pushed the door open, the woman rushed past him, knocking him to the side.

"Come on," she said as she started up the stairs. "We need to leave before he comes back."

"Before who comes back?"

She paused on the steps, hesitating, "Um, my, uh...Mr. C-C-Carlson."

She started heading up again.

"Wait," Ben said. "What does he look like?"

She looked back at him. "What?"

"What does this Mr. Carlson look like?"

"Doesn't matter. We need to get out of here."

"Tell me."

She shot a look toward the top of the stairs as if expecting someone—Mr. Carlson, no doubt—to be standing there. When she looked back at Ben, she gave him a quick description that perfectly matched the dead man in the bed.

"How long have you been down here?" Ben asked.

"Please, can we talk about this someplace else? I can't stay here any longer."

Not waiting for him to respond, she raced up the rest of the way and disappeared into the first floor of the house.

Before heading after her, Ben glanced into the room where she'd been. It was not what he expected. Modern, a big TV, a large bed, a sitting area, even a refrigerator. The kind of apartment a college kid could only dream about.

Resisting the urge to go in for a better look, he ran up the stairs. It wasn't hard to tell which way the girl had gone. The front door to the house was wide open. When he stepped outside, he spotted her in the middle of the street, not far from his Jeep, staring at the house.

"Is this your car?" she asked as he neared her.

"Yeah."

"I need you to get me out of here, okay? Before he comes back."

"What's your name?"

"Me? Uh, Iris. Are you going to take me or what?"

"I'm Ben," he said. "Iris, Mr. Carlson isn't coming back."

"How the hell would you know that?"

"When was the last time you saw him?"

"I don't know. A few days ago."

"Is that how long you've been in the basement?"

"Not even close."

"How long?"

"I don't know," she said, defensively. "Why is this important?"

"Has it been more than two weeks?"

"Yeah. I think we can safely say that."

"Iris, Mr. Carlson's dead."

"Bullshit."

"No, I'm serious. He died of the flu." Ben gestured toward the other houses. "Everybody did."

Her lips parted in a wary grin as she backpedaled. "Right. Everyone's dead."

"They are," he said, matching her step for step. "Just listen. Do you hear any cars? Any voices? Today's New Year's Day. It's beautiful outside. Don't you think there should be people in their yards? At least some kids playing?"

She pointed at him. "Stay right where you are."

"I'm not trying to scare you, but it's the truth. Look around. We're the only ones here."

"I swear, don't you take another step."

He stopped. "I don't know what happened to you in there, but Mr. Carlson *is* dead, and you don't need to worry about him anymore. You're all right. He can't do anything to you now." He nodded back at the house. "He's lying in his bedroom. Been dead for days."

"Oh, I get it. This is some kind of mind game, right? You're one of...Mr. Carlson's buddies he always talks about, aren't you? You're trying to screw with me."

"The only thing I'm trying—"

Before he could finish, she turned and sprinted down the block.

"Help!" she yelled. "Help me!"

Ben stood there for a moment, stunned. He had obviously handled that poorly. The question was, what should he do now? Let her run off and figure things out for herself?

Like you could do that.

With a groan, he took off after her.

15

SANJAY COULD SEE Darshana, Arjun, and Kusum sitting together in the middle of one of the fenced-in confinement zones within the walls of the survival station. Though they were too far away for him to see any cuts or bruises, they didn't appear to have any obvious injuries.

After Prabal had shown up that morning, Sanjay had spent as much time as he could searching for the others before the sun rose too high, and then worked his way back to the building where they were supposed to rendezvous. For hours he hoped Kusum and the others had been able to find someplace to hide, and were simply waiting for night to make their escape, but then, not long after three p.m., he spotted Arjun being transported in the back of a UN-labeled truck.

Sanjay had hurriedly worked his way back to the building he had used earlier to spy on Pishon Chem. From there, he watched as Arjun was escorted into one of the holding areas, where he was greeted by an already captured Darshana. The only good news was that Kusum appeared to still be free.

Knowing he had to risk being seen, he moved back into the city to search for her, ducking into whatever hiding spot he could find every time he heard soldiers nearby. Right before six p.m., several cars raced past on an adjoining street and screeched to a halt a few blocks away. Sanjay moved down an alley until he reached a building close to the spot where the cars had stopped. Using the stairwell just inside, he made his way to the roof, and positioned himself so he could look down on the street.

No!

Kusum was backed against a parked car, facing four UN-clad soldiers.

Her voice drifted up to Sanjay. "I did nothing wrong. You should not treat me like this. I am already heading to your survival station."

"We are merely offering you a ride," one of the soldiers said.

"From the way you are acting, I do not think I want your ride."

"It is only a precaution. I must insist."

"And I am telling you no."

Sanjay looked from one soldier to the next, wishing he could do something. But even if he had a rifle and knew how to shoot it, he wouldn't be able to get all of them before they did something to Kusum.

"You can either walk to the car, or one of my men will carry you," the soldier said.

The back and forth went on for a few more minutes, but ended with the inevitable—Sanjay watching as his wife was driven away.

The rest of the evening he'd spent watching the compound. For the longest time, there was no sign of Kusum. Finally, thirty minutes earlier, she'd been led out of the main building, into the same fenced area where Arjun and Darshana were.

Sanjay was convinced whatever the fake UN personnel had planned for them wouldn't be good, and knew he had to get them out. In fact, if possible, he had to get all the prisoners from both holding areas out, too.

In his favor, he'd spent a lot of time at the compound when he'd worked for Pishon Chem, had even lived at the on-site dormitory, so he was very familiar with the layout. There were three official entrances in all: the front and back gates, and a door along the perimeter wall across from the administration building.

Unofficially, one could always try going over the wall, but the broken glass cemented across the top would make that very difficult. There was, however, another way, also unofficial—a way that had the additional benefit of being located in a remote, seldom used part of the compound. It was an area where previous tenants had dumped things like wooden crates, old machinery casings, rusty empty barrels, and worn tires. Sanjay had no idea how long the junk had been there. He just knew the Pishon Chem people had left it untouched. Behind the piles of rubbish, a dip in the ground near the base of the wall had eroded from years of monsoons until the bottom of the wall had been exposed, and a channel to the outside created. Without much work, Sanjay figured he could widen it enough to get through.

How he would get everyone out the same hole in a timely manner, he'd figure out later.

Right now, he needed to concentrate on getting in.

KNOWING HER PARENTS would forbid her if she told them what she intended to do, Jabala sneaked away from the school, pushing one of the motorcycles they had obtained, until she felt she was far enough away that she could start the motor without anyone hearing it.

She took with her only four items: a large bottle of water, a flashlight, the satellite phone with its charger, and a backpack to carry them all in. After talking to Leon from America, she knew, despite his warning, she had to go to Mumbai. It seemed he had valuable information about the survival stations that Sanjay and Kusum needed to know now. Waiting for them to return might be too late. Anything that would lessen the danger her sister and brother-in-law were facing was worth the risk of the journey.

She didn't let the fact that she didn't know exactly where they were deter her. She was aware of what part of town they would be in, and was confident she could find them.

So she rode into the night, only her bike's headlamp lighting the road in front of her. Everything else was blanketed in an unnerving darkness. To keep her mind off what might be out there, she turned the trip into a game, seeing how long she could stay on the centerline without drifting to the side.

By the time she reached the outskirts of Mumbai, her record was fourteen minutes.

PULLING THE DIRT out of the way wasn't the issue. No, the issue was the large rock sticking out of the ground, limiting the space to squeeze through. Sanjay thought he could move around it, and knew that both Kusum and Darshana would have no problems, but Arjun would never be able to slip through. Chances were, many of the other prisoners would get stuck, too.

He had no choice but to dig it out, wasting twenty minutes he could have been using to free everyone. When it was finally out of the way, he slipped through the hole and into the compound. Moving quietly, he headed around the piles of debris and between two storage buildings. On the other side was the parking area Pishon Chem had used to keep excess vehicles—a couple dozen Jeeps, nearly as many light trucks, and a handful of sedans. At the time, Sanjay had barely given them a second thought. Now he knew they had always been intended for use after the flu outbreak.

Unlike before, the lot was nearly empty. All the Jeeps were gone, as were most of the trucks. The only vehicles left were three pickups and five sedans.

Leapfrogging his way through the lot, he moved from vehicle to vehicle until he neared the main building. This would be the difficult part. He had to run along the side of the building, over to a storage area, and then around an annex before he finally reached the back of the holding areas.

It took him two minutes to reach the annex building and drop to the ground at the corner. Peeking around the edge, he could now see the holding areas. The one to the left was where Kusum, Darshana, and Arjun were located. It was a bit farther away than the other one, and he would have to travel across an open area to get there, but there was no moon tonight and little other illumination bleeding into the area. If he was careful, he should be okay.

Forcing himself to move at half speed, he crawled across the open ground until he reached the first of the double fences. He studied the enclosure. No one was outside, which meant they all had to be inside the only building.

He checked the guard posts he could see from his position. No one seemed to be paying the holding areas any attention. From his shoulder bag, he removed the heavy-duty wire cutters he'd found in a shop several streets away. With one hand gripping the handle, and the other covering the snips to muffle the sound, he began to cut. He went up and over two meters in both directions, creating a flap. After he passed through, he put the flap back in place so it wouldn't be noticeable. He made a similar opening on the inner fence, pulled it out of the way, and entered the holding area.

Please do not let that have been the easy part, he thought.

Hugging the building, he circled around to the door and went inside. From his observations, he'd determined no guards were inside the holding areas, so, as he'd hoped, he didn't find any inside the barracks, either. What he did find was a room filled with twenty bunks, three beds high, the seventeen current residents scattered among them.

A few moved at the sound of the door opening and closing, but most remained as they were, some snoring, some breathing deeply, every last one asleep.

He found Kusum, Darshana, and Arjun at the far end, the women on the same lower level of side-by-side bunks, with Arjun sleeping on the mattress above Darshana.

Seeing his wife, Sanjay had never felt so relieved in his life. Though he had not admitted it to himself, he had known there was a chance he'd never be this close to her again.

He leaned over and gently touched her shoulder. "Kusum," he whispered. "Wake up."

She stirred but remained asleep.

"Kusum. It's me. Wake up."

She blinked and looked at him, half asleep, then her eyes widened.

"Oh, no," she said. "Why did you let them catch you?"

He hugged her and whispered, "No one caught me."

"What? I don't understand."

"I came for you." He pulled the wire cutters out of his bag and showed them to her.

"You broke in?"

He nodded.

The change in her expression was quick and dramatic. First she was stunned and confused, and then she was angry.

"Are you crazy? You could have been killed."

"How could I let you stay here? If I was the one trapped, you would come for me."

"I would not."

"You would," he said. He didn't have to see it in her eyes to know he was right, but it was there anyway. "Now get up so I can get you out of here."

"Not without the others."

"Of course not."

"I don't mean just Darshana and Arjun," she said, correctly sensing that was his intention. "We need to get everyone out of here."

"And we will, but I need to show the three of you the way out first so you can help me. All right?"

This time she was the one who pulled him into a hug.

IT DIDN'T TAKE long for Jabala to realize the empty darkness of the country was preferable to the partially lit silence of the city. The reality of what she was seeing kept fighting with her memories of how things used to be. Even at this late hour, Mumbai had always been active, always full of people.

Not tonight. Not ever again.

The closer she got to the center of the city, the more the

noise created by her motorcycle concerned her. But the thought of getting off and walking terrified her more, so she settled for lowering her speed as much as she dared so that the drone of the engine would be kept to a minimum.

Ten minutes later, she was glad she did. The reduced sound allowed her to hear a car heading in her direction. She killed her engine and moved tight against a taxi parked at the curb, just as the lights of the car came into view.

She was trapped, no way to get around the parked cars and hide without drawing attention. The best she could do was sink down to the street, and act like she was one of the corpses that littered the city. Dropping quickly, she turned her head so that she was facing the parked car, and froze.

The car on the road rushed past her without even the slightest hint of slowing. As soon as the sound of its engine faded, Jabala stood back up, and started to move the motorcycle away from the car, but stopped. She'd been lucky that time, but she might not be so lucky if it happened again.

Like it or not, it was time to walk.

SANJAY AND KUSUM decided the best method for getting everyone out was for the two of them to escort the remaining detainees in small groups to the hole in the wall, where Arjun would help them through from the compound side to Darshana waiting on the city side.

The actual guiding of people to the hole went smoothly. Convincing them they needed to leave was the problem. Most still clung to the belief they were in the hands of the UN, and would soon be given the vaccine. But even the most die-hard of those was troubled by the way they'd been treated since they'd arrived, so while some did put up a fight, in the end they all agreed to go.

When the last person from the first holding area was safely on the other side of the wall, Sanjay turned toward the interior of the compound.

"Where are you going?" Kusum said, grabbing his arm.

"There are still more people back there," he replied,

163

pulling the wire cutters out of his bag. Where did she think he was going?

"No," she said, pulling him toward the wall.

"What do you mean, no? We cannot leave them here. You said so yourself."

"Sanjay, the ones in the other area are all showing signs of the flu. Darshana and Arjun saw several of them brought in earlier."

So that was the difference, he thought. She was right. They couldn't risk escorting them out. While he, Kusum, Darshana, and Arjun had been vaccinated, the people they'd rescued had not. Any exposure to the disease was likely to kill them all.

Still, how could they do nothing?

"Give me five minutes," he said.

"Sanjay, they are sick already. We can't take them with us."

"I understand, and we won't. But I'm not going to leave them locked in there."

Knowing she would continue trying to dissuade him, he pulled from her grasp and hurried around the debris pile. When he reached the second holding area, he immediately set to work cutting an opening in the outer fence. This time, instead of creating a flap, he cut out the entire section and laid it on the ground.

He then did the same for the inner fence. He contemplated entering the barracks and telling them about the way out, but he feared he would pick up traces of the flu and carry them back to the others, so those who were inside would have to find the holes on their own.

He had hoped Kusum had gone under the fence to join the others, but she was still waiting at the wall when he returned.

"Go, go," he whispered, motioning her toward the hole.

She didn't move.

"What are you waiting for? Go," he said.

"What did you do?"

"I cut a hole in their fence, that's all."

She closed her eyes and shook her head in disapproval, but she couldn't help from grinning. When she looked at him again, she placed a hand on his cheek. "You are a good man."

She kissed the corner of his mouth, dropped down, and crawled through the hole.

OMAR WOKE IN a fit of coughing.

"No," he silently pleaded, after the spasms stopped.

He'd seen the symptoms in others countless times in the last week, and though he'd somehow been able to avoid the flu for over a week, he knew his luck had run out.

He'd woken up with a headache the previous morning. That's what finally spurred him into going to the survival station. Until that point, he'd been too afraid to journey across the city and risk exposing himself to the disease. He wasn't quite sure how vaccines worked, but they were still effective even if you were already ill, weren't they?

When he arrived, he tried to mask how he felt, but somehow the soldiers had figured it out, because not only had he not gotten a shot, but they had put him into what was basically a prison, with others who seemed also ill. Oddly, only a dozen or so meters away from their enclosure was another where those who still seemed healthy were placed.

He was angry he'd been locked up, but he could at least understand it. Why the UN would lock up those uninfected made no sense to him. Whatever the reason, it didn't matter anymore. The detention pen he was in was where he'd die.

As he coughed again, someone shouted a weak "shut up."

Thinking maybe a little fresh air would help, he shuffled through the barracks and out the door. He had no idea what time it was. He only knew it was still night.

His need to cough was replaced by an urge to pee. Having no desire to return to the barracks to use the facilities there, he walked around the back of the building and zipped down his pants. He watched the stream of water turn the dirt to mud for a moment, and then his gaze began to wander, his mind all but blank.

Several seconds passed before he realized what he was looking at. Not the chain links of the fence, but a square hole cut into the barrier. He bent down and looked through the hole. There was another missing section on the outside fence.

A way out.

This cage didn't have to be the place where he died.

He could go home and lie down on the bed next to his dead wife.

He almost stepped through the opening then and there, but he remembered the old man, Mr. Kapur, who also talked of a wife he'd left behind. Omar was not so sick that he couldn't take the time to let the man know about the opportunity. What Mr. Kapur decided to do then would be his business.

Decision made, Omar headed back into the barracks, content in the thought that very soon he'd be on his way home.

SENIOR MANAGER DETTLING woke to the sound of someone pounding on his door.

"Mr. Dettling? Are you awake?" van Assen, his assistant asked.

Dettling threw back his covers and sat up. "What is it?"

"Sir, the detainees have escaped."

Dettling, already rising to his feet, froze for half a second. "They what?"

"Someone let them out. There are holes in the fences."

Dettling walked quickly to the door and pulled it open. "Which pen?"

"Both, sir. We caught some from the infected group trying to get out. Four of them are still missing."

"And the others?"

Van Assen looked uncomfortable. "The uninfected detention area is empty. They're gone, sir."

"They can't be gone."

"I have people searching the compound, but so far they

haven't found any of them."

If the uninfected warned others to stay away, the Mumbai recovery operation could turn into a failure. "Have you sent out search parties?"

"Not yet."

"What are you waiting for? Do it! Now!"

JABALA DISCOVERED THE Mumbai survival station purely by accident. She knew she must've been getting close, but when she reached the next corner, she had not expected to see its gates right there in front of her.

She jumped back out of sight, hoping she hadn't been seen, and pressed herself against the side of the building. When she was finally able to get her panic under control, she realized the street was still quiet. They had not seen her.

Slowly, she retreated to the previous block, and turned down the road that paralleled the one the survival station was on. Three businesses down was a restaurant where most of the dining had been done at tables spread under a tattered awning along the sidewalk. She sat at a table in the back corner, where she could watch the street and be able to hide quickly if anyone showed up.

Okay, now what? she wondered.

When she'd left the boarding school, she'd been sure that finding Kusum and Sanjay would not be a problem, but now that she was here, surrounded by the reality of the city, the task seemed impossible. While Sanjay had said the plan was to find someplace where they could watch the survival station, there were far too many buildings in the area. He and Kusum could be in any of them.

What do I do now? What do I...

The world was so quiet, so very quiet. And dark. And warm. And—

Her head jerked up, her eyelids shooting open. For a second she had no idea where she was.

Restaurant. Mumbai.

Right.

She blinked several times. She'd fallen asleep in the chair.

How stupid can you be?

She scanned the street to make sure she was still alone, then paused.

Is that someone shouting?

She sat up and cocked her head.

Definitely. Several people, in fact.

She eyed the street again. Still empty.

Relax, she told herself. The yelling wasn't on her street. It was coming from a few blocks away. She narrowed her eyes, her slowly waking mind sensing that the location should be important.

A few blocks away...a few blocks...

Her brow shot up. The survival station.

As if on cue, she heard the roar of multiple engines coming from the same direction. Wanting to see what was happening, but knowing she had to be smart about it, she went over to the door leading to the inside part of the restaurant. Thankfully, it was not locked. Beyond was a single room with a small kitchen on one side and a couple of tables along the other. There was also a door in the back, exactly what she'd been hoping for.

She undid the locks holding the back door in place, and carefully opened it. The area behind the restaurant couldn't quite be called an alley. Though open to the sky, it was barely wide enough for two people to walk down shoulder-to-shoulder—if they could get over the boxes and trash that filled much of the space. Jabala decided to give it a try, and was pleased to find that after the first stack of rubbish, the area beyond was relatively clear.

The passageway did not go all the way to the end of the street, ending instead at the back of a building Jabala thought faced the street leading to the survival station. If she could get inside, she should be able to see what was going on.

There were three windows on the old and weathered back wall, one on each floor. The ground-floor window was closed, but the one right above it was partially open. The wall had plenty of notches, so climbing up to the window was not much of a challenge. It did take some extra effort, however, to push it open wide enough for her to climb through.

Inside, she found herself in a storage room packed with stacks of dresses and suits and boxes. A window was on the opposite side, overlooking the street, but it was blocked by several bundles of cloth.

Jabala carefully moved the bundle at the end just enough so she could see outside. The survival station's gate was wide open, and she counted eleven soldiers wearing blue helmets with the letters UN large and white on the sides. They stood armed and ready right outside the gate, their attention focused on the city.

Suddenly, several of the men looked back toward their base. When one of them shouted something, the soldiers split into two groups and moved to the sides. A few seconds later, a truck with a dozen more soldiers rumbled out of the gate and onto the road. As soon as it was gone, the men on the ground moved back into place.

Something was definitely going on.

Jabala leaned closer to the window to try to see more of the survival station. That's when she heard the floor creak behind her.

SANJAY'S FIRST INSTINCT was to get everyone out of the city right away, but several of the people they'd rescued were elderly and needed more rest before attempting to hike out of Mumbai. So they took them all to the building where Prabal was waiting.

"Everyone stay inside," Sanjay instructed them. "And, please, remain quiet at all times. We will wait until the sun goes down again before we leave."

Most were still in a state of semi-shock, from both their sudden imprisonment and subsequent rescue. A few wanted to know exactly what was going on. Sanjay promised to tell them everything after they were safely out of the city.

He and Kusum were getting ready to lie down

themselves when all hell broke loose over at the compound.

"What's going on?" Darshana asked, bolting up from where she'd been trying to sleep.

"I will check," Sanjay said. "Make sure everyone stays quiet."

Sanjay headed up the stairs to the roof, Kusum right behind him like he knew she would be. As they peered out at the survival station, Sanjay noted several soldiers moving around as if they were searching for something. Then, from behind one of the buildings, a man in civilian clothes stepped out and began running toward the front gate.

There were several shouts as a handful of soldiers moved in and encircled him a few car lengths from the gate. Though Sanjay couldn't hear anything, he could tell a conversation was going on. The man tried to run again, but two of the soldiers grabbed him. The man kicked and yelled as the soldiers turned him around and started marching him back to the holding area.

Seeing the man's chest heave with a cough, Sanjay realized what was going on.

"It's the ones from the other holding area," he whispered. "They must have found the hole in the fence."

One of the guards shoved the prisoner hard. The man stumbled forward several steps before falling to the ground. As they jerked him back up, there was blood on his face.

"Oh, God," Kusum said under her breath.

"I should not have cut the hole," Sanjay said. "I should not have done it."

For a moment, neither of them said anything, then Kusum pointed toward the back gate.

"No," she said. "Look."

Huddled behind a couple of the vehicles were two men. Even from this distance, Sanjay could tell one was considerably older than the other. Only two guards were on the gate, as most of the other soldiers had moved toward the shouting at the center of the compound.

The younger man peeked around the vehicle, said something to his companion, and the two of them moved across a small open space to the backside of the guard hut. Kusum sucked in a worried breath, but the men timed their move well and the guards did not see them.

The old man picked something off the ground and handed it to the younger one. A few words passed between them, then the younger one cocked his arm and threw the item toward the main part of the compound. Though Sanjay and Kusum couldn't hear the object land, it was clear the guards could. They both turned as one toward the noise, the guard nearest the hut taking a couple steps away from the fence.

The younger man threw something else in the same direction as before. This time the guards came together, talked, and one started cautiously walking in the direction of the sound. His partner followed him for about ten paces before stopping, his back to the gate.

"They are never going to make it," Kusum said as the younger man peered around the side of the hut, clearly intending to try sneaking out the opening.

When the guard took another step toward the center of the compound, the two men eased out from behind the hut and slipped quietly out the back gate into the city.

A muted echo. Metal. Like an empty drum.

Sanjay swung his gaze toward the sound. It had not come from the compound, but rather from an opening behind the buildings across the street from where they were. Though they weren't high enough to see all the way down the opening, they could see much of it, and there was no missing the dark form of a person climbing over a pile of trash.

"Is it one of the soldiers?" Kusum asked.

"I do not think so," Sanjay said.

He had no doubt the soldiers would perform a thorough search once they realized even more of their prisoners had escaped, but he didn't think there'd been enough time for them to be sneaking around like this yet.

"One of the people who escaped?" she asked.

"Perhaps."

"They are going to get themselves caught. We have to help them."

She was right. Whoever was down there was moving toward the building right outside the survival station's main gate. It would be only a matter of time before the person was discovered.

"I will go," he said. Before she could argue, he added, "You need to get the others up and move them to where we had the camp. If that is a soldier and they are searching buildings, they will search this one, too. We cannot wait until tomorrow night to leave."

Kusum looked like she was going to argue, but instead said, "Be very careful. And if they are sick, do not get too close."

"Don't worry about me. I will be fine. Now go."

SANJAY WASTED NO time sneaking across the street into one of the buildings on the other side. Instead of looking for an entrance to the back passageway, he headed up to the very top and ran from one roof to the next until he reached the end.

There, he leaned over the passageway to see if the person was still there. Not surprisingly, the area was now empty, but an open window was two floors below him. As far as he could tell, it was the only thing open along the entire passage. It had to be where the person had gone.

He located the entrance to the internal stairway and made his way down. When he reached the room with the open window, he quietly crept inside. The only light was what trickled in through the windows, and for a moment he thought he was alone, but then something moved. A person stood by the front window, peeking out at the street below.

As he took another step forward, the floor groaned under his feet.

JABALA TWISTED AROUND, her heart thudding in her chest. On the other side of the room was a man.

A soldier, she thought. *They've come to get me.*

She glanced to her right, hoping there was some way she

172

could get out, but the only exit was the one behind the man.

"It's okay," the soldier said. "I don't want to hurt you."

In her panic, she did not recognize his voice at first. But as he spoke the last few syllables, it clicked.

"Sanjay?" she said.

SANJAY FROZE.

The person at the window, a woman, knew his name.

"Sanjay, is that you?"

His eyes widened in surprise. "Jabala?"

He wasn't sure if she let out a laugh or a sigh of relief, but the next thing he knew she was rushing toward him, throwing her arms around him.

"Sanjay! You nearly scared me to death."

It took him a couple of attempts, but he was finally able to remove her arms from around his neck, and push her back enough so he could see her face. "Jabala, what are you doing here?"

"I was looking for you."

"Yes, of course. But why?"

Before she could answer, the roar of another troop truck sped past the front of the building.

Grabbing her hand, he said, "Come on. We need to get out of here. We can talk later."

SANJAY LOST COUNT of how many times they'd had to stop and wait as groups of soldiers passed near them. Sometimes the vehicles had been driving fast toward other parts of the city, sometimes they had gone by at a slow crawl, the soldiers scanning both sides of the street.

Not a minute went by that he didn't worry Kusum and the others would be spotted. It was hard enough for only him and Jabala to stay hidden.

"This way," he said, leading her across the now vacant street into a dark alleyway.

Several moments later, Jabala's foot kicked something,

173

and Sanjay heard her start to stumble. He twisted around and caught her before she could fall.

"You have to be careful," he told her.

"It is too dark," she said. "I cannot see where I am walking."

"Okay, okay. We will go slower," he said. "Keep your eyes open."

Fourteen steps into their reduced pace, something buzzed.

"What was that?" Sanjay asked, looking back.

Jabala was already pulling something from her bag. In the dark, it looked like a black lump. She touched it and held it to her head.

"Hello?" she said.

She had a phone? A *working* phone?

She listened for several seconds. "No," she finally said. "We cannot talk now. Later." She listened again, then, "Hold on." She put a hand over the phone and said to Sanjay, "How long until we will be able to stop?"

"Who are you talking to?" he asked.

"A friend."

"A friend?"

"Sanjay, how long?"

Reluctantly, he said, "We still have a few kilometers to go. Could be thirty minutes. Could be two hours."

Jabala was silent for a moment before removing her hand from the phone. "Leon, please try again in one hour...okay, okay. Good-bye."

As she put the phone away, Sanjay said, "Who is *Leon*?"

"He is in America," she said. "He answered Naresh's radio signal."

"That's the satellite phone from the school?"

"Yes."

"Why would you bring that here? It might get broken or lost."

"I thought it important you talk to Leon yourself. He warned me about the survival stations, that the UN personnel were not who they said they are. Exactly like you have been telling us."

"He said these things?" Sanjay asked.

"Yes."

"What else did he say?"

She told him about the conversation she'd had.

When she finished, he was quiet for a moment. "All right. Let's go. We have already stayed in one place too long."

"But you do want to talk to him, yes?" she asked.

"Yes," he said, silently adding, *Very much.*

16

I HAD HOPED to be on the road for at least a couple of hours by now, but it took me longer than I expected to get ready.

My first obstacle was finding a bag. It's not like I can haul my wheeled suitcase behind me. I needed a backpack, and not a book bag type. If that were the case, I would have found what I needed right away. There are plenty of those lying around. But a backpack I can carry food and clothes and that kind of stuff in is not exactly something most of the other students left behind during the holidays.

For the first time since all this started, I actually left my floor. I have to say, even though I knew logically that if anyone infected had been in the building they were days dead now, and, hopefully, no longer a danger, I was scared to death. I think if a draft had caused a door to swing just a few inches, I would have turned on the spot and kept running until I got back here. The tingling I felt under my skin was near constant, and though I was wearing a heavy jacket and a scarf around my face, I was shivering the whole time.

My search ended two floors below mine. The room was shared by a couple guys who apparently had never been taught how to keep their place clean. I cringed with every dirty shirt I had to move to see what was underneath. The backpack—an honest-to-God hiker-type backpack—was on the floor of the closet buried under several jackets and a duffel bag full of baseball gear. There was a tag on the strap identifying it as belonging to JEROME LARSON. I've probably seen him around, but I don't know the name. I am, however, very thankful that he decided he didn't need the pack over Christmas. I found a bonus, too. A compact sleeping bag that looks like it's meant to work in some pretty harsh weather. Of course, maybe that's a little wishful thinking.

Whatever the case, thanks, Jerome.

For clothing, I went through everything that had been left behind by the girls on my floor, and gathered the best of the lot that fit me—thermal underwear, T-shirts, pants, sweaters, gloves, caps. There was too much to carry, so I ended up having to pare down quite a bit.

Food was next. I decided to only carry enough for three days at a time. I figure it should be easy to find something to eat along the way. Any store or restaurant or house I pass will likely have plenty of canned stuff I can pick through as needed.

After the food there were several small things: toothbrush and toothpaste, soap, deodorant (I went back and forth on that but decided I would wear it for myself if no one else), brush, flashlight, matches, and a pocketknife I found sitting on Norman Gleason's dresser. I also took Kaylee's Sorel boots. They're much better than anything I have.

I can't lie and say I didn't wish I'd found a gun. I know, I know. Pre-Sage Flu, a gun on campus—in my very building—would have scared the crap out of me and pretty much everyone else. I probably would have been the first calling for the gun owner's expulsion. Now I wish somebody had smuggled one in.

Before I finished packing, I made one final look around, in case I found something that might be useful. The only thing I ended up adding was a picture Patty had in her room of the two of us and Josh and Kaylee. I know Josh is dead. When I called his phone and the woman who answered—maybe his mother or sister, I'm not sure—said he wasn't with us anymore, I hadn't realized what she'd meant, but it wasn't long before I pieced it together. I don't know about Patty or Kaylee, though. I guess they're probably dead, too, but I hope not.

So that's pretty much where I am. My plan is to head south to the Beltline Highway, and take that east to I-90. From there I can take the interstate all the way to Chicago. If I find roads clear enough, I'll see if I can find a car I can use. Who knows? Maybe I'll run into someone who can give me a ride. I know I'm supposed to be careful about exposure to others, but exposure to the elements isn't going to be all that great, either. Guess I'll play that one by ear.

BRETT BATTLES

Not sure how far I'll get today. The sun goes down pretty early, and there's no way I'm going to be walking after dark.

I'll write again when I stop.

17

THE THREE MAIN communication workstations had been manned nonstop all morning. Several of the stations in the mobile comm trucks the Resistance had brought from Montana were also in use. Now that most of the so-called survival stations around the world had opened, the Resistance's efforts to save what was left of humanity had gone into overdrive.

Leon and the other communication coordinators knew they wouldn't be able to save everyone, but they would try. The biggest obstacle they were facing was convincing those who were in traveling range of a survival station to not go there. The survivors were desperate for anything that seemed like a way out of the horror, and Project Eden's UN ploy filled that void perfectly. Of course, the Project had known that from the beginning, and had carefully planned out this phase.

Where Resistance coordinators could, they sent in teams, armed not only with proof that the UN did not exist anymore, but, more importantly, with vaccine. This personal touch worked more times than not, but there were still groups and individuals who would not listen to what the Resistance had to say and headed for the stations anyway.

By noon, Leon was in contact with fourteen different groups, but the one that interested him most was Jabala's. She and her friends had apparently figured out on their own that the survival stations were false fronts for something more sinister. How, exactly, still wasn't clear, but he felt particularly connected to them, and wanted to make sure they were all right.

The girl had told him to wait an hour before calling back, but he figured fifty-six minutes was close enough and input her number again. Though the computer indicated the call had connected after the third ring, he could hear nothing from the other end.

"Hello?" he said.

No, not nothing. Breathing, and…something else. A faint, rhythmic tapping sound.

"Jabala?"

"Five minutes," Jabala said, her voice a whispered rush.

The line went dead.

Leon stared at the screen. What was going on? Was she in danger?

He checked the clock to note exactly when he could call back.

At the station next to him, Crystal was saying. "Uh-huh…okay…yes, you're authorized. Keep us informed."

As she was clicking off, the door opened and Rachel walked in.

"How's everything going?" Rachel asked.

"Just got off with our people in Panama," Crystal said. "Their team in Belize is getting bogged down. Apparently there are several pockets of survivors, but getting to each is proving difficult."

"I'm sure they're doing the best they can."

"Rachel, it's the same team that's scheduled to visit that large group in Costa Rica tomorrow morning. No way they can make it now."

"How soon?"

"At least another day. Maybe two."

"When is Project Eden say they'd return to the island?"

"Going by the radio conversation we intercepted, could be anytime in the next forty-eight hours or so."

"No way to rearrange our people?"

"The team's in the field, away from the plane. Even if we order them back, it'd still be a day and a half until they get to the base, load up again, and go to Costa Rica."

"No alternatives?"

"The real problem isn't the medical team or aircraft, it's the pilots. Panama has an extra seaplane sitting there, and there's a med team in Guadalajara that just finished up, but no one to pick them up or fly them to Costa Rica."

Rachel closed her eyes and rubbed a hand across her forehead. "We can't afford to lose anyone," she said in a low voice probably meant more for herself than anyone. She looked at Crystal again. "Do what you can. As soon as a flight team becomes available, send it."

"Yes, ma'am."

Rachel switched her attention to Leon. "You look...concerned."

He hesitated a moment before saying, "I am." He explained what had been going on with the group in India. When he finished, he glanced at the clock. "It's actually time for me to call them again."

"Then do it. And please put it on speaker."

This time the call was answered on the first ring.

"Leon?" Jabala asked.

"Jabala, are you okay? You sounded—"

"We are okay now, thank you."

"Did something happen?"

Over the next several minutes, Jabala told him of her decision to travel to Mumbai in search of her brother-in-law Sanjay, thinking he and Leon should talk. Apparently while she was on her way there, Sanjay and Jabala's sister Kusum had sneaked into the survival station and rescued several of the people being held there, or something like that. It wasn't completely clear. Now they were all together, hiding from soldiers who were pretending to be with the UN.

After sharing a long, surprised glance with Rachel and Crystal, Leon said, "Perhaps I should talk to Sanjay."

"Of course. One moment, please."

A few seconds later, a male voice said, "Yes?"

"Is this Sanjay?" Leon asked. The man sounded younger than Leon had expected.

"Yes. And you are...Leon?"

"Right. Your sister-in-law tells me you've had quite an adventure this evening."

"I am not sure I would call it an adventure," Sanjay said, no humor in his voice.

"I'm sorry. I didn't mean to make light of it."

"It is okay. I am tired."

"Of course. I'll try not to keep you long. Jabala said you actually went into the survival station."

"That is correct. But it was not that difficult. I knew about the hole under the wall from before."

"That's right. You worked for Pishon Chem."

"I did, well, until I found out what they were going to spray was not an anti-malaria chemical." He explained about finding his cousin Ayush dying of exposure to Sage Flu; about getting Kusum, Jabala, and their family out of Mumbai; about sneaking into the Pishon Chem compound, and forcing the managers to give him vaccine.

"When we first heard about the survival stations, we were excited," Sanjay went on, unaware of the stunned listeners at Ward Mountain. "But when the location was finally announced, and I realized it was the same facility used by Pishon Chem, I became suspicious. I knew we needed to check first before sending everyone there. So my wife, three of our friends, and I came here. When I saw that the people who seemed to be running the operation were the same people in charge of Pishon Chem, I knew these were not UN representatives, and that whatever they had planned could not be good." After seconds of silence, he asked, "Are you still there?"

"Sorry," Leon said. "It's just, well, your story is surprising."

"You do not believe me?" Sanjay asked, his tone growing defensive.

"Absolutely, we believe you," Leon said. "You've been through a lot, that's all."

"Has not everyone?" Sanjay asked.

"Yes, that's true." Leon paused. "So when you realized these people weren't the UN, I assume that's when you snuck back in and helped the survivors they'd collected escape."

Sanjay took a moment before responding. "There were two holding areas inside. One for those who were not obviously infected, and one for those who were. I brought everyone who was not infected out. I...cut a hole in the fence for the others, but left it for them to discover. I did not want to risk picking up the disease and spreading it to anyone who had not been vaccinated yet."

The last came out as almost an apology.

"You did the right thing," Leon said.

"I do not know about that, but, I, uh, I did what I had to."

"Are you going to take everyone out of the city to your boarding school?"

"The school?" Sanjay said, suspiciously. "How did you know about the school?"

"Jabala mentioned it, but don't worry, she didn't tell me where. And even if she had, the last thing we want to do is harm you."

"Who exactly are you?"

"We're a group of people who have been fighting those behind Pishon Chem for a long time. Though we tried, we couldn't keep the virus from being released. Now our goal is simply to keep the survivors alive."

"And the others? Who are they?"

"They call themselves Project Eden. And they have been planning this for a long, long time."

"But why? I don't understand."

"I don't understand it, either. All I know is that they want to control those they chose to survive, and direct the future as they see fit. I'm sure this is all difficult to believe, but—"

"Not as difficult as I wish it was," Sanjay said. "You wanted to know what I am going to do? I'm going back."

"Going back where?"

"To Pishon Chem," Sanjay said. "To the survival station."

"Why would you do that?" Leon asked, not trying to keep the surprise out of his voice.

"Because we have no more vaccine, and the people who escaped today will need it. The only place I know to find it is inside those walls."

Leon was about to tell him that he might be able to get some vaccine to them in a few days when someone touched his arm.

"HELLO, SANJAY. MY name is Rachel."

"Hello." His reply came back tentative, as if unsure why he was being passed off to someone else.

"Sanjay, no one here thinks it's a good idea for you to reenter the survival station."

"What choice do we have? We are out of vaccine."

"We have vaccine," she said. "It will just take time to get it to you." She glanced at Leon. He held up three fingers. "Three days at the earliest."

"Three days is a long time," he said. "This flu is everywhere, yes?"

"The risk of exposure is still very high, if that's what you mean."

"Then I do not see how I have any choice."

She hesitated. "I said we don't think it's a good idea to go, but if you need the vaccine now it could be your best chance. That's something you will have to decide. What I will promise you is that we will get vaccine to you no matter what you choose to do, in case you run into others later."

"If anyone dies because I did not go back for more vaccine, it will be as much my fault as that of those who have spread the disease."

"Sanjay, that's not true."

"Of course, it is true. How many people have died?"

"We…we don't know."

"Here in Mumbai there were millions and millions people. Now maybe I have seen one hundred still alive. One hundred people out of so many. Is it the same everywhere?"

She hesitated. "Yes."

"Then I must go."

THE RANCH, MONTANA
1:44 PM MST

THE TRIP SOUTH had been anything but pleasant. The Dash 7 Combi aircraft belonging to the research station on Amund Ringnes Island was a hearty, four-propeller plane, but it was not immune to the heavy turbulence that kept Pax and the others strapped in their seats most of the time. Its limited flight range of a thousand miles in the best weather conditions also meant stops at deserted airports in Cambridge Bay, Yellowknife, and Edmonton for fuel.

Edmonton was the most disturbing. More than a million people had lived in and around the city. The airport had been used by large commercial airliners. Thousands of passengers had passed through its terminal every day. But during the stop, not a single person was seen.

As soon as the plane crossed the US border, Pax made his way up to the cockpit.

"Strap in," the pilot told him, pointing at the auxiliary jump seat. "Catching up to another storm."

The pilot's name was Ian Lourdes, and he was dead right about the storm. Not more than a minute after Pax clicked his restraints into place and donned the headset hanging next to the seat, the plane was buffeted by a layer of unsettled air.

Lourdes glanced back at Pax. "We're about fifteen minutes out if your coordinates are correct."

"They are," Pax said.

"I sure as hell hope so. If they're not, we won't know until we're too low to do anything about it."

Pax had given the flight crew the exact GPS coordinates for the end of the runway at the Ranch. With the storm, it was likely to have a fresh layer of snow, but it wouldn't be the first time the Combi had landed in similar conditions on this trip.

"Getting low on fuel again, too," Lourdes said. "You sure there's enough there to get us up in the air again?"

"More than enough." Pax hoped he was right. While the Ranch did normally maintain a large supply of aircraft fuel, there was no telling how many flights had been moving in and out in the wake of the outbreak.

Right before they began their descent, the pilot flipped on the intercom and said, "Buckle up. We're heading down."

"I should radio in now," Pax said. "We don't want to surprise anyone."

The copilot, Frank Kendrick, flicked a couple of switches and said, "Go for it."

"Bravo Four, this is Pax," he said. "Bravo Four, this is Pax. Come in."

Static.

"Bravo Four, come in. This is Pax."

Nothing.

"Bravo Four, we are approaching your runway. Do you read?" He looked over at Kendrick. "You sure you have me dialed in right?"

Kendrick read off the frequency. It was the same one Pax had given him.

"Bravo Four, please come in."

"They're not going to shoot at us if we try to land, will they?" Lourdes asked.

"We'll be fine. Don't worry about it," Pax said. The truth was, he had no idea what the hell was going on. The Ranch should have answered by now.

"You're *sure* the runway is where you said it is?" the pilot asked. The only things they could see were clouds.

"Exactly where I said it is."

Lourdes nodded once, not looking reassured.

"Bravo Four, this is Pax. We are about to land. Please respond."

Dead air.

As Pax started to try again, they dropped out of the clouds into a swirl of snow. Pax craned his neck to get a better look out the window. They were at the Ranch all right. He recognized the valley.

"You're dead on," he said. "Runway's just ahead."

"I don't see it," Kendrick said.

"It's there. Trust me."

"Don't have much of a choice now," Lourdes said.

"Five hundred feet," Kendrick announced, reading off the altimeter. "Four seventy-five. Four fifty."

The countdown continued as they neared the runway.

"Bravo Four, Bravo Four, this is Pax. We are coming in now. Bravo Four, do you read?"

"Two seventy-five. Two fifty. Two twenty-five."

"Bravo Four! Bravo Four! Why aren't you answering?"

"One fifty. One twenty-five. One hundred."

There was no distinction between the runway and the meadows surrounding it. As long as Lourdes stuck to the coordinates, Pax knew they'd be all right, but the knowledge didn't keep him from clenching up as the wheels sliced through the snowdrift and hammered onto the ground. The plane shook with the impact, but stayed moving in a straight line as the momentum slowed and finally died.

"Told you it was there," Pax said, smiling.

He instructed Lourdes to bring the plane around and taxi to a spot to the side about halfway back. There, tucked behind a stand of trees, was the fuel supply. It was also where the road to the Lodge began.

He couldn't understand why no one was waiting for them. Even if the Ranch had somehow not heard his radio calls, a team should have been there to see who was on the plane.

When the plane stopped, he told the others to remain on board and climbed down the retractable staircase. He pushed his way through the snow away from the aircraft, raised his arms, and waved them back and forth over his head.

"It's Pax!" he yelled. "Rich Paxton! You can come out!"

The only movement he saw was snow falling.

"Hello? Can you hear me? Tell Matt that Pax is back!"

Silence.

He tried a few more times before returning to the plane.

"I guess we're going to have to hike in," he said. He looked over at his men. "Tom, you're with me. The rest of you help get the plane fueled up."

Decked out in the same winter gear they had used up in northern Canada, Pax and Tom Grady set off for the Lodge.

The road, usually plowed in the winter, was now buried under two feet of snow, more in some places.

"I don't like this," Tom said.

Pax made no reply.

The Lodge was a bit over a mile away, about a ten-minute hike on a nice summer day at a strong and steady pace. Under current conditions, it took them twice as long before they could see the trees thinning ahead, signaling the meadow where the Lodge was located.

Knowing they were close, Pax couldn't help but pick up his pace. He was anxious to see his friends again, to find out what had been going on. But as he stepped out from the trees, he stopped.

The Lodge was gone. It should have been *right there*, but in its place was a pile of snow-covered, charred timbers.

He looked toward the dorm building off to the side. Not there. Only another pile of debris.

"Oh, my God!" Tom said, stepping out behind him. "What happened?"

The answer to that was clear. The Lodge and the dorm had been destroyed. How and why, Pax had no idea.

"This way," Pax said. He cut across the meadow toward the woods on the other side.

Had anyone been in the buildings when they went down? Were his friends—

Stop it! he told himself. Those were questions that would only drive him crazy. What he needed was more information.

By the time they reached the woods again, both men were panting but they kept going, weaving through the trees and slogging up the hill to the Bunker's emergency entrance. It took Pax a few minutes before he found the configuration of trees he was looking for, but there was no need to pace off the correct distance to find the hatch. It was unburied and wide open.

Keeping his fear in check, he knelt next to it and looked

inside. Snow had piled up directly below the opening, but otherwise the tunnel was dark.

He reached into the opening and felt along the wall near the ladder. When his fingers knocked against the switch, he flipped it up. Lights located along the top of the tunnel instantly drove the darkness away. At least the power was still working. That had to mean something, didn't it?

"I'll go down first," he said. "If it looks okay, you follow."

"Got it," Tom said.

Pax descended the ladder, letting himself drop the final few feet to the ground. The tunnel stretched away for a while before bending out of sight. The part he could see was empty.

"Clear," he yelled up at Tom.

As soon as Tom joined him, they set off for the Bunker proper.

Any hope Pax had that everything was still all right vanished when they reached the partially open blast door. The area beyond was too quiet. If nothing else, they should have heard the soft hum of the ventilators feeding fresh air into the underground space, but there was no noise at all.

Emergency lights, triggered by motion sensors, flickered to life as the two men stepped into the main part of the Bunker.

"They're gone," Tom whispered.

Or dead, Pax thought but kept to himself, saying instead, "Let's take a look around."

Behind every door they opened and every corner they turned, Pax expected to find bodies, thinking that somehow the latest strain of Sage Flu had turned out to be resistant to the vaccine he and his friends had been given, but the dorms and the common areas were blessedly empty. They checked the storage rooms at the back of the kitchen. When Pax had looked in them last, they'd all been full. Now they were empty.

Their next stop was the weapons storage area. It, too, had been cleared out. Pax was starting to understand what had happened, at least a little bit.

"Comm room," Pax ordered.

As they stepped inside the Bunker's nerve center, Tom said, "Oh, my God."

Most of the computers were gone, but the monitors and all other equipment still in the room had been destroyed. Chunks of glass and metal and plastic littered the floor. Pax stepped carefully through the mess and over to the communication director's desk.

Standard operating procedure: upon abandoning a facility, the location of the next destination was to be left, when possible, in one of three specific places around the communication director's workstation.

Pax found what he was looking for in position number two. Etched along the upper lip of the electrical socket cover were seven characters: 113-S78.

The number eight meant nothing, as did the three and the second one. They were decoy numbers. The real message was: 1-S7.

Nevada. They'd gone to Nevada.

Pax closed his eyes and said a prayer of thanks that his friends were apparently still alive. When he opened them again, he said, "Let's get back to the plane. There's nothing else here to see."

18

AFTER TWENTY MINUTES of looking for Iris, Ben began to wonder if maybe he should have left. If the girl didn't want to be found, she wouldn't be. There were a million places where she could hide. He could search for a month and never come within a block of her.

But he couldn't stop thinking about the fact she was alone out there, even more so than he was. As terrifying and gut wrenching and mind numbing as living through the outbreak had been, at least he had known what was going on. Iris had clearly been unaware the world was dying around her.

He continued on for a few more blocks before finally deciding it was time to use his Jeep to cover more ground. The walk back took him thirty minutes. When he reached his vehicle, the first thing he did was pull a bottle of water out of the back and down the whole thing in one long gulp. Out of habit, he walked toward a recycling bin sitting at the curb, and had the lid open before he realized what he was doing. No one would ever collect the contents of the can. He tossed the bottle in anyway, figuring it was still better than dropping it on the street.

Instead of returning to his Jeep, however, he detoured to the Cape Cod house. Iris had all but said she'd been held captive there by this Mr. Carlson guy, but something about it—her actions, the whole setup—didn't quite fit. Maybe if Ben could figure out what had happened, he'd have some clue about where she had gone. It was a long shot, but he thought it worth a try.

He headed down to the basement first, wanting to get a better look at the room she'd been trapped in. After blocking the door with a chair so he wouldn't trap himself down there, he went inside. His impressions from earlier had been dead on. A lot of money had been spent in this room. Whoever had paid for it really wanted the person living there to be comfortable. He looked around for any personal items that might tell him a little more about Iris, but other than clothes and some simple jewelry, he came up empty.

Upstairs, he returned to the bedroom of the man he assumed was Mr. Carlson. He retrieved the wallet he'd seen earlier in the dresser and flipped it open. A driver's license with a picture of the dead man indicated his name was Marvin Bernard Carlson, age forty-seven, with an address matching that of the house. There were a few business cards with the same name. Apparently Mr. Carlson worked as a manager for H&R Block. Insurance card, AAA card, a couple of credit cards, and a wallet-sized copy of one of the portraits on the wall. It was the one with the girl at her youngest.

Ben walked over to the portraits. He hadn't realized it before, but in none of the pictures was the girl truly smiling. He noticed something else this time, too. Yes, she was a few years older now, but the girl was Iris.

A trip to the other bedroom confirmed it had been Iris's room. PROPERTY OF IRIS CARLSON was written inside the covers of several books on the shelves. He wondered what was going on here, but then decided he probably didn't want to know.

He exited the house and walked over to the Jeep.

"Where did everybody go?"

Iris stood half hidden behind a tree in the yard directly across from her house, her gaze firmly planted on the Cape Cod. Had she been there when he first came back? Probably, he thought.

"It's like I told you before," he said, keeping his voice calm. "They're gone. There was a massive flu outbreak, and almost everyone is dead."

"You're not dead."

"No."

"I'm not dead."

"No," he said.

"And...Mr. Carlson?"

Ben decided now was probably not the time to call her on her deception. "He's dead."

She looked at the house. "In his bedroom."

"Yes."

Her lower lip began to tremble. She sucked it between her teeth until the shaking passed. "I need to see."

"I'm not sure that's a good idea."

She tore her eyes from the house and looked at Ben. "I *need* to. Don't you understand?"

He nodded. "Sure. I understand." When she didn't move, he said, "Would you like me to go with you?"

"Yes, please. I don't think I can go alone. "

Staying a few paces in front of her, he led Iris into the house and down the hallway. When they passed the first bedroom, he sensed her hesitate behind him, and thought she might go inside. But Iris apparently decided against visiting her old room, and soon joined him at the door to the master.

Ben covered his nose and mouth with his shirt. "You might want to do the same."

As soon as she did, he opened the door.

"It's not pretty," he said.

"I don't care."

"You want to go in first?"

She shook her head.

Ben walked into the room and stepped to the side. Iris remained in the hallway for a few seconds before finally entering the room.

"That is Mr. Carlson, isn't it?" he asked.

Only a nod as she stared at the corpse.

They stood there in silence for over a minute, before Iris abruptly turned and walked out. Ben started to follow her, but stopped and returned to the dresser. He hesitated, feeling guilty for what he considered doing. But he thought it might help him figure out Iris, so he opened the drawer, retrieved Mr. Carlson's wallet, and slipped it into his pocket.

He found Iris outside, sitting on the curb.

"I'm heading south," he said. "If you want to come with me, you're welcome."

At first he didn't think she had heard him, but then she looked up. "I'd like that. Thank you."

CENTRAL CALIFORNIA
12:47 PM PST

MARTINA KNEW THERE had to be some unwritten rule about driving hung over. At first she thought it would be a good thing—the fresh air rushing past her, the bright morning sun keeping her warm. What she hadn't taken into consideration was the helmet pressing in on her head, keeping that fresh air away and intensifying the heat to the point she could feel sweat dripping down her neck. From the looks on her friends' faces, they weren't doing much better. She was pretty certain none of them would be drinking again anytime soon.

She had purposely set a slower pace today, worried that in their diminished capacity they might not see a pothole or a branch in the road. Turned out the reduced speed was a good thing.

They were on Route 166, the often windy and narrow highway that separated the San Joaquin Valley from the coast, when they dipped around a bend and had to come to a sudden halt because the road in front of them was blocked.

Martina's first thought was that there had been an accident—by the looks of it, a big one, involving over half a dozen vehicles. But then she realized that while the nearest two cars appeared to have run into each other, the ones behind them seemed to have been placed there on purpose. They were in even rows, perpendicular to the road, stretching from one shoulder to the other.

"How are we supposed to get around that?" Riley asked.

Craig popped the stand on his bike and hopped off. "I got

this. Just need to push a few of them out of the way."

He walked around the accident to the car in the first row, and leaned inside to put it in neutral. The moment his head disappeared inside, the crack of a rifle rang out from the trees beyond the blockade.

Craig jerked out of the car and dropped to the ground.

The girls stared, momentarily stunned.

"Down!" Martina yelled as another shot went off. "Everyone! On the ground!"

She hit the pavement a second before the other two.

"Why are they shooting at us?" Noreen asked. "We didn't do anything!"

"Craig?" Riley called out. "You all right?"

"Yeah, I'm okay," Craig called back. "Scared the crap out of me, that's all. Are you guys all right?"

"Yeah," Riley said. "We're okay."

"Those were warning shots," a male voice called from the trees. "Next one won't miss. Now get on your bikes and go back the way you came. This road is closed!"

"We're just trying to get to the coast," Martina shouted back. "Not trying to cause any problems!"

"Plenty of other ways to get there. You're not coming through here!"

"Okay, okay! No problem! Please don't shoot at us again, all right?"

"If you turn those bikes around and get out of here, there won't be any problems."

"I'm going to get up," Martina said.

Riley reached out and grabbed Martina's wrist. "No. What if it's a trick?"

"I think he could shoot us where we're lying if he wanted to. And even if he can't, what are we going to do? Just stay here?"

Riley reluctantly let go as Martina pushed herself to her feet.

When the rifle remained silent, Martina said, "Okay. Everyone up."

Noreen was the first to join her, and then Riley stood.

"My friend's going to come back from the car, okay?" Martina shouted.

"He shuts the door first," the man responded.

"Craig," Martina said, dropping her voice a few decibels. "Do as he says."

"Hell, no. I'm not getting up," Craig said. "He's going to shoot me."

"He's not going to shoot you," Martina said.

"You don't know that."

"Craig, just shut the door!"

"Uh-uh. No way."

Martina closed her eyes for a second, frustrated. She guessed the roadblock was there to keep the man with the rifle and anyone else with him safe from people who might be infected. If she and the others did what he wanted and left, it would all be fine. Like the man said, there were plenty of other highways to the coast.

"Sir!" she shouted. "My friend's a little worried if he moves you might shoot him."

"He has to close the door, that's all. Don't want it left open for anyone else to get any ideas."

Martina raised her hands and took a step forward.

"What are you doing?" Riley whispered.

"If you'll allow me," Martina shouted, "I'll close the door. Then we'll be on our way."

The man said nothing for several seconds, then, "If you try anything funny, me or one of my friends will take you down."

He's alone, she thought.

"I won't try anything," she said. "Going to do exactly what I told you I would."

She took another step forward, and then another.

"Martina," Riley said. "Don't!"

"You two get on your bikes and turn them around. I'll be right back."

She could hear Riley start to protest again, but Noreen cut her off.

"Come on," Noreen said. "Let's do what she said."

197

Martina kept her pace consistent all the way to the car. When she reached the door, she looked down at Craig. "After I close it, get up, and we'll walk back."

"No. He'll shoot us in the back," he protested.

His fear was obviously keeping him from thinking clearly.

"If you don't get up, we're going to leave you here," Martina said.

She shoved the door closed and turned back toward the motorcycles. She was five steps away before she finally heard Craig get to his feet and scramble after her.

When they were all on their bikes, she shouted, "We're sorry we disturbed you! Didn't realize this way was cut off!"

"You do now," he replied.

"You know, you can come with us if you'd like," she said.

"What the hell?" Craig whispered. "Are you crazy?"

"Thanks for the offer," the man shouted, "but we're good here. Best you get on your way now!"

"All right," Martina said. "Good luck to you!"

As they headed back into the central valley, Martina wondered how many others were holed up like the man on 166. Must be hundreds or even thousands scattered all over the place. People just trying to survive. Would they chance a trip to a survival station to get inoculated? She figured some would, while others would probably be too scared to venture from the safe haven they'd created.

Well, there was one good thing that came out of the encounter. Her headache was gone.

19

WITHOUT THE SNOWPLOWS, the Resistance convoy would have never made it out of Sheridan. Twenty miles south, the going became easier, much of the road covered by only a few inches of snow. After they passed Douglas, there were miles of the interstate completely clear, so they were able to make it to checkpoint three—the Central Avenue/US 85 exit in Cheyenne—in just under six hours.

At a gas station near the base of the off-ramp, they fueled up the vehicles and settled in to wait for Hiller and Rick.

Chloe took the opportunity to locate some solitude behind the station. She was lucky there had been so much snow when she fell off the roof the night before. Her injuries could have been a whole lot worse. Still, having her wrist in a sling and her cracked ribs taped up meant she'd been relieved of her driving duties, something that pissed her off more than the injuries themselves.

Driving would have been good. It would have focused her mind on the road instead of keeping her constantly aware of the others inside the cab.

Aware of Ginny.

Chloe had tried to sleep, but she could still see the girl when she closed her eyes. Not as she currently was, sitting in back with Brandon and Josie, but on the roof where Chloe had first seen her. A pair of eyes peeking above a scarf, her name hanging in the air between them.

Why did this girl bother her so much? What was it about her?

Chloe was sure she'd never seen the girl before. Well, not in this part of her life. But what about in the other part? The memories from then had been lost to her for years. Which, of course, meant if Chloe had known Ginny before, the girl would have been a toddler at best, and would have looked different enough that seeing her now should not have triggered such a strong response.

So what was it?

The name, yes, but not *that* name, she thought. What that meant, she didn't know. She also felt it was more than something to do with the girl's name.

Her face? Her eyes? The way she wore her clothes?

The harder Chloe thought about it, the further the answers seemed to move away.

"You all right back here?"

She turned in surprise.

"Sorry," Ash said. "Didn't mean to startle you."

"It's fine," she said, then narrowed her eyes. "Should you be walking around?"

"Should you?"

She allowed herself to smile.

"You looked pretty lost in thought there," he said. "Everything okay?"

"Sure. Why wouldn't it be? I mean, other than the world going to shit."

"Other than that, yeah." He leaned up against the building. "All that riding can't be good for us."

"You were in the army. You should be used to it."

He grunted a laugh and said, "You never get used to it." He shoved his hands into his pockets. "So you're the one who found the cat, huh?"

"Sorry about that."

The cat had been a surprise to them all, Brandon keeping it under wraps until they'd been on the road for nearly half an hour. It had hissed a few times and so far was only letting the kids touch it.

"Well, we couldn't very well leave it there, I guess," Ash said.

She didn't say anything. Because of her fall, she'd forgotten all about that cat. If she'd remembered, she could have been the one who brought it along.

"Brandon said you seemed to freeze up there."

"Up where?" she asked, knowing perfectly well what he meant.

"Last night."

She looked at the storage sheds sitting side by side at the back of the station lot. "It was cold. We were all freezing."

"I don't think that's what he meant."

She shrugged. "I don't know what he was talking about."

"He said you appeared to be staring at Ginny right before you slipped."

"It was dark up there. Not sure how he could tell who was looking at who."

"Well, *I've* noticed you've tried very hard not to look at her today."

"Is there a point to this?"

"Only that I'm your friend, and you seem troubled, so that worries me."

"Then let me ease your mind." She pushed off the building. "I'm not troubled, so you don't need to worry."

Without waiting to hear what he had to say next, she started to walk away.

As she came around the building, Matt said, "Ah, there you are. Have you seen Ash?"

"Right here," Ash said, rounding the corner behind Chloe.

"You guys have a minute? I'd like to talk to you."

"I'd have to check my schedule," Ash said, "but I could probably move some meetings around."

"We'll use my Humvee," Matt said, not even cracking a smile.

ASH WAS THE last to climb into the vehicle.

"How are you both doing?" Matt asked, once they were all seated and the door was closed.

"Better than I was last week," Ash said.

Matt looked at Chloe. It seemed to take her a moment before she realized he was waiting for her to respond.

"Uh, worse than I was last week."

Matt studied them, as if assessing his next words. "I'm considering taking a little detour before heading to Nevada."

"Detour where?" Ash asked.

"New Mexico."

"I assume there's a reason why."

Another pause, briefer this time. "As you know, in the past, we were able to get some of our people placed inside Project Eden, to help us know what was going on."

"Didn't really do a lot of good, did it?" Chloe said.

It looked for a moment as if Matt would snap at her, but the tension in his face quickly disappeared and he sighed. "No, you're right. It didn't help us stop them before. But that could change now."

"What do you mean?" Ash asked.

"Project Eden may have altered the course of human history, but I'll be damned if I allow them to direct which way we go next. What you two did at Bluebird was a big step in that direction."

"We failed at Bluebird," Ash said.

"Yes, the virus was still released, but you eliminated the Project's directorate, and that was *not* a failure. With the directorate gone, a new set of leaders should have been put in place."

"What do you mean, *should* have?" Chloe asked. "They seem to still be operating pretty damn effectively."

"The Project has always functioned under a group-leadership model, with one person acting as principal director," Matt said. "This director is supposed to work in concert with the other directors. If it hadn't been for this structure, they would have never made it this far. When it became apparent that the directorate at Bluebird was gone, procedures were put into motion to form a new directorate.

202

Only, apparently, what happened is that the new principal director hijacked the process, and turned the set of directors below him into a rubber stamp committee.

"Right now, the bulk of the Project is operating exactly as planned. As soon as they have eliminated the survivors they feel are unnecessary, they'll unite the remaining population and start the final phase—the next coming of man, if you will. But instead of the whole directorate deciding things, it will be just this one man."

"A dictatorship," Ash said.

"Exactly." Matt frowned. "I'm not saying I'd be happier if a committee was running things. As long as Project Eden is in charge, it doesn't matter to me who's calling the shots." He paused. "What does matter, though, is the opportunity this presents to us. What happened at Bluebird was a rare thing. Having the full directorate in the same facility at the same time was an act of arrogance. If they had lived through Implementation Day, we would have never seen them all in one place like that again. It made them vulnerable, and they paid the price."

Ash saw where this was going. "A single leader has the same vulnerability, only constantly."

"Yes, he does," Matt said. "Hence the trip to New Mexico. One of our people inside was able to get us a message that the current principal director, a man named Perez, is operating out of a Project Eden facility near Las Cruces, New Mexico. I'm going there, and I'm taking him out."

"But isn't this the same problem?" Chloe asked. "If we get rid of him, won't someone else take his place?"

"Possibly," Matt said. "But it will be a big blow nonetheless, more so because he's been operating so independently. And we need to start somewhere. After he's gone, we'll go after the next set of leaders and the next and the next. Each time we succeed, the Project becomes more unbalanced. They have already taken so much from us. We *cannot* let them rule the future."

"You're sure this Perez person is in New Mexico?" Ash

asked.

"Absolutely."

"How are we going to get in?" Ash asked. "We can't just walk up and knock on the door."

"There's a way," Matt said.

"What way?"

"It would be better if neither of you knew that."

"Why not?" Ash asked.

Matt eyed them both. "Because when we reach southern Colorado, the two of you and the kids will head to Nevada."

"The hell we will," Chloe said. "If you're going after the Project, I'm going, too."

"I need people who can fight," Matt said. "Not people I have to worry about because they're already injured."

"You need me." Chloe glanced at Ash. "You need both of us."

"Yes, I do," Matt said. "But as you were, not like this." He grimaced. "I know how much both of you have done, that you've both earned the right to be there. But be honest with yourselves. You're going to be more of a burden than help, and you know it."

"And you're not going to be?" Chloe said, motioning to his bad knee.

"I have to be there," he said. "You don't."

"Bullshit. You...I can..." She was so worked up, she looked like she was going to launch herself right at Matt and rip out his throat. Instead, she threw open the door and charged out of the truck.

Matt's head drooped. "I'm sure you understand," he said to Ash.

"Oh, I understand the reasoning, but your logic is flawed."

"I just want—"

Ash cut him off. "Injured or not, when the mission is critical, you always want your best people with you, and you've got no one better than Chloe and me." He leaned forward a few inches. "The fact that you don't see that makes me very concerned for those who will be going with you."

He opened the nearest door and piled out, his exit not quite as graceful as Chloe's, but his point made.

IT WAS ANOTHER seventy minutes before the snowplow driven by Hiller pulled into the gas station parking lot.

Matt was the first to greet him. "Any problems?"

"Not with the kid," Hiller said. "He's been out the whole time. But this thing…" He nodded his chin at the truck. "Not sure how much farther it can go."

"We'll leave it here, then."

"What do you want me to do with Rick?"

"Let's put him in Ash's truck. At least when he comes to, his sister will be there."

"Sure," Hiller said. "I'll get one of the other guys to help."

"I can do it," Matt told him.

Hiller looked unconvinced, but he headed back to the plow with Matt limping along behind him. Together they eased Rick out of the passenger seat. With one of the boy's arms over each of their shoulders, they carried him toward the Humvee Ash and his family had been riding in. They were a little over halfway there when Matt saw Ginny running toward them, her eyes wide.

"Rick? Rick, oh my God!" As she neared, her steps faltered. "Rick?" She looked at Matt. "What's wrong with him?"

"He's sleeping, that's all."

"He looks sick. Is he sick?" she asked, panicked. Instead of backing away like most people would, she moved closer to her cousin.

"He's not sick. He's asleep."

"Are you sure?"

"I'm sure," he said. "Can you open the back door for us?"

With a nod, she hurried over to the Humvee and did as requested.

After Rick was situated and the doors were closed again,

Matt turned to the others standing around. "Everyone load up. I'm hoping we can make it all the way to Denver before we stop for the night."

He watched them walk off and climb into their vehicles. They were good people—great, even—all willing to do whatever needed to be done.

For how many of them, he wondered, would this be the last call to action?

20

PRIMARY DIRECTOR PEREZ read the report, his displeasure increasing with each word.

In Mumbai, India, someone had taken it upon himself or herself to release the survivors who had already shown up at the survival station by cutting holes in the detention-area fences. Perez's initial question was why would anyone even consider doing this? The survival stations were places of refuge as far as anyone on the outside was concerned, and those in the holding areas would believe what they'd been told, that their confinement was merely a precaution designed to keep as many people alive as possible. No way any of them would want to leave prior to receiving the promised inoculation.

To Perez, this meant it had been an inside job.

Though not acknowledged to the Project Eden general membership, it had long been known among those in charge that some members were not quite as dedicated to the cause as everyone else. They were sympathetic to those outside the Project, willing to risk everything the Project stood for to avoid what they considered unnecessary deaths. Perez was sure the person who'd cut through the fences was one of these people, and that he or she was part of the Project personnel assigned to Mumbai.

When he finished reading, he called Claudia on the

intercom. "Who's the director in Mumbai?"

"Mr. Dettling."

"Dettling?" he said. Perez was good with names, and had at least a passing knowledge of most of the people running Project operations around the world, but Dettling didn't sound familiar.

"That's Pishon Chem," she reminded him.

Right. Pishon Chem.

There had been a problem there on Implementation Day. The previous senior manager, Herr...Schmidt, had died of complications from an injury he'd received. If Perez remembered correctly, the injury had occurred in the semi-chaos of a loading zone being used to distribute KV-27a to the unsuspecting men hired to spray the city with it. Schmitt had been punctured in the shoulder by a loose railing on one of the trucks or something like that. By the time anyone realized what had happened, he'd lost too much blood to be saved. Dettling had been the next man in seniority, and was immediately promoted.

"I want to talk to him. Right now."

"Right away," she said.

One minute later Perez's phone rang.

"I have Mr. Dettling for you," Claudia announced. "Center screen."

"Put him through."

The center monitor filled with a head shot of a tired-looking, middle-aged man with thinning hair.

"Principal Director," Dettling said. "This is an honor. What is it I can do for you?"

"You can start by telling me what the hell is going on over there."

Dettling hesitated. "I assume you mean the detainee issue."

"Yes. The detainee *issue.*"

"Uh, um, most of those who had been housed in the infected enclosure were still within the compound so we've been able to round them up."

"And the uninfected?"

"We're, um, still looking for them."

"How many have you reacquired so far?"

Another pause. "None yet, sir."

"None? As in zero?"

"Yes, sir."

Perez stared into the camera, letting an oppressive silence grow between them.

After several seconds, Dettling shifted nervously in his chair and said, "Sir, I promise you we will—"

"Have you caught the one responsible?"

"Not yet. I'm sure we'll find him when we find the others."

"And what makes you think that?"

Dettling's eyebrows moved toward each other, his forehead wrinkling. "I'm, uh, not quite…I don't know—"

"Why would you assume the person who cut through your fences is with the others and not still there in your compound?"

"Our compound? You mean, you think it could be one of the infected detainees?"

"Mr. Dettling, prove to me you're not an idiot and tell me you are looking into your own personnel."

"My personnel?" Dettling said. "You mean the Project people here?"

"It certainly wouldn't be anyone where I am, would it?"

"Of course not. It's just…I didn't—"

"No, you didn't, but now you will. Check them."

"Yes, sir. Of course."

The intercom buzzed. He hit the speaker button

"Sir," Claudia said. "It's time for your Madrid call."

"All right," Perez said. He hung up and looked back at the camera. "Mr. Dettling?"

"Yes, sir?"

"The next time we talk, you will tell me the mess is cleaned up."

"Absolu—"

Perez hit the key that terminated the call.

21

AFTER RETRACING THEIR path back into the San Joaquin Valley, Martina and her friends headed north again on the I-5 until they reached Highway 58. Because of their experience with the man back on 166, they kept their speed down as they traveled through the mountains, and whenever they came to a blind turn, they slowed to almost a crawl. But there were no roadblocks this time. In fact, they saw very few cars at all.

By the time they reached the 101 freeway, the sun was nearing the horizon. Martina pushed her friends a little farther, but when they crossed into the Paso Robles city limits thirty minutes later, it was too dark to continue.

They found a motel just north of what appeared to be the local fairgrounds, and scrounged some food from a place called Margie's Diner down the street before calling it a night.

"What do you think they're doing?" Noreen asked, as they lay in their room waiting for sleep to take them.

"Who?" Martina said.

"Jilly and the others. I'll bet the UN's put them up in a nice place with hot meals and clean clothes and showers."

"We've got a shower here," Martina said. "And if you want clean clothes, we can stop at Target in the morning."

"Not the same."

Quiet for a moment.

"How many people do you think there are?" Riley asked.

She and Martina were sharing a bed tonight.

"I don't know," Martina replied. "A hundred? Two hundred?"

"Maybe a thousand," Riley said. "Can you imagine what it would be like to see a thousand people in one place right now? I'd love that."

Silence again.

"Do you...do you think my dad and sister are there?" Riley asked.

"I hope so." It wasn't really an answer, but Martina didn't want to tell her friend what she really thought.

This time the silence went on for several minutes, and Martina started to think she was the only one still awake.

Then Noreen whispered, "What's going to happen?"

"We find Ben," Martina said.

"No, I mean, you know, what's going to *happen*? Next year. The year after that. The rest of our lives. What are we going to do?"

Martina was quiet for several moments before giving Noreen the only answer she could come up with.

"We live."

ISABELLA ISAND, COSTA RICA
10:40 PM CST

WHEN THE RESORT had simply been a resort, the bar was where everyone gathered in the evenings. The nights had been filled with laughter and celebrations then—accounts and lawyers and managers in vacation mode, letting loose in ways they never did back home. Since those on the island had become isolated, there was little laughter and no celebrations, but attendance at the bar remained high.

Surprisingly, few abused the new open-bar policy, most choosing to have only a drink or two at most, and many none at all. It was simply the place where some people could pretend everything would be okay, while others could at least feel they weren't alone. It was where many started their day, and most ended it.

Since the radio contact with the UN plane the day before,

the mood of the residents gathered at the bar had turned hopeful. Soon the UN would bring them the vaccine, and everyone might be able to get off the island and look for loved ones who might have survived.

A favorite guessing game at the bar was: When would the UN arrive?

"I'd bet it won't be more than a couple more days at most. They know we're here. They can't leave us unprotected for long."

"The fact we *are* here is why they won't be getting to us for a while. We're contained. Safe. Why waste time on us while there are probably others in more danger?"

"We're in plenty of danger. Plenty!"

"I don't think it will be much more than a week. That's what they said, right? A week? Hey, Robert, they said a week right?"

Robert had been nursing a cold glass of water at a table along the railing of the deck. The conversation had been going on over at the bar. He'd been trying to ignore it, but had known at some point they'd try to pull him in. It had happened with others several times already.

He looked over and said, "They told us it could be a few days, maybe more."

"Could be," one of the men in the group pointed out to his friends. "Could be a few weeks, too."

Just like that, Robert was once more forgotten. He returned his gaze to the dark rolling sea. Of all the people at the bar, he was the only one who seemed to be still worried. Not about the UN and the vaccine, of course. He was happy about that. But until everyone was inoculated and started leaving the island, Robert was in charge of making sure they were all fed and safe. It was a responsibility that seemed to grow heavier every day.

"You should never drink alone."

He looked up and found Estella standing next to his table.

"Don't know if this qualifies as drinking," he said, picking up his glass. "Water."

"Drinking is drinking." She pulled out the other chair, scooted it closer to his, and sat down.

Ever since their morning on the beach the day before, he'd begun to notice her around more. He wasn't sure if she'd always been there, or if her presence around him was something new. He had to admit he didn't mind.

"So when do *you* think they will come back?" she asked.

"They'll get here when they get here," he said.

"A smart answer."

"Don't know if it's smart, but it certainly saves me a lot of grief."

She cocked her head. "Grief?"

"Uh, keeps me from, let's see, um, having people get mad at me for no reason."

"Ah, okay. I understand."

She raised her glass toward his. As they clinked, he noted she was either drinking a tumbler full of straight vodka or was also having water.

She took a sip, and put her glass down. "You are a busy man."

He raised an eyebrow. "Do I look busy?"

"You do." She tapped her temple. "Inside, you thinking very much."

"Well, hazard of the position, I guess."

Again, her head cocked.

Before she could ask, he said, "Part of doing my job."

A nod and a smile.

"What do you do back home?" he asked, wanting to move the spotlight away from him.

Her face clouded. "I do not do anything now, I think."

"I mean before," he said.

"I worked at a university. In the library."

"You're a librarian?"

"Why do you sound surprised?"

"You don't strike me as the librarian type."

"Strike you as the librarian type?"

"It means—"

"I know what it means. You do not strike me as the

bartender type."

"I'm not a bartender anymore."

"And I'm not a librarian now, either."

He smiled and looked back out at the sea.

A minute passed, or two or three—he wasn't keeping track. When he heard Estella's chair scrape against the ground, he looked over and watched her rise to her feet.

"Thanks for joining me," he said. "It was nice." He meant it. For a few moments as they'd talked, he'd been able to forget about everything else.

She looked down at him, the corner of her mouth turned up ever so slightly, and then held out her hand, palm up.

"Come," she said.

He smiled, ready to tell her, thanks, but he had too much on his mind. Before he knew what he was doing, though, his hand was in hers and he was on his feet, all thoughts of the island and the others and the vaccine and the UN fading away.

WALSENBURG, COLORADO
9:55 PM MST

THE RESISTANCE CONVOY reached Denver as the sun was going down, but since there was only a light dusting of snow on the freeway, they pushed on, not stopping until they reached Walsenburg three hours later.

Their home for the night was a Best Western north of town. Ash, Brandon, and Josie took a room on the second floor, while Ginny and Rick chose one about as far away as possible on the first. That hadn't been Ginny's idea. She and Josie and Brandon had begun to form a bond, and Ash knew the girl would have liked to stay near them.

Rick, on the other, had spent a good part of the trip glaring at Brandon and rubbing the hand that was missing a finger. Ash knew he would have to keep an eye on that situation. Though Brandon had become very good at taking care of himself, Rick was several years older than Ash's son and twice his size. Ash had no doubt the kid was planning some kind of retribution.

"You all right?" Ash asked Brandon, once he and his

214

kids were alone in their room. While his son had not outwardly let Rick's unwanted attention affect him during the trip, Ash was concerned that inside was a different story.

"Yeah, why?" Brandon asked.

"Rick."

"Rick? I can't help it if he's a jerk. If he didn't want to get hurt, he shouldn't have been shooting at us."

Ash put a hand on his son's shoulder. "True. Probably best, though, if you keep your distance. Don't think he's looking at things in quite the same way."

"How's Brandon supposed to do that when we're all in the same truck?" Josie asked.

It was a good point, and one Ash had been thinking about. "I'll see what I can do about that in the morning," he said.

They ate dinner in their room, sharing cans of pears and ravioli and lima beans, and got ready for bed. Ash was finishing brushing his teeth when someone knocked on the door.

"I'll get it," Brandon said.

As the door opened, Ash heard Matt's voice from the hallway. "Hey, Brandon. Your dad around?"

Ash stepped out of the bathroom. "What's up?"

"Can I borrow you for a minute?" Matt asked.

"Sure." He pulled on the shirt he'd just taken off and told his kids, "Be right back."

Stepping out of the room, he saw Matt wasn't alone. A few feet away, Chloe was leaning against the wall.

"What's going on?" Ash asked.

"Not here," Matt said, and headed down the hall.

Ash glanced at Chloe, silently asking if she knew what was up.

"More bullshit, I bet," she whispered as she pushed herself off the wall and followed Matt.

Matt stopped about ten feet short of the end of the hallway, in an area where none of the rooms were being used. When Ash and Chloe joined him, he said, "I didn't want to spring it on you in the morning, so I'm going to tell you now.

This is where we part."

"Matt, it's not a good idea," Ash argued.

Ignoring him, Matt said, "The 160 heads west from here. You'll take that. Here." He pulled a folded map out of his pocket and held it out to Ash. "The route to the base in Nevada is marked. You'll take one of the plows and your Humvee. Head out when we do in the morning, so you beat the storm."

"You're making a mistake," Chloe said. "You need us."

"We've gone over this already," Matt said. "I'm not going to argue about it again."

Ash had yet to take the map from him.

"Chloe and I are the only ones here who've ever actually been in one of Project Eden's facilities," Ash said. "There's a good chance you're going to need what we know."

"Take it," Matt said, waving the map. "Get the kids to Nevada where they'll be safe."

With extreme reluctance, Ash took it from him.

Looking relieved, Matt said, "I sympathize. I really do, but trust me, this is not a mission you want to be on, especially in the condition you both are in." He forced a smile. "Now go get some sleep. I'll see you in the morning." Then, looking as if he couldn't get away fast enough, he walked stiff-legged to the stairs and headed down.

"This is stupid," Chloe said when she and Ash were alone. "Even with one hand I'm better than anyone he's got."

Ash didn't doubt that was true. His own condition, though, was not quite as accommodating. He knew he'd be struggling to keep up with the others, but that didn't mean he shouldn't be part of the team. If what Matt had planned would truly deliver a major blow to the Project, Ash needed to be there. *That* would be protecting his kids. Driving them to Nevada would be running away.

"You're thinking it, too, aren't you?"

He looked up and saw Chloe staring at him. "What?"

"That you're going to New Mexico whether Matt wants you to or not."

He hesitated. "The kids," he said. "I can't just leave

them."

"Your kids aren't kids anymore," she said. "We find a good place for them to hide and they'll be more than capable of taking care of themselves until we get back."

"I don't know." He rubbed his eyes. "I want to. I…I don't know."

"I do know," she said. "I'll see you in the morning."

As he watched her walk back to her room and disappear inside, he tried to figure out what would be the right thing to do, but this wasn't his decision alone.

When he returned to the room, Brandon and Josie were lying down but still awake.

"What did he want?" Josie asked.

Ash walked over to the empty bed the kids had left for him, and sat on the corner. "I need to talk to you both about something."

EASTERN NEVADA
9:17 PM PST

THE AMOUNT OF fuel left at the Ranch had not been nearly as much as Pax had expected, so they'd only had enough to get the Combi to Idaho Falls, where they were able to finally fill up their tanks. By the time they got back in the air, it was after seven thirty p.m.

Pax was sitting in the cockpit auxiliary seat, headset on, when they neared their destination.

"Bravo Eleven, this is Pax," he said, using the call sign for the Nevada base. "Bravo Eleven, please come in."

Static.

"Bravo Eleven, this is—"

"This is Bravo Eleven," a female voice cut in. "Please restate your call sign."

Grinning broadly, Pax said, "It's not a call sign. It's my damn name. It's Pax. Rich Paxton."

For a moment, there was no response, then, "Pax? Are you kidding me?"

Recognizing the voice, he said, "Is that you, Crystal?"

"Yes! Pax, oh my God! We thought—" She paused.

"Hold on."

When the static stretched to several seconds, Pax said, "Bravo Eleven, you still there? Crystal?"

"Is it really you?" A female voice, though not Crystal's anymore.

"Rachel," Pax said. "It's great to hear your voice."

"You're alive."

"Hell, yes, we're alive!"

"All of you?"

"Yeah, my whole team."

"Thank God. When we lost contact with you, we couldn't help but think something happened. Where are you?"

"Should be touching down on your airstrip in about ten minutes."

"Are you serious?"

"I hope so. If not, you're going to have to pick us out of the desert."

"I can't believe it. We've really missed you around here."

"Been busy, have you?"

Her tone turned serious. "You don't know the half of it."

"Well, I guess you can fill me in when we get down."

"Yeah."

"If you could do us a favor and light up the landing lights, that'd be great."

"Of course."

Seconds later, a double row of lights popped on in the sea of darkness below them.

RACHEL PUSHED OPEN the truck door and hurried toward the plane, making it almost all the way there by the time Pax climbed out.

They threw their arms around each other, Pax lifting her into the air as they hugged.

"I can't believe it's really you," she said. "I wasn't sure if we'd ever see you again."

"There were a few days there I wasn't sure about that

myself," he said. He kissed her cheek and set her down, then looked around. "I take it things haven't exactly been normal around here."

She almost laughed. "Oh, Pax, I've missed you."

She hugged him again, and started walking with him toward the truck.

"Matt too busy to make it out to say hi?" he asked.

"He's not here."

She could feel Pax tense.

"He didn't—"

"He's fine," she said, cutting him off. "Just out on a mission."

"What kind of mission?"

"I'll fill you in on everything later."

"What about Ash and Chloe? Were they able to make it back?"

"Yes, both of them."

"That's something, anyway."

When they reached the truck, they climbed into the back and waited for the rest of the team to get there. Rachel recognized all but two of the men.

When she mentioned this to Pax, he said, "No, that's my mistake." He waved the men over. "Rachel, I'd like you to meet Ian Lourdes and Frank Kendrick. They work with the research facility that put us up on Amund Ringnes Island."

"Researchers?" she asked, confused by why they had come.

"Pilots," Pax said.

Of course. Someone would have had to—

Pilots.

"Gentlemen, it's a pleasure to met you," she said. "I can't thank you enough for bringing our friends home. I'm guessing you both are pretty tired."

"Exhausted," Frank said.

She smiled and asked, "*How* exhausted?"

SALINAS, CALIFORNIA
9:41 PM PST

EDEN RISING

IRIS HAD FALLEN asleep within moments of lying down.

Ben, on the other hand, was wide awake. In what was surely the most eventful couple of weeks in human history, today had been a banner day in his small part of it. Leaving his childhood home, given the current circumstances, would have been traumatic enough, but throw on top of that finding Iris like he had, and then hunting for her after she ran off, was plenty to place the day squarely on top.

He pushed off his mattress and headed down the carpeted aisle.

His initial plan had been to find two rooms in a motel, but the first place he checked was full of the dead. Iris, who by that point refused to leave his side, had been so freaked out she wouldn't even let him check any other motels. Houses seemed to be out of the question, too. So Ben began looking for anyplace they could sleep halfway comfortably.

"There! There!" Iris had shouted as they were driving around on their search.

"You don't have to yell. I'm right here," he told her.

But when he looked to see what had caught her attention, he could almost forgive her outburst. A mattress store. Perfect.

The place turned out to be stocked not only with mattresses, but also sheets and blankets and pillows. It was the jackpot of non-hotel/non-home places to sleep.

He made his way to the back of the store, grabbed a can of soda out of the machine he'd jimmied earlier, and headed back up front, where he sat down on a bed in the window display.

Outside it was as dark as he'd ever seen it. Salinas had apparently lost its power. No street lamps, no lit signage, no emergency lights on in buildings. As strange as the darkness was, he had a feeling it would become the norm from now on, so he knew he'd better get used to it.

He popped open the can and took a sip. The soda was cool, but only because the store itself was cool. That was probably something else he'd have to get used to—not always being able to have a cold drink when he wanted one.

220

Or heat. Or air conditioning. Or ice.

Those were only a few items on the monstrous list of things he'd have to get used to, he thought. The truths and expectations he'd grown up with were gone.

He stared out into the pitch-black night.

This is the new reality. This is it.

JILLY PULLED HER blanket tight to her neck. The room was heated, but she was shivering.

We should have all stayed together, she thought. *We should have gone with Martina.*

On the bed below her, Valerie muttered something in her sleep, "taking it time," or "taking it, Tim," or maybe something else entirely. Whatever it was, Valerie sounded panicked. She twisted one way and then the other before falling silent again.

Jilly had no idea if she spoke in her own sleep, but she wouldn't doubt it.

From the moment they'd arrived at the survival station set up inside Dodger Stadium, Jilly had had a weird feeling about things. The UN officials they'd met with had given them only kind words and smiles, but something felt off.

Each girl had been taken into a room and interviewed individually.

"And you're from Ridgecrest, too?" Jilly's interviewer asked.

"Yes."

"Pretty amazing you were all able to survive."

"I guess." On the way to L.A., the girls had decided to keep quiet their belief that they were immune. They didn't want to chance not being given the vaccine in case they actually needed it. They agreed that if asked whether they'd had the Sage Flu during the spring outbreak, they'd say no.

"Were you and your friends together the whole time?" the interviewer asked.

"For the most part."

A notation on the page, then, "Did you see any others? Survivors, I mean."

The girls hadn't discussed this point. Should she tell the woman about Martina, Noreen, Riley, and Craig? "I didn't see anyone," she said. If the other girls wanted to tell their interviewers about Martina, so be it. She didn't feel right doing it.

The questions went on for over half an hour. At the end, Jilly was led through several stadium tunnels and out onto the baseball field, where two identical fenced-in areas were set up. They looked very much like the prisoner-of-war camps she'd seen in history class.

"Quarantine," her escort had said. "Just until we're sure you aren't showing any signs of the illness. At that point, you'll be given the vaccine."

"And then I'll be free to go?"

He looked surprised by her question. "Well, of course, that's a choice you can make. But we do have relocation zones where we are consolidating survivors. You'd be much happier there." When she didn't say anything, he went on. "Anyway, you don't have to make that decision now." His friendly smile was back. "There are books and movies inside the barracks building. You'll find something to occupy your time."

But Jilly didn't read any of the books. She didn't watch any of the movies, either. None of her teammates did. Though they hadn't discussed it, she sensed they all were feeling the same way she was. That something was wrong here.

Jilly turned on her side, the uncomfortable thoughts refusing to go away. When sleep finally came, it wasn't like a wave that pushed her deep beneath the surface, but more like a gentle swell, lapping over her face for a moment or two, but never enough to keep her under for long.

FROM THE JOURNAL OF BELINDA RAMSEY
11:57 PM CST

SO TIRED. WALKED until dark, but have only made it a few miles out of town, I think. I don't know for sure.

Found a farm just off the highway. Too scared to go into the house, so am in the barn. Plan was to have something to eat, then figure out where exactly I am. Guess I must have lain down. I don't remember doing that. But I do remember the last time I checked my watch it was almost 7 p.m., so looks like I've been out for about five hours.

Still exhausted, though. Forcing myself to eat and jot this down. Eyes are already getting heavy again, so am sure I'll be sleeping soon.

Until tomorrow.

January 2nd

World Population
961,001,699

22

FOR THE FIRST time since 1804, Earth's human population dipped below one billion.

23

SANJAY KNEW HIS best chance of getting back inside the Pishon Chem compound unseen was to go while most of the troops stationed at the survival station were spread throughout the city, looking for escaped survivors. He asked Kusum to come with him, knowing he would need someone as backup, and she was the one he trusted most. Besides, she wouldn't have let him go without her.

They made record time on their return trip, and worked their way through the neighborhood surrounding the compound until they were once more standing next to the hole at the back wall. They paused there, listening, in case a guard had been stationed on the other side. All was quiet.

As soon as Sanjay passed underneath the wall, though, his heart sank. Someone had moved a couple of barrels over the hole's exit. He put his hand on the bottom of one of the barrels and tested its weight.

Empty.

He tried the other. Also empty.

Not quite the disaster he had feared.

Careful to not tip over the barrels, he inched the first one to the side, and then did the same with the other. After they were out of the way, he poked his head out and looked around. The area was as deserted as it had been when he and Kusum came through earlier.

He crawled back out the other side. "Okay," he

whispered to Kusum. "Be very careful."

She rolled her eyes and waved impatiently for him to go back under.

After they were in the compound, they put the barrels back in front of the hole. To the casual observer, it would look like the barrels were still in place. Sanjay then led Kusum around the scrap piles and headed toward the administration building.

The vaccine he had stolen for Kusum and her family had been located in a medical storage room near the first-floor conference room. He thought they must have more of it there. If not...

No! It is there, he told himself.

They passed between the dormitory buildings and over to the back entrance to admin.

"You stay out here," he whispered to Kusum.

"Why? So someone walking by can see me?"

"What? No. Someone needs to keep an eye on things out here. And since I am the one who knows where the vaccine is, I need to be the one who goes inside. There," he said, pointing at a few parked vehicles a dozen meters away. "Hide behind those cars. You will be fine."

SENIOR MANAGER DETTLING had lost track of how many times he wished someone else had been put in charge of the Mumbai location, but never had he wished it more than after his ass chewing by the principal director.

Just get me through this so I can help with the rebuilding.

That's what he'd been looking forward to. This killing, this culling of humanity, as necessary as he realized it was, still gnawed at his soul.

This was why he had conspired with the other Pishon managers to hide the real cause of Herr Schmidt's death. He couldn't blame that boy Sanjay for shooting the senior manager in the shoulder so he could steal some vaccine for his family, any more than he could blame one of his own people if one were responsible for cutting the holes in the detention-area fences. The possibility of it being an inside job hadn't occurred to him, but the principal director seemed convinced. Hell, under the right circumstances, Dettling himself might have cut the holes.

The director wanted a witch hunt, wanted him to serve up whoever had done this—if indeed it was one of Dettling's people—and undoubtedly pack him off for punishment elsewhere. Dettling didn't think he could do that. He ran a hand through what was left of his hair, trying to think of some way out of this.

It was the picture on the wall that provided him the answer. It was a shot of the Pishon Chem managers with several of their Indian team members. A PR picture taken by a local newspaper that probably never had the chance to run it. But it had been important to keep up appearances, so the team had posed, smiling.

One of the managers in the picture was Bernard Weathersbee. He'd been one of Dettling's lieutenants until he was severely injured in a truck accident less than twenty-four hours after the spraying had begun. Weathersbee had held on for over a week, but finally succumbed to his injuries yesterday morning.

Dettling made a quick check of the logs. No, the death had not yet been reported to the directorate.

He thought for a moment. Yes, it might work. He felt bad blaming his friend, but it was better than pointing the finger at someone who would suffer for it.

When the escapees were finally caught, Dettling would serve up Weathersbee, saying he'd been killed during the search. Satisfied, he left his office in search of van Assen to help set the plan in motion.

AS SANJAY NEARED the conference room, the door across the hall began to open. With nowhere else to go, he slipped inside the unused office he'd just passed.

Leaving the door open a crack, he watched as Mr.

Dettling, one of the Pishon Chem managers Sanjay had known, emerged from the senior manager's office. If Sanjay had been a few feet farther down the hall, Dettling would have seen him and recognized him for sure.

Sanjay's pulse raced.

Relax, he told himself. *You're almost there.*

He waited to make sure Dettling didn't immediately come back, then he reentered the hallway and slinked past the empty conference room to the unmarked door of the medical supply room. He tried the knob, hoping it was unlocked, but he wasn't that lucky. And he couldn't break into it. Besides the fact the door was sturdy, the noise would draw attention. What he needed was the silver key with the J on it. That's how he'd gotten in last time.

He looked back at the senior manager's office. Had Dettling come from a meeting with the man? Or was it empty, the senior manager attending to business elsewhere? Sanjay had been armed with a gun the previous time he was in the gray-haired man's presence. He'd even had to shoot the senior manager in the shoulder to convince him to cooperate. Now, the only things he had were the wire cutters he was still carrying and his own two hands.

You do not need a gun, he told himself.

The senior manager was old and weak and dismissive. Sanjay could easily get the key from the man. He was sure of it.

He checked the hallway Dettling had turned down to make sure it was empty, and crossed over to the office. Slowly he pushed the door open, ready to rush in if the manager started to yell.

But no one was inside.

Hoping the manager had left his keys behind, Sanjay raced over to the desk. There were no keys sitting on top, so he started pulling open drawers. Nothing in the center drawer or in the top drawers on either side.

The bottom drawers presented a problem. Both were locked. He finally figured out that if he left the center drawer open, the locks would release. He hit pay dirt in the bottom left drawer. A cardboard box stuffed in the back contained three key rings, each holding a couple dozen keys. The first set he checked had the silver J key, so he didn't bother with the other two. Putting everything back so no one would know he'd been there, he returned to the hallway.

The key slipped easily into the medical supply room door, like he knew it would. A turn to the left resulted in a click as the latch pulled away. Sanjay stepped inside, closed the door, and turned on the light.

He was here. He'd made it.

Knowing he had precious little time, he hurried over to the glass cabinet where the vaccine had been last time. When he took it then, he'd identified it by its orange tint, the selection confirmed by the look in the senior manager's eyes. Now, after filling dozens of syringes with the vaccine when he and Kusum had inoculated the others in their group, he had seen more than enough bottles to recognize the drug's name if he saw it again.

KV-27a/V/ASH VARIANT.

He had no idea what it meant, but that wasn't important.

Starting on the top shelf, he worked his way to the bottom, checking every item. No vaccine. He moved to the bottom cabinet, but it was empty.

This is where it was, he told himself. *Could I have taken it all?*

He looked around, searching for another cabinet like the ones he'd checked. But he already knew there were no other similar cabinets. As he twisted to the left, his gaze fell on a stack of boxes in the corner that had not been there before. Printed on the side in black was /V/ASH.

It wasn't the full name he'd seen on the vials, but part of it.

He pulled the top box off the stack and set it on the counter. It was just under a half meter square and almost the same high. The seams were sealed with black and yellow striped tape.

He pulled the wire cutters from his pocket and sliced down the middle of the tape. Inside the box were four smaller containers that looked identical to the ones full of vaccine he'd stolen. Trying not to get his hopes up, he opened one of the small boxes. It was full of vials containing an orange-tinted liquid. Holding his breath, he pulled one out and looked at the label.

KV-27a/V/ASH VARIANT

He opened another of the smaller boxes. It, too, contained the vaccine. *All* the boxes must've contained the vaccine.

His excitement was momentarily tempered by the thought that maybe the survival station was exactly what it was supposed to be. That maybe anyone coming in would get one of these shots.

But why would the same people who had brought the plague down on everyone be the ones who started handing out the cure?

That's when the likely truth dawned on him. It was horrible. Almost worse than unleashing the disease itself.

The cure *would* be handed out, but only to those the Pishon Chem people—whom Leon had referred to as Project Eden—deemed worthy of it.

Sanjay put the vials away and secured the top of the box. No, he would not allow this Project Eden to make that decision. If someone needed the vaccine, no matter who they were, Sanjay would make sure the person received it.

KUSUM CHECKED HER watch again. It was closing in on thirty minutes.

She stared at the door Sanjay had disappeared behind, willing him to open it and step through. When he finally did, she let out a gasp of surprise.

Realizing he was having difficulty closing the door because of the box he was carrying, she jumped out of her hiding spot and ran over. As she neared, she realized it wasn't just one box, but two.

"Let me," she whispered, putting her hand on the doorknob.

With relief, he let go and watched her quietly close the door.

"Is this all vaccine?" she asked.

"Yes."

"This is so much more than before."

"This is not even half of it. There are six more boxes."

"Six more," she said. "How can we carry that many?"

"We cannot, but we can hide what we cannot take with us, and come back for them later. Better in our hands than in theirs, yes?

Instead of taking the boxes from him, she grabbed his face and kissed him. "You are a surprising man, Sanjay."

"Not surprising. What other choice do we have?"

"That's exactly what I mean."

"Take these," he said, shoving the boxes toward her. "Carry them over to the hole and come right back."

She transported the first two boxes, and then boxes three and four.

When she returned for the next pair, he said, "I will bring the last two. Take these and the others out of the compound, then start taking them to the building we used before. The sooner we can finish, the better."

Kusum nodded. "Do not be long."

"I'll be right behind you."

DETTLING FOUND VAN Assen at the security office near the main gate, monitoring the search efforts. He motioned for him to come outside where they'd have some privacy.

"Any progress?" he asked, after he'd led his assistant around the side of the building.

"Unfortunately, no," van Assen said.

"What do you think the likelihood is we'll find any of them?"

His assistant seemed reluctant to reply, but finally said, "We'll be lucky if we find one or two. It's a huge city, and they know it better than us."

"I agree," Dettling admitted. While it would have been

nice to find them, the important thing now was the assigning of blame. "I need your help on a delicate matter."

Van Assen had proven to be a very trustworthy and competent assistant, who was of a similar mind to Dettling on most matters concerning the Project, so the senior manager had no reservations about filling him in on his plan to placate the principal director.

"We can do this quietly," Dettling said when he finished outlining his plan. "The report will go straight to the directorate. No one else here needs to know about any of it."

"Of course," van Assen said. "I'll handle the staging and the pictures immediately. There are plenty of empty rooms on the basement level. We can say we cornered him in one of them. He then put up a fight and, unfortunately, was killed in the process."

Dettling kept his expression blank, but inside he felt relieved. Van Assen understood exactly what he wanted. Everything was going to be just fine.

"I think, perhaps, it would be good if we continue the search for a few more hours," van Assen suggested. "The fewer people here at the compound while I take care of this other matter, the better."

"Yes, I agree."

"Well, then, I suppose I should get to work."

SANJAY ENTERED THE main building and returned to the medical room for the fourth time that evening. As he picked up the last two boxes, his gaze fell on the set of keys he'd put on the counter.

For a few seconds, he wondered if he should return them to the senior manager's office, but thought that the missing vaccine would be noticed long before the missing keys, so he left them where they were.

As he'd done each trip before, he used the wall to help him hold the boxes while he turned the knob, and started to open the door.

That's when he heard the footsteps.

VAN ASSEN RETURNED to the admin building and made a stop at his office. There, he retrieved a pair of gloves, a camera, and his set of keys. While he could have grabbed the Glock 9mm pistol in his drawer, he knew it would be better if the shots that "brought Weathersbee down" were not from the gun assigned to him.

The main weapons arsenal was located back in the security building. There was, however, a weapons locker—albeit a less–equipped one—near Mr. Dettling's office. He headed there next, and was considering which firearm would be best when he heard a door open behind him.

He turned quickly, a thousand excuses for why he needed to be in the locker running through his head, but no one was in the hallway. As far as he could tell, all the doors were shut.

But it had definitely been a door. He closed the weapons locker door and tiptoed over to the nearest office. Placing his ear close to the surface, he listened for anyone inside. Not hearing anything, he moved quietly to the next office, but it was more dead air.

He knew he had heard a door, and it had been in *this* hallway. Not counting Dettling's, there was one more office, the conference room, and a few storage rooms. He headed for the office.

When he reached the door, he stopped and listened again.

KUSUM WAS ALMOST caught while transporting the first two boxes to the safety of the building outside the compound.

She was only a block away from her destination when a car came around a bend. She barely had time to dodge into a narrow gap between two stores.

The car drove slowly down the road, flashlight beams shining out the open windows onto buildings and parked cars.

Kusum knelt down, intending to go all the way prone with the boxes beside her when she remembered the distinctive yellow and black tape. If they saw that, they would stop for sure. She snatched up a pile of food wrappers and newspapers and covered the exposed ends of the boxes, hoping that would be enough. Then down she went.

A few moments later, through the corner of her eye, she saw the wall beside her light up, less than an arm's length above her head. She tensed, ready to make a run for it if the light dipped any lower, but the car kept moving, and the muted glow of the flashlight beam quickly faded.

She waited until she couldn't hear the car anymore, and then jumped to her feet and ran the rest of the way.

She hid the two boxes in a storeroom of a first-floor shop, concealing them behind a stack of dresses and children's clothes. Then she headed back to the compound to help Sanjay bring the others.

But when she arrived, Sanjay wasn't there yet.

She nearly crawled into the hole, thinking he might need help, but stopped herself.

He's being careful, she told herself. *He'll be fine.*

She wasn't sure if she believed that or not, but she knew if she went back in, there was as much of a chance she'd make things worse than better.

She grabbed two more boxes and started back for the building.

He'll be here when I get back.

He'll be here.

BOTH THE OFFICE and the conference room were empty. Van Assen even went ahead and checked Dettling's office. No one there, either.

So, which door had opened?

He looked around the hallway again.

One of the storage rooms? No one should be in any of those, not this late at night, and especially not on a night like they were experiencing. But those were the only places he hadn't checked.

There were four of them: the weapons locker he'd been in, a maintenance closet, the medical storage room, and the telecom equipment room. The medical storage room was closest, so he went there first.

SANJAY HEARD FOOTSTEPS approaching the storage room. Not knowing if the door had automatically locked when he shut it, he grabbed the knob and held it tight.

He realized too late that he should have put the boxes down first so he could use both hands, but there was nothing he could do about it now.

The steps stopped right outside, and then the knob shook, but it didn't turn. It was locked, he realized with relief. As soon as the other person let go, he did, too, and thought, *Go look somewhere else.*

But instead of steps moving away from the door, he heard the rattle of metal, followed by the sound of a key slipping into the lock.

VAN ASSEN INSERTED the J key into the doorknob and turned it. As he stepped forward, something grabbed his arm, yanked him inside, and shoved him to the floor.

As he looked back, he saw the culprit flee the room. But the man wasn't one of the Project's people; he was an Indian. And he was carrying two boxes sealed with yellow and black tape.

Van Assen pushed himself to his feet and rushed over to the back corner where the eight boxes of vaccine had been stored.

They were gone.

Every last one of them.

SANJAY SPRINTED DOWN the hallway toward the exit, knowing the man he'd thrown to the ground would be after him in seconds. He'd recognized the guy. The man had been one of Dettling's subordinates, but Sanjay had never known his name.

Faster! he ordered himself, sure that a hand was about to clamp down on his shoulder.

He knew he should have dumped the vaccine—it was slowing him down—but the idea of leaving any of it behind was not acceptable to him.

"Hey! You there! Come back here!" the man yelled behind him.

Sanjay kept running until he reached the door. As he banged it open and rushed outside, he would have collided with Mr. Dettling if he hadn't spun at the last second out of the way. While the move saved him from hitting the man, the top box slipped from his grasp and fell on the ground.

"What the hell? What's going on?" Dettling said. As Sanjay leaned down and picked up the box, Dettling narrowed his eyes. "Sanjay?"

"Leave me alone," Sanjay said as he started to run again. "Leave all of us alone. Haven't you and your Project Eden friends killed enough?"

VAN ASSEN SHOVED the door out of the way. When he exited the building, he was surprised to find Mr. Dettling standing just outside, staring at the receding form of the intruder.

"He's got the vaccine!" van Assen yelled.

Dettling had no reaction.

"Mr. Dettling, did you hear me? He has the vaccine!"

"The vaccine?" Dettling said, as if not comprehending the words.

"Yes! He's taken all of it!"

More silence.

Whatever was wrong with Dettling, van Assen wasn't about to let it take him down, too.

Pushing past his boss, he headed after the thief.

SANJAY DIDN'T EVEN bother trying to hide. The faster he got out of there, the better chance he had of remaining free.

He weaved his way through the compound and into the back junk area. When he reached the barrels sitting in front of the hole, he risked a look back. He didn't see anyone, but knew he couldn't count on that for long.

He shoved the first box into the hole as far as it would go, then used the second one to push the first, and then he followed it. The first box cleared the other end, but the second seemed hung up on something. He pulled it back a few centimeters and wiggled it forward, hoping to avoid the obstruction. For a second, it felt like it would get stuck again, then it was free, and...

...pulled from his grasp.

As the hole above him cleared, he saw Kusum looking down. "What took you so long?"

"Go! Run! They are chasing me!"

Instead of running, though, she grabbed his arm and helped him out.

"Come on, come on," he said, grabbing two of the boxes.

Kusum picked up the other two that were there, and they ran.

VAN ASSEN'S ENCOUNTER with Dettling ended up causing him to lose the intruder. He ran in the direction he thought the man had gone, but could not find him. When he ran into the junk area, he noticed that the barrels covering the hole by the wall had been moved.

Dammit!

Without hesitating, he dropped into the hole and squirmed under the wall. It was a tight fit, but he was just able to make it. When he climbed out the other side, he whirled around.

But there was no one there.

DETTLING STARED INTO the night.

Sanjay. My God.

The last time he'd seen the kid, Sanjay was holding a

gun as he forced Dettling and several other managers into a storage room. And now here he'd been again, not only saying words that Dettling had often thought himself, but actually using the name Project Eden. Where could he have heard that?

Dettling knew he should have been running right behind van Assen, knew they should be doing everything they could to retrieve the vaccine, but the final straw had broken him.

What have we done?

He numbly walked into the building and down to his office. From one of the desk drawers he pulled out a bottle of whiskey, intending to drink himself into a stupor. He was halfway through the bottle when he thought about the gun in his other drawer.

The first shot went wide as his head swayed from the alcohol.

He was smarter the second time, and had the gun's barrel firmly planted against the top of his mouth when he pulled the trigger.

"I DO NOT see anyone," Kusum whispered.

"Neither do I," Sanjay said.

They were lying on the roof of the building where the boxes were hidden, scanning the streets between them and the compound.

"I think we are okay," he said.

She slapped his shoulder. "Not okay. Why did you let him see you?"

"Because I thought it would be more fun that way."

She slapped him again.

"We need to talk about you hitting me so much," he said.

"What is there to talk about? If you stop doing stupid things, I will stop hitting you."

"And you are the judge of whether the things I do are stupid or not?"

"Of course."

He frowned. "I am not sure I am enjoying marriage so

much."

"You are enjoying it fine." She turned on her side. "Now come here and put your arms around me."

He snuggled into her. "We really should be going," he said. "The sooner we can get all the boxes to where the others are, the sooner we can leave the city."

"Soon," she said. "But not yet."

24

THE VEHICLES HEADING south into New Mexico were lined up in the hotel parking lot, their engines running. Ash, Josie, Brandon, Chloe, Dr. Gardiner, and Ginny stood outside the lobby shaking hands and wishing everyone good luck. Rick was up in his room. According to Ginny, he was sulking about being kidnapped, but wouldn't fight continuing on with them.

"Be safe," Ash said to a couple of the men coming out of the hotel.

"You guys, too," one of them said.

"Take care."

"Same for you."

Lily Franklin came out. "Wish you guys were coming with us," she said.

"I hope you're bored to death and don't need to patch anyone up," Ash said.

"You and me both."

Matt came out with the last two men. "Davis and Sorrento here will be your drivers," he said.

The two men didn't look happy about being left out of the raid, but they nodded to Ash and Chloe.

"If you guys get going here pretty quick, you might be able to make it all the way to Salt Lake City tonight," Matt said. "But don't push it. Stop when you're getting tired."

"We'll be fine," Ash said.

"Anything else you need?"

Ash shook his head. "Don't think so."

"No," Chloe said. "Think we're good."

"All right, then. I guess we'll be off."

Before he could turn away, Ash held out his hand. "Good luck."

"Thanks, Captain," Matt said, shaking it. "If we can pull this off, we all might have a chance."

"Then I suggest you pull it off."

After Matt had climbed into his Humvee, Ash said to Chloe, "You could have loosened up a little. At least said good-bye."

"Yeah. I could have."

In a mighty roar, the convoy turned onto the road toward the interstate.

As soon as the last truck disappeared onto the on-ramp, Ash said, "Ginny, get your cousin. It's time to leave."

ASH ASSIGNED RICK to ride in the snowplow with Davis, which seemed to suit the kid fine. The rest of them piled into the Humvee. For the first time since they'd left the Ranch, Ash took the front passenger seat.

Sorrento, a skinny guy in his late twenties, seemed to have shrugged off the disappointment of missing the main mission, and smiled as he checked to make sure everyone had a seat.

"All right. Let's get going," he said.

"Just a second," Ash told him.

Sorrento paused, his hand ready to shift the truck into gear.

Ash sat motionless for a moment, running everything through his head again.

"Captain?" Sorrento said.

Ash glanced at him, and then picked up the handheld radio they were using to communicate between their two vehicles. He switched to the same band Chloe had set the radio in the plow to—one they were confident Matt would not be using—and clicked the talk button.

"Davis?" he said.

"Yes, sir," Davis said. "Ready to go when you are."

"I think for this first part, you just follow us," Ash said. "If we run into any problems, you can swing around and take care of them."

"Okay, sir. If that's what you'd like."

Ash looked at Sorrento. "Let's hit it."

Sorrento put the Humvee in gear and drove them toward the parking lot exit.

"Go left," Ash told him.

Sorrento slowed the vehicle. "Sir?"

"Change of plans. We're taking the interstate."

"The exit for 160 is only a mile or so down," Sorrento said, confused. "It's actually quicker if we go through town."

"We're not taking 160."

"We're not? But Mr. Hamilton said—"

"I don't care what Matt said."

"Okay, but if you're thinking we should go through Albuquerque and head west from there, that's kind of the long way around."

"We're not going to Nevada," Ash said. "Not yet, anyway."

Sorrento looked completely lost now. "I'm not sure I—"

"We're going south."

"But Mr. Hamilton thinks we're going to Nevada."

"That, he does."

The truth of Ash's intent seemed to slowly dawn on Sorrento. Brow unfurrowing, he tilted his head back. "We're going to follow them?"

"Now you're getting the picture," Ash said. "Won't be a problem, will it?"

Sorrento eased off the brake and smiled. "Not at all, sir."

"Hold on," Dr. Gardiner said from his seat behind him. "Did I hear you right? We're heading into New Mexico?"

The Humvee rumbled onto the street and turned toward the interstate.

"That's correct, Doctor."

"No, no, no! We're going to Nevada. That's where my family is."

"Don't worry. We'll get you there eventually," Ash said. "At the moment, your services may be needed elsewhere."

"Uh-uh. No way. I didn't sign up for this."

"You didn't sign up for anything," Chloe said. "We saved your ass. *I* saved your ass. You and your family would already be dead otherwise."

"This isn't the old world anymore," Ash said. "We don't get to sit around in our living rooms while someone else fights our fights."

"I don't consider what I've been doing just sitting around a living room," the doctor argued.

"No, that's true, but there's more work to be done. What Matt and the rest of the team are planning will go a long way to saving a lot of people. They'll be putting themselves in harm's way, which means they will very likely need medical attention, probably more than Lily can handle on her own."

"So we're following them because they might need *me*?"

"No," Chloe said. "We're going because they will definitely need Ash and me. You are an additional benefit."

Davis's voice came over the radio. "Weren't we supposed to take that?"

Ash glanced outside. They had just passed the US 160 exit off the I-40.

He picked up the radio. "Change of route," he said. "I'll explain when we take a break in a while."

"All right, sir."

Ash looked back at the doctor. "Is this going to be an issue?"

He knew Gardiner was a good man who was still trying to come to grips with all that had happened. The doctor wanted to be with his family, to know they were safe. But these days, the best way to keep loved ones safe often meant risking one's life. Ash was sure that on some level, the doctor understood this.

A few moments later, his hunch paid off.

"No," Gardiner said. "Not an issue."

"ROBERT, YOU UP?"

Someone knocked rapidly on Robert's door.

"Hey! Come on. Wake up!"

Robert forced his eyes open and checked his watch. It was already after seven. He couldn't remember the last time he'd slept that late.

"Robert! Wake up!"

He recognized Renee's voice now.

"Just a minute," he said.

Estella stirred beside him, her body draped over his side. "What's going on?" she whispered.

"I'll check."

He extracted himself from the bed as Renee began pounding on the door again.

"I'm coming," he said.

He grabbed his shorts off the floor and pulled them on as he moved out into the small living room that made up the rest of his apartment. Since he was now in charge, he could have moved into Dominic's larger place, but that seemed wrong.

"Robert!" Renee yelled.

He pulled the door open and stepped onto the threshold in case she had been planning on coming inside. But the moment she saw him, she turned and started walking away.

"Come on," she said, hurriedly. "We've got to go."

"What's going on?"

"Another plane," she said. "They just radioed and said they'll be here soon."

"The UN?"

"Yes."

"Give me a second."

"I'll be in the radio room."

Robert ran back inside to grab his shirt and sandals.

"What is it?" Estella asked.

"The UN. They're coming back."

She pushed herself up. "With the vaccine?"

247

"I don't know. I would think so. Look, I'll, um, meet you at the bar in a little while."

"Sure. Okay."

Robert went over to the bed, gave her a deep kiss, and ran out of the room.

AFTER GIVING THE plane instructions to land in the lagoon, Robert and Renee—and pretty much all the rest of the island residents—headed down to meet it.

The plane buzzed overhead as it did a flyby of the lagoon before coming in and landing smoothly on the calm waters. The engine noise increased again as the aircraft taxied across the bay to the main pier, where Robert and Renee were waiting. A few of the others were also on the pier, while most remained on the beach, with a mix of wary and excited looks on their faces.

As the plane pulled up next to the dock, Robert counted six people inside—four men and two women. He grabbed a rope and tied the front of the pontoon to the dock while Renee did the same at the back.

The plane's door opened, and the first visitors the resort had received since the outbreak climbed out.

Leading them was a smiling woman with brown hair and tan skin.

Robert offered her his hand and helped her down. "Welcome to Isabella Island."

"Thank you," she said. "We're very glad to be here." She had a hint of a Hispanic accent but her English was perfect. "I'm Dr. Vega, but please call me Ivonne."

"Robert," he said. "Robert Adams."

The other woman was next, introducing herself as Helena Chavez, a nurse, and then one of the men, a doctor named Peter de Coster.

"The others will join us in a little bit," Ivonne said. "They need to unpack the supplies."

"We can get some people to help them out, if you'd like," Robert offered.

"That would be great."

He asked for volunteers and saw almost every hand shoot up. He picked out three, who quickly made their way to the plane.

"We will need someplace to set up," de Coster said.

"Of course," Robert said. "The bar will probably be best. Plenty of room there, and that's where people tend to hang out anyway."

"Sounds perfect," Ivonne said.

"Follow me."

As they walked along the path back to the resort, Renee said, "I can't tell you how glad we are that we didn't have to wait long for you to come back."

"We're glad we could make it," Ivonne replied.

"Can you tell us what's going on out there?" Robert asked. "How bad is it?"

Ivonne's smile faltered. "About as bad as you can imagine. Billions have died already."

He stopped walking. "Did you say billions? With a b?"

"Yes," she said.

Robert couldn't get his head around the number. Did that mean whole countries were gone? Continents? Was that possible?

"That can't be right," he said.

"I wish it wasn't, but there's no part of the planet that hasn't been touched." She paused. "Except, perhaps, your island."

"No," he said, still stunned. "We've been touched."

Dr. de Coster's eyes widened. "The disease is here?"

"Not anymore."

"How can you be sure?" he asked.

Robert told them what had happened to Dominic.

"No one else has come down with the flu?"

"Not a one," he said.

Ivonne smiled. "Sounds like you dodged a bullet."

"Dominic didn't."

"Of course. I'm very sorry about your friend."

They fell into silence for several seconds.

EDEN RISING

De Coster finally spoke. "You were going to show us where we could set up?

"Right," Robert said. "This way."

I HAD TO go into the farmhouse this morning. I know I said I didn't want to, but the one thing I hadn't taken with me when I left the dorm was matches, and I really wanted to light a fire to warm up. There's a side door that leads straight into the kitchen. I looked through the windows first. If I'd seen even a hint of a body, I would have just dealt with the cold. But the room looked empty, so—with apologies to the homeowners—I broke a window so I could unlock the door.

I have to say that as I stepped inside, I was tempted to keep going until I found a fireplace, or, even better, a warm bed. That was before the smell hit me, though. It was so strong and putrid, I stumbled back outside and thought for sure I was going to throw up. I don't know how I kept it down.

Again, I thought about abandoning the search for matches and going back to the barn. But the thing is, this wasn't going to be the last time I smelled death—far from it, I'm guessing. And if I let it keep me from what I need, then I might as well give up now. I'm not saying I'm ready to extend this newfound bravery to actually seeing bodies yet, but I'll deal with the smell.

I buried my nose under as many layers of my scarf as I could wrap around, and then went back inside. I could still smell the bodies rotting elsewhere in the house, but it wasn't as potent as

250

before. Searching through the kitchen, I found a large container of matches, an unopened box of Ritz Crackers, and a sharp knife that could come in handy if I ran into any unfriendly animals. Honestly, the knife is really just something that makes me feel safer. Not sure, really, how I would handle an attacking animal. It did get me thinking about guns again, though, and whether there were any in the house. I've never shot a firearm before, but I know a gun would be real protection. Of course, that would have meant moving beyond the kitchen, still something I was not mentally prepared to do.

As much as I would have liked to build a fire inside the barn, I was afraid some of the sparks might burn the place down. "Girl Survives Plague Only to Die in Fire." Hell of a headline, even if there would be nobody to read it. Or, I guess, write the headline in the first place.

I cleared an area out front that was covered by the barn's eaves and mostly snow free, if not exactly dry. I then gathered some loose pieces of wood and dried hay from inside, and arranged them in the way my dad used to when we went camping. The first match broke in my hand, but the second got things going, and soon I was warming my hands by the small blaze.

I wanted to get an early start this morning, so I knew I couldn't sit there for long. I still hadn't made a journal entry, though, and that was something I promised to do every day, so I went back in the barn to retrieve this book.

I barely remember last night. I was really tired, so I didn't get a chance to look around. But now I noticed a workshop down at the far end. I figured there might be something there that was good to have, so I headed over to check. Didn't make it all the way, though. As I was passing one of the animal pens the owners had turned into storage areas, I noticed several large objects covered with tarps.

I grabbed one of the covers and threw it off, and I'm not going to lie—I started to laugh. A snowmobile. In fact, there were four of them. Guess who's not going to have to walk anymore?

I was concerned at first that I might need to make another trip into the house to find the keys, but I found a ring with keys for all four in one of the drawers under the workbench. The good news is, all four engines started on the first try. There's no real bad news, but my problem is, I have no idea which one would be the best to take. I've decided to go with the one that looks newest. I'm hoping that means its engine is in the best shape.

I found several gas cans stored in the same area, and used what was left in one of them to fill the tank. I've strapped two of the cans that are near full to the back end with ropes and bungee cords. If I don't run into any trouble, I'll definitely be able to make it across the border into Illinois before nightfall. If I push it, I might even make it all the way to Chicago.

Here's hoping for no trouble.

SALINAS, CALIFORNIA
6:50 AM PST

BEN WOKE WITH a start. He'd been dreaming. Of what, he couldn't remember, but his heart was pounding and his breaths were short and fast. As the rush receded, his body began to relax and his head sank back into the pillow. He lay there for a minute, trying to remember what it was that had caused such a panic, but whatever had occupied his unconscious mind was gone for good.

He glanced over at the bed where Iris had been sleeping, but it was empty. He sat up and looked around. He didn't see her anywhere in the showroom.

Restroom, he guessed.

Ben pulled on his shoes and headed to the back of the store, needing to use the facilities himself. After making a stop in the men's room, he knocked on the door to the women's.

"Iris? You in there?"

No answer.

He pushed the door open a few inches.

"Iris?" When she didn't respond again, he said, "I'm coming in."

A quick check of the stalls confirmed what he'd suspected. She wasn't there.

Great.

She'd probably run off again. The question was, should he once more try to find her?

"No," he told himself a moment later. She knew what was going on now. Maybe she just wanted to be alone. If that was the case, so be it.

He walked back into the main showroom, thinking the sooner he hit the road, the sooner he'd reach Ridgecrest, where, God willing, he'd find Martina. After he'd repacked the few things he'd taken out of his bag, he unzipped the pouch where he kept his keys. But his keys weren't there.

"Son of a bitch!"

Slinging his bag over his shoulder, he ran toward the front of the store, but long before he got there, he could see through the big plate-glass windows that his Jeep was not where he'd left it.

"Dammit!"

He burst out the main door and ran out into the parking

area. No Jeep anywhere.

"No! No! No!"

He jogged over to the street and looked both ways. Nothing moved in either direction, nor could he hear the sound of an engine, even in the distance.

He yelled in frustration. It was *his* Jeep with *his* things in the back.

Oh, God, he thought. The photo of his family, his mother's favorite, it was still under the driver's seat.

And the earrings. The ones he'd bought for Martina. They were to be the first ever Christmas gift he'd give her.

All of them, gone.

He stared down the road, numb.

25

PEREZ MADE HIS way through NB219 to the barracks section used by the security forces. As he stepped into the common area, the men who saw him first immediately jumped to attention, with the rest soon doing the same.

"I'm looking for Mr. Sims," he said. "Anyone know where I can find him?"

"In his room, sir," one of the men said. "Keep going straight. B-09."

"Thank you."

The door to Room B-09 was open a few inches. Perez looked inside and saw Sims unpacking his bag.

"Mr. Sims," Perez said as he rapped a knuckle on the door.

Sims whirled around. "Principal Director," he said, surprised. "Did I get the meeting time wrong?"

After spending the night in Denver, Sims and his team had arrived back at NB219 less than fifteen minutes earlier. He was due in Perez's office for a debriefing at the top of the hour.

"No. I had something that finished up early. Thought I'd save you the trip."

In truth, Perez had canceled a previously scheduled video conference so he could make this personal appearance. In his mind, Sims was the second most important person in the Project. He had become the hammer that reinforced the principal director's rule. So Perez knew it was necessary to make sure their working relationship was solid. Small things, such as dropping in like this, went a long way toward solidifying loyalty.

"Thank you, sir, but you didn't have to do that."

"Not a problem," Perez said. "I take it you didn't find anything after your last report."

"No, sir. Those first tracks we saw were it. There was a big storm up there. I'm pretty sure they're riding it out somewhere. Once the weather clears up, we can go back out and look for them again."

Perez had received a report on the storm. It was the same one, though diminished, that was expected to hit northern New Mexico in the next hour or two, and could possibly make it all the way down to Las Cruces at some point during the night.

"If you do go back, what do you think your chances are of finding them?"

"Fair, I guess."

"Give me a percentage."

"Well, if the weather clears up in that area like it's supposed to tonight, and we leave before first light tomorrow, I'd say we have maybe a forty-percent chance. If we have to wait twelve hours or a full day more, it would go down to single digits and probably not be worth it."

Perez wasn't sure a forty-percent chance would be worth it. "Touch base with me this evening. We'll make a decision then."

"Yes, sir."

"Anything else to report?"

"No, sir. That's it."

"Very good." As they shook hands, the principal director said, "Tell your men I'm very pleased with the work they are doing."

"I will. They'll appreciate that, sir."

26

"TRY AGAIN," RACHEL said.

"Okay," Crystal said, "but the result's going to be the same. Either their radio is off, or Matt's not answering."

"He's got to answer."

"I realize that, but I can't make him pick up."

Rachel's jaw tensed. She needed to reach her brother, and try to talk him out of this insanity one last time. "Keep at it, Crystal," she said. "You can make it every ten minutes, but don't stop. They've got to check in at some point. When you do reach them, no matter where I am or what I'm doing, let me know. I *must* talk to Matt."

"I'll do my best," Crystal said.

ROBERT MADE SURE he was the very last person in line to receive an inoculation from the UN doctors. Renee had tried to take the position for herself, but settled on second to last at his insistence. Together they watched as the others went behind the screens that had been set up, and come back out a few minutes later, a few rubbing their arms and all of them smiling.

After Estella received her shot, she paused when she reached Robert. "It doesn't hurt too much," she said.

"I'm happy to hear that," he said.

She touched his hand. "Lunch after you're done?"

"Sure."

She walked off, and he could feel Renee staring at him.

When he looked at her, she said, "Oh, really now."

"Please don't start." Robert wasn't in the mood to participate in any teasing. He was happy they were all being vaccinated, but he was still coming to grips with how many people Ivonne had said were dead.

Renee seemed to sense his frame of mind and didn't say anything more.

Slowly, they continued moving forward until they were the last two in line.

After a few minutes, Helena, the UN nurse, stepped around the end of the screen and motioned to Renee. "Señorita, please come back."

The two women disappeared behind the screen, leaving Robert the only one left.

He glanced out at the sea. It was another postcard day in paradise—blue sky, light breeze, and sunshine. It was the kind of day guests coming to the resort always hoped for as they flocked to the water, and took to the Jet Skis and snorkeling boats and surfboards. But that was Before. In the After, the water was empty and the beach deserted.

"Robert?"

He turned and found Ivonne smiling at him.

"Your turn."

Renee was still there, sitting in a chair next to Dr. de Coster.

"Please sit here," Ivonne said, pointing at the empty chair next to where she was set up.

After Robert followed her directions, she placed a strip of plastic against his head. When she pulled it off, she looked at it, and then noted something on the pad of paper. "Temperature's normal," she said. "Your arm, please."

She wrapped a blood pressure cuff around his bicep, placed a stethoscope against his arm, and pumped up the device. Again, she wrote down the results.

"Feel any unusual aches or pains?" she asked, her fingers probing under his jaw and down his throat.

"No, I'm fine. I told you, we're all fine," he said.

A disarming smile. "I'm sure you are. It's procedure only."

"Sure. I guess that makes sense."

She opened a plastic packet and removed a swab attached to a long, wooden dowel. "If you would open your mouth, I want to take a sample from inside your cheek."

The testing went on for another few minutes, ending with two vials of blood being drawn before she pulled out a prepared syringe with orange-tinted liquid inside.

"This won't hurt much, but you may feel a little uneasy in the next few hours. It doesn't happen to everyone, but if it does, don't worry. It will pass quickly."

She jabbed the needle into his arm and pushed down the plunger. At first, it felt like he had a knot under his skin, but even before Ivonne put a small, round bandage over the injection point, the sensation had gone away.

"That's it. You're all done," she said with a smile, and looked over at Helena. "Next one, please."

"He was the last," Helena said.

Ivonne leaned back in her chair and began rolling her head over her shoulders. "Finally." She noticed Robert looking at her. "Yours is the largest group we've had to deal with at one time."

"We're the largest?" he said, surprised yet again.

"By far," Dr. de Coster said. He'd finished with Renee a few minutes before, and she had left to join the others. "The average is three or four people. Our biggest group previous to yours was seventeen."

"It's a miracle that all of you are still here," Ivonne said.

To Robert, it wasn't so much a miracle as him and Dominic making hard choices and sticking by them.

He touched the bandage on his arm. "How long until we're safe?"

Something changed in her expression. She glanced past Robert at de Coster. When she looked back, she said, "You're the one in charge here, correct?"

"Well, there are a few others who try to help keep things in order," he said.

"Perhaps you should have them join us."

Robert suddenly felt very uncomfortable. "Why?"

"There are some things we need to discuss."

NOT WANTING TO cause any unnecessary concern among the rest of the island's survivors, Robert decided the meeting would be held in Dominic's apartment, located in a part of the resort few others ever went.

In addition to Renee, Robert asked Enrique Vasquel and Chuck Tyler—the two people who'd been helping him and Renee the most—to attend the meeting. Ivonne, Helena, and de Coster were joined by the older man who had ridden in the back of the plane with them.

"Are we talking about how we're getting off the island?" Chuck asked. "I assume that's why we're here."

"Perhaps I should introduce our colleague first," Ivonne said, motioning to the man from the plane.

"No need to be so formal," the man said. "Name's Richard Paxton, but you all can call me Pax. And it's a damn pleasure to meet you. What you've all done here is pretty amazing. I am definitely impressed."

"Um, thanks," Robert said. "I'm a little confused, though. Ivonne made it sound like there was something important you guys needed to talk to us about."

"There is," Pax said. "And it starts with an apology. Robert, my friends here and I, we have deceived you. We are not, nor have ever been, associated with the United Nations."

A stunned silence.

"I know that's a bit of a surprise, but—"

"If you're not the UN, then who are you?" Robert blurted out.

"Screw that," Chuck said, clamping a hand over the bandage covering his inoculation. "What the hell did you put into us?"

"The vaccine for the Sage Flu," Ivonne said. "We didn't lie about that."

Chuck rose out of his chair, clearly not believing her. "Jesus! Maybe you're wondering how we're still alive. Maybe that's why you took our blood. Maybe you think we can save you!"

"Hold on," Pax said. "No need to get all riled up. First off, as you can see, we're not sick, either."

Chuck's face twisted into a grimace. "That doesn't mean anything. Maybe you're just not showing signs yet."

"Secondly," Pax went on, "taking your blood would tell us nothing. There are too many people alive here for all of you to be naturally immune. You're still breathing because you've kept the sick away. That's it."

"You're talking bullshit," Chuck said.

He walked quickly to the door and pulled it open. Standing right outside were the two pilots.

"Out of my way," Chuck said.

"Best if you go back inside and finish listening to our friends first," the larger of the two pilots said.

"Or what?"

"Now, Chuck, nobody wants any trouble here," Pax said. "We're just talking. Come on back and have a seat. Afterward, you can run around and shout that the sky is falling to your heart's content. You have my word on that."

"Your word?" Chuck scoffed.

The friendly smile Pax had been wearing disappeared. "My word."

Robert rose to his feet. "Chuck, come on back. It's better to hear what they have to say than not, don't you think?"

"What are they going to tell us that'll be worth listening to?"

"Well, we won't know until they're done, will we? I promise you, if I think it's all bullshit, I'll be the first to say you were right, and then you and I can escort them back to their plane and kick them out of here. Deal?"

Chuck considered Robert's suggestion for a moment. He shot a glance at the blocked door, and then, his face hardening, he returned to his seat. "All right," he said, his gaze now fixed on Pax. "Tell us what the hell's going on."

"Thank you," Pax said. "I appreciate you giving us the time." He said nothing for a moment, looking at Robert and his friends. "Yes, we did lie about being with the UN, but we're not the only ones who have done that. You see, there is no UN anymore, not since the flu hit."

"But that's not true," Renee said. "The message on TV, on the radio. The secretary general."

"Gustavo Di Sarsina," Pax said.

"Yes!"

"I watched the video myself last night on my trip south. Pretty convincing. The thing is, Di Sarsina is not the secretary general, and the message is not from the UN."

"Oh, come on!" Chuck said.

"He said there are survival stations," Renee argued. "Places people can go."

"He's right about the latter, but calling them survival stations is a bit disingenuous," Pax said. "It's a long story, if you're willing to listen."

"We've got time," Robert said.

US 101
CENTRAL COAST OF CALIFORNIA
10:44 AM PST

MARTINA AND HER friends had been on the road for over an hour. The temperature was cool but not unbearable, the sky clear and wide. The freeway north of Paso Robles consisted of two ribbons of asphalt, each two lanes wide. One was for northbound traffic and the other for south, with about a thirty-foot-wide strip of grass between them.

The four travelers had already come across several accidents, the worst of which had forced them to ride off the road to get around it. So, in the interest of not dying, they were once more keeping their speed down to forty miles an hour. It wouldn't get them anywhere fast, but by Martina's figuring, they would still make San Mateo before nightfall.

They had just come over a small rise when the sun

glinted off something in the distance.

Glass, probably, Martina thought, either another accident or an abandoned car at the side of the freeway. A few moments later it winked out, masked by the undulating road. She'd almost forgotten about it when the glint appeared again, only it had shifted position. A different car? Or...

Was it moving?

She slowed.

The glint shimmered and dipped.

It *was* moving.

Martina let her bike roll to a stop.

"What's up?" Noreen asked as she and the others stopped next to Martina.

"I think there's a car heading this way."

They all looked down the road.

"I don't see anything," Riley said.

"It was there a moment ago," Martina said.

"That sun reflection?" Craig asked.

"You saw it, too?"

"For a second, but it disappeared pretty quick. You saw it moving?"

"I think so," Martina said.

Riley cocked her head. "You hear that?"

Martina and the others listened. Above the sound of their idling bikes was a low whine.

"That's an engine," Craig said. "I'm sure it is. I think you're right."

"Should we try to flag them down?" Riley asked.

"I don't know if that's a good idea," Noreen said. "The only other person we've come across shot at us. Maybe this guy will try to ram us with his car."

"She's right," Martina said. "We have to be careful. Maybe we should stay right here and watch it drive by. We can get a look at whoever's inside. If they seem okay, we can catch up to them and get their attention. If not, we keep going on our way."

The others seemed to like this idea.

After killing their engines, they climbed off their bikes

and walked over to the shoulder so they'd have a better look when the car drove by.

It wasn't long before Martina could see the approaching vehicle was red. It looked more like a truck than a sedan, but it was still too far away for her to tell. Maybe an SUV or a station wagon?

It disappeared into a dip, and when it came up again, it was considerably closer.

Not a station wagon or an SUV.

It was a Jeep. A red Jeep.

Not unlike Ben's red Jeep.

A few seconds later, Martina realized it didn't have just a passing similarity to Ben's Jeep. It looked almost identical, and a few seconds after that she thought, *Not almost.*

She whipped around and raced back to her bike.

"Hey! What are you doing?"

She wasn't sure which one of them had yelled at her, but she didn't care. All she could think about was Ben, and that he was right there on the other side of the road. She fired up her bike and raced onto the grass separating the lanes.

When she reached the southbound side, she stopped and began waving both arms over her head. "Ben!" she yelled. "Ben!"

Behind her, one of the other bikes pulled up.

"What the hell, Martina?" Noreen asked.

"That's Ben's Jeep," Martina said, her gaze still on the approaching vehicle. "I know it is!"

The Jeep was only a few moments away now, but given that it hadn't started to slow, she realized Ben hadn't seen her yet. She stood up, one foot on the ground, the other on the bike's footrest, and waved again. "Ben! It's me!"

That did it. The Jeep began to decelerate.

"It's him," Martina said to Noreen, a huge smile on her face. "It's Ben."

She was starting to hop off her bike when the Jeep sped up again.

She waved her arms faster. "Hey, Ben! Stop! It's me!"

As the vehicle blew past her, she realized two things:

first, it was indeed Ben's Jeep, the license number and the dent in the front fender being proof of that; and second, the person behind the wheel wasn't Ben.

The driver—a woman with wild brown hair—glanced stone faced at Martina before looking back to the road. Martina had met a few of Ben's friends, but this woman wasn't one of them.

But whoever she was, Martina was certain the woman knew where Ben was.

Without thinking twice about it, she fishtailed into the southbound lanes and raced after the Jeep.

27

MATT KNEW HE and his team had caught a break. Bad weather was coming—there was no missing the wall of gray clouds following them southward—but so far they had been able to stay ahead of the storm and make excellent time.

As the town of Alamogordo came into view, Matt said, "We'll stop here for a bit."

"Yes, sir," Hiller said. He'd taken over driving Matt's Humvee. "Any place in particular?"

Matt checked his notes. "East on 10th Street. Should be a big market four or five blocks in on the left."

"Got it."

Matt shifted in his seat and looked out the side window at an ocean of shrubs and dirt. Though it had been a long time since he'd been in this part of the country, it looked exactly the same.

How naïve he'd been back then, enough to become a member of Project Eden without fully understanding what the organization's real mission was. He had been an engineer, working on what he then considered a dream job, helping to build secret underground facilities throughout North America.

It had been interesting.

It had been cool.

It had been a huge mistake.

Plumbing, that had been his specialty. He'd spent six years of his life overseeing the installation of pipes and vents and toilets and sinks and showers.

The horror he helped create.

The unimaginable he helped bring about.

There was no forgiving his participation. It didn't matter that as soon as he and several close friends who were also members figured out what was truly going on, they began planning how to get out. Nor did it matter that Matt had dedicated every moment of his life since to fighting Project Eden.

Blame for the deaths of the billions lay at the hands of anyone who had ever helped the Project.

Lay at his hands.

He knew nothing he could do would ever change that, knew he wasn't fighting Project Eden to right his own sins. He was fighting them because he had to, because not to fight wasn't an option.

His convictions could only take him so far, though. The resistance organization he'd built to combat the Project had achieved no more than minor victories at best. Even the destruction of Bluebird had not stopped the Project from unleashing its genocidal pandemic.

But as he'd told Ash, eliminating the previous directorate was a start.

And now Matt had a chance to add to that.

And by God, it was a chance he would take.

THEY PARKED THEIR vehicles near the entrance to the Lowe's Marketplace grocery store. Matt tasked his men with checking inside and stocking up on any useful supplies.

"Hiller," he said, before the team leader could walk off with the others.

"Yes, sir?"

"I'd like you to come with me."

With Hiller beside him, Matt limped his way toward the gas station at the opposite end of the parking lot. Three long days of riding had stiffened up his leg more than usual, and left him with a dull, constant ache radiating from his knee.

If Rachel had been there, she wouldn't have let him even leave the truck.

His sister. His beautiful, loyal, wonderful sister. What a mess of her life he'd made. She hadn't been part of the Project, hadn't known anything about it. He had let her believe he was dead for nearly a year, but it had been the only way to ensure that the Project forgot about him.

And what did he do when he finally contacted her? Pulled her into his madness.

Yet one more thing I'll never be forgiven for.

As they neared the station, he told Hiller, "Stay here and make sure no one disturbs me."

"Yes, sir," Hiller said.

Matt walked past the pumps, pulled the satellite phone out of his pocket, and checked his watch. The correct window of time had just opened up, but, to be safe, he waited another thirty seconds before dialing the number.

The line was answered after half a ring.

"Yes?"

"It's me," Matt said.

"Tell me something I don't know," C8 said. "Like why the hell you think you need to come here yourself?"

"Because you can't do what I can."

A pause. "It's an unnecessary risk," the man said.

"Not to me."

C8, like most of the Resistance's other moles, was not someone who'd infiltrated the Project from the outside as Matt had always portrayed it, but a man who'd been a member since when Matt himself had been a part of the organization.

"When will you be here?" C8 asked.

"I'm an hour away right now."

"What?"

"I told you I was coming."

"I know...I just...I thought..."

"This is an opportunity we can't afford to miss."

"I realize that."

"So you can get me inside?"

A slight hesitation. "Yes."

"Tonight?"

A much longer pause. "Yes."

"Where do I meet you?"

MATT WALKED BACK to Hiller, the sat phone once more in his pocket.

"Everything all right, sir?" Hiller asked.

"Yes. All good."

As Hiller turned to head back to the others, Matt put a hand on his arm.

"One moment," he said.

"Oh, I'm sorry. If your leg's bothering you too much, I can go get the truck and bring it over."

"Thank you, no. I actually need to talk to you."

"Of course," Hiller said. "What can I help you with?"

"We're going to stay here in Alamogordo for a little while."

Hiller's brow furrowed. "What about Las Cruces?"

"We'll get there, but not until it's dark," Matt said. "We won't go together, however. I'll leave first. You and the rest of the men will follow twenty minutes behind me."

"You're going alone, sir? I don't understand."

"You don't understand because you haven't been given all the details. And I'm afraid it'll have to stay that way for now." He gave Hiller the directions to a shopping center in the south side of the city. "You'll wait there in case you're needed."

Hiller was clearly uncomfortable with the plan.

"This is a unique opportunity," Matt explained. "But one that needs to be handled in a very specific way."

"With you going in alone."

"Correct."

"Sir, I can't lie to you. I don't like this. Have you talked this plan over with anyone?"

Matt appreciated the kid's concern, but it was a waste of time. Taking a harsher tone, he said, "If I have or have not talked to anyone about this, it is not your concern. This is what we will be doing. Understood?"

A reluctant "yes, sir."

"Thank you," Matt said. He put a hand on the man's shoulder. "I've been at this fight a lot longer than you, so don't worry, I know what I'm doing."

"I wasn't trying to suggest—"

"I know you weren't." Matt made a show of looking around the parking lot. "Now, while we're waiting for the sun to go down, I need you to do something for me."

"Yes, sir?"

"I need a car."

THE CLEAR ROADS were a blessing and a curse. Back in the snows of Colorado and Wyoming, following Matt's group would have been a simple matter of keeping eyes on his vehicle's tire tracks, but in New Mexico, where the snow was only now threatening to fall, there were no ruts to show the way. So while Ash and the others could travel quickly, they had no idea if the convoy was still in front of them.

"Why don't you call him?" Gardiner said.

"Do you really think he'd tell us where he is?" Chloe asked.

"Maybe someone else will answer."

"Not if I know Matt," she said. "Hell, he probably turned the damn phone off."

"What about Rachel?" Josie suggested.

"Who's Rachel?" Ginny asked.

"Matt's sister," Brandon told her.

"Maybe she knows where he is," Josie added.

"I doubt it," Chloe said.

Ash pulled the satellite phone out of the bag between the two front seats. "Maybe not, but it's a good idea, Josie. We'll give it a try."

He punched in the number for Ward Mountain.

The call was answered with, "Can I help you?"

"Crystal?"

270

A slight pause. "Yes?"

"It's Daniel Ash. Wondering if I can speak to Rachel."

"Captain Ash? Definitely! I've been trying to get ahold of you guys for her all day. Hang on. I'll go find her."

Ash looked back at Chloe. "They're getting her."

"My money's on she doesn't know anything," Chloe said.

Over two minutes passed before Rachel picked up the other end.

"Ash. Thank God," she said.

"Afternoon, Rachel."

"Please tell me you're heading back to Nevada," she said.

"I know that's what Matt thinks we're doing, but we're not. We're trying to catch up to him, but hoping you might be able to tell us exactly where he is."

"What?" she said, confused. "You're with him, aren't you?"

"No," he said, surprised by the question. "Matt left Chloe and me with the kids and told us to head to Nevada."

"And he went to New Mexico," she said, sounding as if it were inevitable.

"Yeah. Didn't you know that?"

"He said he was going to go, but I was hoping he would come to his senses."

"His senses? You don't think he should have gone?"

"Of course not. He's in no condition to be out in the field, especially if he's going inside that damn place."

"So I take it you *don't* know where he is."

"Somewhere near Las Cruces, I would guess."

"Yeah, well, we knew that much. We're hoping to avoid showing up at the wrong time and making things worse."

"I don't understand why you guys aren't with him right now," she said. "I mean, I get it with the kids, but someone else could have brought them here. You and Chloe should be with Matt."

"That's what we thought, too, but Matt was concerned about our injuries. Didn't think we'd be up for it."

Dead air, then, "Oh, God."

"What?" Ash asked.

"Look, I'm...sure he was concerned about your injuries, but I have a feeling that's not the main reason he didn't bring you along."

"Well, then why?"

"Because either of you would have stood up to him, kept him from doing what I think he's going to do."

"And what's that?"

"God, I hope I'm wrong."

"Rachel, what?"

"I think he's going into that facility *alone*."

"Are you kidding me?"

"I'm sure he thinks he's the only one who can do this."

"Why would he think that?"

She hesitated. "Because he's been there before. And because he thinks it's his responsibility."

"Why would Matt have been in a Project Eden base?" he asked.

"It was years ago," Rachel said.

"I didn't ask when. I asked why."

A long pause. "Because he was part of the crew who helped build it."

Ash put his hand over the phone and looked at Sorrento. "Pull over. Now!"

As soon as the Humvee was at the side of the road, Ash hit the speaker button. Chloe needed to hear this, and, as much as he wished he could keep it from everyone else, there was no other way.

"Rachel, tell me how Matt was involved in the construction of Project Eden's Las Cruces facility."

Eyes throughout the truck widened in surprise.

"Please don't ask me that," Rachel said.

"Too late."

A sigh, then in a low, defeated voice, "It wasn't just Las Cruces. He helped build a lot of different Project Eden bases. That's why our facilities are so good. He saw what they had done, and tried to create something even better."

"Was he on an outside construction crew, or was he a member of the Project?"

"Ash, please understand, he didn't realize what he was getting into. It was a job offer with great pay. When you joined the Project back then, they didn't always tell you everything up front."

"He was in the Project."

"Yes."

"Is he *still*?" Ash asked.

"How can you ask that? After all he's done? After all that's happened to us?"

She was right. Matt's actions in the last several years would not have made sense if he were still in the Project. But it was a necessary question, so he wasn't about to apologize. "When did he get out?"

A few seconds passed before Rachel said, "There was a group of them who figured out what was really going on, and realized they had to do something about it. Most remained in the Project to do what they could from the inside."

"Your sources," Chloe said.

"Yes. Many of them."

"And Matt?" Ash asked.

"He and a couple others volunteered to leave the Project so they would be freer to fight it. No one just leaves the Project, though. To get out, they would have to die. Matt's death was the easiest, from what I was told. With the help of others who were remaining behind, he set it up to look like he was killed in a construction accident at one of the facilities. The other two were going to fake a plane crash, only something went wrong and they both lost their lives.

"Matt lay low for a while to make sure no one suspected anything. While he was doing this, he obtained a new identity, the one you know him by, and had some plastic surgery done so he could walk down the street without being nabbed. Once he was sure they weren't looking for him, he started up the Resistance."

Ash wasn't sure what to say. It made sense, of course. How else would Matt have known so early about the Project's existence and the need to stop them? What bothered Ash wasn't that Matt had been a member of Project Eden, but the fact he'd hidden it from everyone.

"What about you?" Chloe asked. "Were you part of the Project, too?"

"No. Never. I didn't even know what it was until...well, until Matt came back from the dead. That's when I gave up my old life and promised I'd help him. And that's all I've done since then."

No one in the car said a word as they absorbed what Rachel had told them.

Ash finally broke the silence. "How's Matt planning on getting into the facility?"

"I don't know specifically. C8 will get him in."

"C8?"

"That's his inside contact."

"Does C8 have a real name?"

"I'm sure he does, but I don't know what it is," Rachel said testily.

"I should have phrased that better," Ash said. "I apologize."

Rachel made no reply.

"All right," Ash said. "So he's going in alone with this C8 guy, and will try to take out the principal director. Have I got that right?"

"Yes," she said. "But, Ash, you've got to stop him."

"I'm not sure I want to stop him. If he really can accomplish what he told us he's planning on doing, I don't think that's an opportunity we can pass up."

"He can't do this alone. You've got to keep him from going. We can find another way."

"We *could* find him and convince him, forcibly if necessary, to take Chloe and me with him."

"I guess you could," Rachel admitted. "Not a great answer, though."

"We still have our original problem," Chloe said. "How are we going to find him?"

Ash thought for a moment, then said, "He'll have to

leave the others somewhere." He turned to Sorrento. "Hand me that New Mexico map." The driver gave it to him and Ash opened it up. "Where exactly is this base?"

"A few miles north of Las Cruces," Rachel said.

"Off the interstate?"

"Not far from it."

"Seems likely that Matt's won't want to chance putting the others right next to the base. So he'll probably keep them in a town where they can blend in and hide if necessary. Las Cruces itself is an option." He studied the map. "If he's coming in from the north, maybe he'll park everyone in Truth or Consequences, and if from the east, um, Alamogordo. So we have three choices."

"What if they're not in any of them?"

"One step at a time," Ash said. "Rachel, we need to get moving here. We'll contact you again as soon as we find them."

"Please do."

After the phone was stowed away, Chloe said, "So where do we start?"

"Truth or Consequences," Ash said, pointing at the small town on the map. "We're already heading that way. If they're not there, we'll backtrack north a bit and cut over to Alamogordo." He showed both routes to Sorrento.

"Got it," Sorrento said.

Chloe looked like she wanted to say something but was hesitating.

"What is it?" Ash asked.

She nodded discreetly toward the children.

"Right," Ash said.

"Right, what?" Brandon asked. Apparently the nod had not gone unnoticed.

"I think we can find something here in Albuquerque to keep you all occupied."

"Dad, no," Brandon said.

"Uh-uh," Josie agreed. "We're staying with you."

"Not this time," Ash said.

"We're not kids anymore," Brandon said.

"Maybe not, but you're still *my* kids. And this time, you're staying here."

WARD MOUNTAIN NORTH, NEVADA
1:03 PM PST

RACHEL HAD FELT the others staring at her as she talked to Ash. Maybe she should have cleared the room again, but by the time the idea came to her, it was too late. It was probably better this way anyhow. It was time people knew the truth. Besides, it shouldn't change anything.

At least, she hoped not.

After the call disconnected, she looked around at the disbelieving faces.

"Yes," she said. "Matt was in the Project. I'm sorry you weren't told before, but there it is. You can ask all the questions you want later. Right now, there's still work to be done."

28

BEN'S JEEP WHIPPED around another abandoned car without slowing.

She's going to get herself killed, Martina thought for the millionth time.

In the three hours she had been following her boyfriend's car, the brown-haired woman had kept the Jeep's accelerator pressed to the floor. Only once had Martina been able to get close to the vehicle. That had been near the beginning of the chase. When the woman noticed her, she jerked the vehicle into Martina's path, missing the front tire of the motorcycle by only a few feet. After that, Martina decided the better tactic was to stay several car lengths back and wait for the woman to eventually stop.

South they went, through Paso Robles, San Luis Obispo, Santa Maria, and Santa Barbara. As they sped down the stretch of the 101 squeezed between the mountains and the ocean, north of Ventura, Martina began to wonder if she would end up chasing the woman all the way to Los Angeles.

The answer turned out be no. A few miles farther on, as they came around a bend, she heard a loud pop and saw the Jeep jerk left and right before slowing. The culprit was a piece of metal in the road that had ripped open one of the vehicle's front tires. Martina would have hit it, too, if she hadn't already clamped down on the brakes.

Before the Jeep came to a complete stop, the woman jumped out and ran down the middle of the road. Martina weaved her bike around the Jeep and caught up to the woman in seconds.

"Stop!" Martina yelled.

The woman looked at her, wild-eyed. "Leave me alone!"

"Stop, dammit. I only want to talk to you!"

The woman yelled something incomprehensible, then sprinted forward in a burst of energy.

Groaning in frustration, Martina brought her bike to a halt, pushed down the kickstand, and hopped off. The woman may have had a few seconds' lead, but Martina was an active college athlete. Twenty steps down the road, she clamped a hand on the woman's shoulder and forced her to stop.

"What the hell's wrong with you?" Martina asked. "Why wouldn't you stop?"

The woman struggled to get away, but Martina held on tight.

"Let go of me! Let go!"

"Relax, I'm not going to hurt you!"

"Let go! I'm not going back. I swear to God I'm not!"

"Going back? Listen, lady, I'm not taking you anywhere. I just want to know how you got Ben's Jeep and where he is."

The woman stopped twisting around and looked at Martina, surprised. "Ben?"

"Yes! Ben. That's his Jeep. How did you get it? Did he give it to you?"

"You know Ben?"

"I'm his girlfriend."

"His girlfriend?"

"How did you get his Jeep?" Martina asked again, her patience all but gone.

"He, um, he didn't need it anymore."

There was sudden defiance in the woman's voice, and Martina knew in that instant Ben hadn't given it to her.

She gave the woman's arm a jerk. "What do you mean, he didn't need it anymore?"

"He's dead," the woman said, sticking out her chin. "He

didn't need it anymore because he's dead."

Martina's grip on the woman's shoulder slipped as every cell in her body went numb. "You're lying," she managed, her voice cracking.

"I'm not," the woman said quickly. "He's dead. I'm sorry, but he didn't need the Jeep anymore." She nodded back toward the vehicle. "You want it? Take it. I don't care."

Martina continued to stare at the woman. "He can't be dead. He can't be. How...how did—"

"The flu. Everybody's dying from the flu. Don't you know?"

"But that's not possible. If it didn't take me, it shouldn't have taken him."

The woman crossed her arms. "I don't know what to tell you. He's dead. Can I go now?"

Martina's mind reeled as she tried to think of an alternative answer, something that would make what the woman said not true.

"His body," she said, grabbing on to a sliver of light. "Did you actually see it? Do you even know Ben?"

"Of course I know him. I...I went to school with him in Santa Cruz. So, yeah, I saw his body."

Martina's peripheral vision began to dim. She swayed and half fell, half sat on the freeway.

"You're wrong," she whispered. "You've got to be wrong."

She repeated it over and over.

When she finally looked up, wanting to ask the woman where his body was, the woman was gone.

Martina jumped up and ran back to her bike. "Hey! Hey, where did you go?

She had to find the woman. She needed to know where Ben's body was. She had to see it for herself.

She started the engine and drove slowly away, her eyes searching both sides of the road.

"Hey! Come back! Where is he? You've got to tell me where he is!"

Her mind was so focused on the woman and Ben that she

didn't realize her friends had yet to show up.

"EVERYONE QUIET, PLEASE," Robert said, his hands raised high in front of him. "We can't all talk at the same time."

"Do we even know if this shot they gave us works?" someone shouted.

"Who are these people? I mean, it sounds like a bunch of bullshit to me," another said.

"What if they're right? What if there is no UN?"

"Please," Robert said again, raising his voice. "Quiet down!"

All one hundred and twenty-nine Isabella Island survivors were gathered in the restaurant dining room at the very top of the hotel, the same room where Dominic had told them all about the outbreak, what seemed like years ago to Robert.

When the roar subsided to a rumble, Robert said, "I realize this isn't what you expected to hear, but I felt it important to tell you exactly what we were told. Before you go forming too many judgments, though, let's consider some facts. We all saw the shipping containers on TV. We saw the boxes releasing Sage Flu. We saw people dying, and governments going into emergency mode before the news finally went off the air. I don't think it's a stretch to say things only got worse after that.

"The thing is, we know this wasn't a natural occurrence. Someone did this. Someone with a huge, well-organized operation. So you've got to think whoever these people are, they've planned on still being around. To me, it makes sense that they would want to run whatever was left."

"Sounds like you've already made up your mind to believe this guy," a guest named Phil Gatner said. "What if they're the ones who put the virus out there? What if *they're* the ones who want to kill us?"

"I guess it's possible," Robert admitted. "But it's been
280

hours since we received our shots, and if they wanted us dead, we would be already."

Several people shouted questions and comments.

Robert raised his hands again. "Please! One at a time."

PAX HOVERED OUTSIDE the restaurant door for the first several minutes of the meeting. He had offered to speak to everyone himself, but both he and Robert agreed it would be better coming from someone the people of Isabella Island knew.

Pax did, however, decide to stay on the island while the medical team moved on to help others. Since this was the largest single group the Resistance had found so far, making sure they did everything they could to stay safe was a priority. He hoped the fact that he was willing to remain here by himself would convince them to take his warning seriously.

When it was clear the meeting was going to last awhile, he wandered out to the deck.

Pax loved the mountains. He couldn't get enough of the Rockies, felt at home anytime he saw them, whether in Alberta, Montana, Wyoming, or Colorado. But the view here of the palm trees and the beaches and the sparkling sea did give the scenery up north a run for its money. He felt he could probably get used to it. It was hot here, too. That was a bonus that would take no getting used to at all.

He leaned against the railing, a gentle breeze blowing across his shoulders, and wondered if there might be other islands like this one, where groups had survived because of their isolation. The more he considered it, the more he thought there had to be. The Project Eden assholes had missed this place. They were bound to have missed others.

He hoped he was right.

For several more minutes, he watched the waves break near the shore and the water lap against the tan beach. He was starting to push himself up, thinking he should go back and check how the meeting was going, when something on the horizon caught his attention.

"THERE'S NOT ENOUGH information," Maureen Johnston said. "How are we supposed to decide what to believe without all the facts?"

"Exactly how are you expecting us to get all those facts?" Kim Sutter countered.

"I don't know. I'm just saying we need to make the correct decision."

"What are you, an idiot?" Kim said. "That's not going to happen."

"Hey!" Robert said. "Let's try to keep it civil, okay?"

"I'm sorry," Kim said. "But, Robert, *you* know there's no way to know all the facts."

"We're only hearing people out right now," Robert said. "Who was next?"

Several dozen hands shot up. Robert pointed at a German guy named Herman Wolfe.

"In my opinion, we are missing a very important point," Wolfe said. "If there is no United Nations, then what will take—"

The door at the back of the room flew open and Pax ran in.

"Robert, may I see you for a moment?" he said.

"We're still in the middle—"

"Please."

Pax looked distressed, so Robert nodded and said to the group, "You all have plenty to talk about amongst yourselves. We can pick this up when I come back."

Loud conversations immediately broke out all over.

When Robert reached Pax, he said, "What's going on?"

Pax put a hand on his back and started leading him to the door. "Not here."

They walked out of the dining room and into the open-air lobby.

"Where do you keep the radio?" Pax asked.

"Downstairs, behind the bar."

"Are all your food supplies up here in the restaurant?"

Robert shook his head. "No, in the kitchen by the bar."

"Okay, then we're going to need a few people."

"Will you tell me what's going on?"

"I will, but first grab four or five folks you trust, and let's get down to the bar."

Robert returned to the dining room and rounded up Enrique, Chuck, Estella, and Manny Aguilar.

"What's going on?" Renee asked as he was leaving again.

"I'm not sure. Just keep everyone occupied. I won't be long."

Pax led the group down to the bar, and let Robert show them the rest of the way to the radio room.

"All right, fire it up," Pax said. "There's a plane out there. We need to find out who they are."

"A plane?" Chuck said. "More of your people?"

"Let's hope so, but I doubt it."

Robert activated the radio and pushed the talk button. "This is Isabella Island calling unidentified aircraft. Do you read me?"

Static.

"Try again," Pax said.

"Isabella Island calling unidentified aircraft. Come in, please."

No response.

"You sure you have it set right?" Pax asked.

"This is the same frequency we used to talk to your plane and the one that said it was from the UN the other day," Robert told him.

Pax looked like it was the answer he was expecting but didn't want. "Do you have any duct tape? Plastic sheeting?"

"What?"

"Do you have any?"

"Um, there's probably duct tape in the maintenance room, but no sheeting that I know of. Pax, what the hell's going on?"

"What about tarps?"

"Yeah. We have tarps, but—"

"You and I will go to the maintenance room." Pax turned

to the others. "You four grab as much food as you can and take it up to the restaurant, things that will be easy to make and can stretch for a couple of days for everyone. You probably have time for two trips at most."

"You've got to tell us what's going on!" Robert said.

"That plane," Pax said. "I'm pretty sure that's your 'UN' friends coming back. And I can guarantee you if it is, they're not bringing you vaccine."

THE ISABELLA ISLAND survivors nearly went into full revolt when they saw all the supplies being carried in.

"Listen up," Pax said. "I realize many of you don't believe a word I told Robert, but here's your chance to get your proof to see whether I'm lying or not. We have a plane heading this way. If it just flies by and doesn't cause any problems, then you can lock me up or put me in a boat and shove me out to sea."

"What do you think they're going to do?" someone asked.

"If I'm right, your island is about to be doused with the Sage Flu," Pax said. "Now, if some of you would be so kind as to help us seal up the room, that would be appreciated."

"That's ridiculous!" someone yelled.

"Why are we even listening to him?"

"What if he's telling the truth?"

Robert jumped up on a chair. "Seems to me we'll know soon enough if he's lying or not, so it's not going to hurt us any to do as he asks. Who's going to help?"

Several hands shot up. After Robert divided them into groups of three, they began working their way through the room.

They were nearly finished with the last window when they heard the drone of the approaching plane. Pax applied the last bit of tape, and then he and Robert went over to where the others were sitting.

The sound of the plane continued to grow louder and louder until it passed not more than a hundred feet directly above them. After it flew by, one of the survivors cocked his head to the side, and then several others did the same.

The sound was soft, almost nonexistent, like the gentlest of rains.

Pax moved over to one of the windows and peeled back the corner of the tarp. Liquid dripped down the outside of the glass. As he motioned for Robert to join him, the plane approached the island again.

"Don't get too close," Pax said. "Just a quick look."

He lifted the flap again.

"Is that it?" Robert asked.

Pax nodded. "All wrapped up in a nice little liquid delivery system the people you thought were from the UN developed for stubborn locations like yours."

The plane flew overhead again, spattering more of the liquid onto the window.

Pax looked up toward the noise. "Another fifteen minutes and they'll have covered every inch."

"Why would they do that?" one of the guests asked.

"They're in charge now," Pax said. "You're excess humanity, and not part of their plan."

Robert was quiet for a second. "The flu won't hurt us, though. We've been inoculated."

"You have, and chances are you'd be fine, but you only received your shots a few hours ago. It's better if we let your immunity build up a bit more. Besides, that's quite a concentration they're dumping out there right now. We need to let it thin."

"So how long do we have to stay in here?"

"I'm not sure. I'll check in with the medical team. They can give us a timeline."

Robert scanned the room "You think this place is safe?"

"Safer than being out there."

29

ASH HAD BEEN positive they would find the Resistance convoy in Truth or Consequences, but they had searched all the logical places the others could have been, and there was no sign of them.

Having no choice but to move on, they headed for Alamogordo, a trip that took them two and a half hours. When they arrived, they began working their way through town.

"Try this one," Chloe said as they approached 10th Street.

"Yes, ma'am," Sorrento said, and took the turn.

"Anything?" Ash asked a few moments later.

"Nothing over here," Chloe said.

"I don't see anything," Gardiner threw in.

Ash looked toward the back of the truck. "What about you?"

"All looks the same to me," Rick said.

Ash hadn't wanted to bring the kid along, but leaving him behind with Brandon didn't seem like a good idea, either. Davis would have probably been able to keep Rick in check, but Ash thought it was better not to tempt fate. When Brandon asked why Rick was allowed to go but he wasn't, Ash had said, "Because he's sixteen and you're not."

"Hey, what's that?" Gardiner said.

He was sitting behind Sorrento, his gaze locked on a parking lot, left of the vehicle. While Sorrento slowed the truck, both Ash and Chloe adjusted their positions so they could see out Gardiner's side.

"What are you looking at?" Chloe asked.

"Up there, near the building. Gas cans, I think."

He was right. In the floodlights that still lit up the parking lot, Ash could see over a dozen cans stacked side by side.

"Let's check it out," he ordered.

Sorrento pulled into the lot and stopped. As Ash and Chloe hopped out, they were greeted by a blast of frigid air, the temperature having taken a drastic downturn since their last stop. The only question now was whether they would have a wet snow or an icy rain when the storm decided it was time to open up.

Chloe knelt next to one of the cans and tilted it toward her. "These look like the same type we picked up in Sheridan." She unscrewed the cap and gave it a sniff. "This one was full recently."

"Looks like they were here," Ash said.

"Only one way they could have gone."

"Yep."

NB219
7:49 PM MST

WICKS READ THROUGH the report again, but still found he couldn't focus on the words, his mind understandably preoccupied. Knowing it wouldn't be any better if he tried again, he clicked the box indicating he'd read and approved it, and sent it on its way.

He glanced at the clock in the top corner of his screen. It was time to go. He opened the bottom desk drawer, reached underneath it, and pulled off the envelope he'd taped there. He stood up, stuffed the envelope in his pocket, and left his office.

"Mr. Wicks!"

Wicks looked back. Adrian Bernstein, one of the true believers who worked under him, was leaning out of his office.

287

"What is it?" Wicks asked.

"I just received some additional stats from western Africa. I assume you want those included in the report."

"I was under the impression it was already included."

"I didn't realize you were going to send it out early. I thought I had another hour."

"Well, you didn't," Wicks said. "I've been called into another meeting. I don't have time to deal with this. Write up an addendum and send it out."

"Yes, sir. Of course," Bernstein said. "Would you like that broken down as—"

"Adrian, don't make me do your job for you."

Wicks walked quickly away before the other man could speak again.

He took a route he knew would be less trafficked so he could increase his pace without drawing undue attention. As he neared the elevator, though, he heard steps coming from the other direction. It was too late for him to head back into one of the corridors that led off the elevator lobby without being noticed by the approaching person, so he continued on.

Reaching the elevator, he realized he had a serious problem. While his own ID pass was right there in his pocket, the one he needed to swipe in front of the reader to call the elevator was still in the envelope in his pocket. How was he supposed to retrieve it without being noticed? He stared at the elevator, paralyzed by indecision.

"Evening."

Wicks jerked back at the sound of the voice. Standing next to him was a gray jumpsuit-clad security guard named Cliff Eames.

"Didn't mean to scare you," Eames said.

Wicks attempted a disarming smile. "My fault. Lost in thought."

"Call the elevator already?"

"What? Oh, uh, no. I…"

"No problem. I got it."

Eames flashed his ID badge in front of the reader. Less than thirty seconds later, the door for car number two opened and the two men entered.

"Business up top?" Eames asked.

Wicks had prepared for this question, only in his mind it hadn't been a security guard who asked, but one of the warehouse workers.

Again with the smile. "Inventory discrepancy on one of my department reports. Needed to stretch my legs, so thought I'd check it out myself. You going on duty?"

"Monitoring room tonight."

"Sounds like fun."

"Boring, more like it."

When the door opened at the top, Wicks motioned for the guard to go first and said, "Don't work too hard."

"I'll try not to."

Wicks spent a few minutes walking down aisles and acting interested in some of the items stored there. When he reached the auxiliary exit, he finally removed the badge from the envelope. He'd cloned it several days earlier from an ID belonging to a manager in an entirely different department, after receiving the message he would be having a guest.

Two other items were in the envelope: a key fob-sized signal scrambler, which, when activated, would interfere with the links to security cameras within a twenty-five-foot radius of the device; and a piece of paper with information he'd waited far too long to obtain.

He turned on the scrambler, opened the door with the cloned card, and headed down the tunnel to the outside.

NEAR FORT MEADE, MARYLAND
10:07 PM EST

"WHY ISN'T THIS working?" Bobby yelled in frustration.

"You've checked everything?" Tamara asked.

"Of course I have, like twenty thousand times."

"You're obviously missing something."

He looked at her as if contemplating whether gutting her or ripping her head off would be the more enjoyable task.

"I'm just saying the answers has to be there somewhere," she told him.

"No kidding," he said.

"Okay, okay. I didn't mean to upset you. Look, why don't you take a break for a few minutes. Clear your head. I've got a Coke that's still cold if you want it."

He sighed and nodded. "Yeah, all right. Toss it here."

Surprisingly, Bobby had been able to get the uplink working for North and South America, portions of Europe, and nearly all of Asia. He also told Tamara he felt confident he could bust in on the current signal. That was not something he could test, though. They'd have to save that until they were ready to go, in case the Project Eden techs could figure out a way around it and block any future attempts. That would be disastrous.

The problem he was having was one of input, something that should have been easy to solve. But no matter what he did, he couldn't get the system to accept the video file he was trying to feed it.

"Maybe if I rerouted the playback machine again," he said, then took a drink. Not only had he tried that at least four times, he'd also worked through a dozen different playback machines.

If only it was as easy as their old stand-ups had been, Tamara thought. Back then, in their news days, all they needed was a camera and the van that linked them to the satellite and they could broadcast from anywhere.

She leaned back. "Bobby."

"Yeah."

"We did bring the camera, didn't we?" They had recorded the file in Washington, DC, with the deserted White House in the background. While that image would add dramatic flare, it was the message that was important.

"It's out in the car," he said. "But if you think recording the message again might work, forget it. It's not the file. I've tried it on a bunch of computers, and it plays perfectly."

"No, I was thinking maybe we could do it live."

"Live?" His eyes lost focus for a second as he fell into thought. "Probably would need to...and then...yeah, yeah...and..."

"Will it work?" she asked.

He stared at nothing for another moment before turning to her, the start of a grin on his lips. "Yeah. I think it might. It means you'll have to keep talking until I figure out how to get the playback going, though."

"I can do that."

LAS CRUCES, NEW MEXICO
8:13 PM MST

UNLIKE ELSEWHERE IN the city, where parking lots and streets were all but empty, the lot serving the Mountain View Regional Medical Center and the road feeding into it were packed with cars. It was the same pattern Matt had seen in other towns, vehicles left behind by the desperate who had rushed to medical facilities only to die there.

It was heart wrenching and depressing, but the hospital was also the perfect rendezvous location. Matt parked the car Hiller had obtained for him in Alamogordo and waited. If someone from Project Eden happened to be in the area, they would drive right by and never know he was there, hidden among all the cars.

He'd been there for an hour, and had spent most of it staring out the window, trying not to think about anything. But of course that was impossible. He knew the dead in the cars surrounding him, in the homes he'd driven by to get there, in everything everywhere. Each body represented someone he should have saved. Someone he had failed.

He could have done so many things differently, small things that would have rippled out and brought about entirely different results. He could see that so clearly now. But there was no going back. There were no do-overs, no second tries. The billions who lay at his feet would always be there.

When he heard a motor in the distance, he climbed out of the car, removed from the back seat the duffel bag containing the special presents he'd brought for the principal director, and walked over to the parking lot entrance.

The car approached, lights off. Nearing the entrance, it slowed, and then stopped entirely as the driver caught sight of

Matt. For several moments the two men stared at each other across the dimly lit space between them—the presumed dead, former Project Eden member and his friend who had stayed, both older now but neither as wise as they wished they had been.

Curtis Wicks made a U-turn. As soon as he stopped at the curb, Matt opened the door and climbed in.

"Hello, Curtis," Matt said.

"I...I don't know what to call you," Wicks said.

"I've been Matt for so long, I don't think I could answer to anything else."

Wicks held out his hand. "Good to see you, Matt."

Matt shook it. "You, too, my friend. You, too."

"WHAT ABOUT THERE?" Sorrento asked.

The Humvee had just entered the Las Cruces city limits.

Ash looked through the light snowfall at the set of interconnected buildings Sorrento was pointing at. It appeared to be a school with several large parking areas. Perfect place for a convoy to hide.

"Yeah. Let's take a look."

THE PASSING HOURS hadn't made Hiller like the situation any more than he had when Mr. Hamilton told him what was going to happen. Sure, Mr. Hamilton was the boss, but going off on his own? That was crazy. What could he possibly accomplish by himself? He should have, at the very least, taken one of the men with him.

But Hiller had been trained to follow orders, and Mr. Hamilton's orders were to wait thirty minutes after he left Alamogordo, then proceed to the Las Cruces shopping center where they now were, and wait.

"Be ready," Mr. Hamilton had said. "If I need you, I'll call, but if nine p.m. comes and I haven't, don't hang around. Get to Ward Mountain as quickly as possible."

Hiller checked his watch. There was less than an hour to

the deadline.

No, he didn't like this one bit.

NB219
8:16 PM MST

MATT FELT HIS chest constrict as they pulled to a stop near the warehouse that sat above NB219. It had been a long time since he'd been so close to a Project Eden facility, and even longer since he'd been near this one, back when it was still under construction.

"We have to hurry," Wicks said. "I have to be in my office in ten minutes. And it won't look good if I'm late."

He led Matt to the auxiliary entrance, located one hundred feet from the side of the warehouse. Meant primarily for emergencies, it was below ground, the door situated in a cutout that had been made to look like part of an arroyo. To open it, Wicks placed an ID card against a reader attached to the frame, and they were in.

A tunnel sloped gently upward, taking them all the way to the warehouse level. Another door, another reader. After the lock clicked open, Wicks held up a hand, telling Matt to stay put while he slipped through the doorway.

Matt was beginning to feel his friend had been gone too long when the door opened and Wicks waved him inside.

"We're all clear," Wicks whispered. "Here, put these on." He was holding out a dark gray jumpsuit and matching baseball cap. "It's what security wears."

Matt put the duffel on the ground and donned the suit. After he zipped it up, he pulled on the hat, wearing it low so the bill would shade his eyes.

"Okay," he said, picking up the duffel.

Wicks led him through the packed warehouse, and made Matt wait again in one of the aisles while he summoned the elevator. As soon as the doors opened, Matt walked as briskly as his bad leg would allow, from his hiding place and into the car with Wicks.

"When we get out, follow me," Wicks instructed. "But not too close. Don't make it look like we're together."

As Matt followed Wicks off the elevator two minutes later, he had another overwhelming moment of dread. He was actually here, in the belly of the beast. Suddenly the plan he'd made seemed ridiculous, impossible. There was no way it was going to work.

Stop it! he told himself. *Take things one step at a time.*

While the warehouse level had seemed deserted, down in the heart of NB219 plenty of people were passing from one hallway to another through the elevator lobby. Matt almost forgot to check for the panel but caught himself in time. It was there, all right, a few feet to the left of elevator car number one. Exactly where he remembered it.

Though he was increasing his physical discomfort, he did everything he could to minimize his limp as he followed Wicks down the hallway. Unfortunately, this required him to walk at an even slower pace than usual, so he fell farther and farther behind. When Wicks finally noticed, he was almost out of sight, and had to slow his own pace considerably until a more comfortable distance between them had been restored.

Matt was fairly sure no one had noticed him, but he was more than a little relieved when Wicks led him into an empty office and shut the door.

"Take this," Wicks said, handing him the ID card he'd used to get them into the warehouse and to call the elevator. "It'll open any door except to the principal director's suite."

"How am I supposed to get to him, then?" Matt asked.

"You don't have to get into his suite. There's a planning meeting at eleven p.m. in the conference room two doors down from here. No one's using this office so you can stay in it right until the meeting starts."

"You're sure he's going to be there."

"He's the one who initiated it. Wants to know where things are on the preparations for the recovery phase."

"All right. Good."

Wicks looked at his watch. "I need to leave."

"Curtis, wait a second," Matt said.

He set the duffel on the desk, unzipped it, and pulled out a plastic-wrapped package.

"You'll find sixteen devices inside. Place them wherever you can, out of sight. The wider dispersion the better. There's a sticky side, remove the plastic, and they'll stay where you put them."

Wicks hesitated a moment before taking the package. "Do I really need to do this?"

"Yes," Matt said. "You do."

WICKS TOOK A deep breath. "Right. I'm sorry. Of course, I'll do it." He took the package from his old friend.

Before heading for the door, he remembered the envelope in his pocket. He pulled it out and removed the piece of paper inside.

"Here," he said, setting it on the desk.

Matt picked it up. "What is it?"

"Something you asked me to look into a long time ago."

Matt unfolded the paper, read the words printed on it, and then looked at Wicks. "Is this—?"

"Yes."

"But you said it didn't exist."

"I lied. I was scared and I lied. I'm sorry."

He turned to leave.

"Hold on," Matt said.

Wicks wanted to keep walking, but forced himself to look back at his friend.

"When the time comes," Matt said, "you'll want to be miles away from here."

30

W<small>ICKS</small> ARRIVED AT his office just in time for his meeting with two of his team members—Adrian Bernstein and Evelyn Courser. Predictably, they were already waiting outside his door.

"Did you take care of the western Africa problem?" he asked Bernstein as he led them inside.

"Yes, sir," Bernstein said. "It's all done. Again, I'm sorry that—"

"It's done," Wicks said curtly. "That's all I care about."

"Yes, sir."

As Wicks moved around his desk, Bernstein and Courser started to sit down in the guest chairs.

"Don't," he said. "This needs to be quick."

"Quick, sir?" Bernstein said. "But, uh, we're supposed to be prepping you for the eleven o'clock meeting."

"Do you think I don't realize that? Unfortunately, I've been pulled into something else I need to deal with, so my time has become limited. I assume you put together notes?"

"Yes, sir," Courser said.

"Then I suggest you highlight anything you were planning to point out, and send them to me. I'll go over the notes before the meeting."

Neither of his people looked happy with that solution, but Bernstein said, "If that's what you'd like."

"It is *not* what I'd like," Wicks said. "What I would have liked was to take the full time for this prep meeting, and not be yanked around by those who have nothing better to do."

"Of course," Courser said.

"Right. No problem," Bernstein threw in.

"Good. Then get to it."

As soon as they were out of his office, Wicks shut the door and locked it.

Back at his desk, he opened the package Matt had given him. The devices were rectangular boxes made of some kind of plastic material. They were about three inches long by two wide, and another half inch thick.

Whatever their purpose, he knew it couldn't be good, and the sooner he got rid of them, the better. He pulled his laptop bag out of the cabinet behind his desk, emptied out the pens and papers inside, and carefully transferred the devices into the wide center section.

When he finished, he took a deep breath, pushed himself up from his desk, and headed out.

MATT KNEW IF things went wrong, he couldn't be found with the piece of paper Wicks had given him. If that happened, the Project might be able to trace it back to Wicks and eliminate any possibility of the message finding its way to the Resistance. So he spent several minutes memorizing the three words it contained, and then crumpled the paper so he could easily get rid of it.

Having kept a second set of devices like those he'd given Wicks, Matt headed down to the conference room where the meeting was supposed to be held and placed two of the small boxes in there. One would have been more than enough, but he didn't want to risk failure.

Using his rusty knowledge of the facility's layout, he made his way as close as he dared to the NB219 director's suite, which he assumed had been taken over by Principal Director Perez, and hid half a dozen devices along the corridor.

As he made his way back, he placed all but one of the remaining devices where he could, and returned to his office hideout. There, he removed three more items from the duffel bag. The first was a mobile phone with a single, remote-control application on it. The second was a set of five one-pound bricks of an extremely powerful plastic explosive that had been strapped together. And the third, a detonator.

After slipping the phone into his pocket, he inserted the business end of the detonator into the explosives, and put the whole thing back into the bag. As an afterthought, he reached into the bag, wedged Wicks's message between two of the bricks, and left the office again, headed for the center of the complex.

LAS CRUCES

MATT'S GROUP HAD not been at the school. Nor had they been at the business park a few miles west. Nor in the lot of the Big Kmart near the interstate.

Thinking it unlikely his friend would have wanted his group stationed to the north, closer to the Project Eden base, Ash had directed Sorrento to go south on a road that paralleled the I-25.

"Looks like a big shopping center coming up," Sorrento said.

It appeared to be an indoor mall, with a wide parking lot already blanketed with a thin layer of snow. The portion of the lot they could see was empty.

"Take us in and around," Ash said.

Sorrento drove their truck into the lot and headed to the south end. As they made the turn around the mall, they were lit up by four sets of headlights.

"Hold on!" Sorrento yelled as he slammed on the brakes.

"Get out of your vehicle right now!" someone yelled from beyond the lights.

Ash whipped his hand up to shield his eyes from the glare.

"Get out now!" the voice ordered.

"I think those are Humvees," Chloe said.

Ash squinted his eyes and could just make out the shapes of two of the vehicles. Chloe was right. He also spotted something else. Behind them and off to the side was the shadow of another vehicle. Not a Humvee. A cargo truck.

He reached for his door.

"What are you doing?" Chloe asked.

"It's them," he said.

"Are you sure?"

"Yes."

He pushed out the door and stood in the opening, still on the truck. "Matt? Matt, it's Ash!"

Hushed voices on the other side, then the lights cut out.

Ash squeezed his eyes shut, trying to readjust to the sudden darkness. When he opened them again, he could see someone stepping out from between the trucks.

"Captain Ash?"

Recognizing the voice, he said, "Hiller?"

"Yes, sir."

Hiller took a few more steps forward and Ash could make out his face.

"We thought you were going to Nevada, sir," Hiller said.

"Change of plans. " Ash hopped to the ground. "I need to see Matt."

"Um, Mr. Hamilton's not here."

"Please do not tell me he went to the base."

"He did."

"Alone?"

"I tried to get him to take one of us with him, but he wouldn't go for it."

Ash swore under his breath as he looked out into the storm.

"Where is he?" Chloe said, getting out of the truck.

"We're too late," Ash said. "He's gone."

"That son of a bitch. What does he think he's doing? How the hell is he going to handle this on his own?"

Ash looked back at Hiller. "Do you know what he had planned?"

"No, sir. He just told us to wait here, and if he didn't call in by nine p.m., we were to head for Nevada."

"Tell me he took a gun with him, at least," Chloe said.

"I don't know. The only thing he had was a duffel bag."

"What was inside?" Ash asked.

"No idea."

Ash rubbed a hand across his chin. With a frown he said, "As much as I wish we could go blazing in and pull him out of there, it's not an option. But sitting around here and waiting isn't, either." He looked at Chloe. "You and I are going to move in close. Hiller, I need two of your best men to come with us."

"That would be me and Lin," Hiller said.

It didn't surprise Ash that Hiller would want to come along. "Okay, the two of you pull together some weapons and whatever gear you think we might need. Chloe and I will appropriate one of those cars over there." He nodded toward the part of the lot where a handful of cars were scattered. Any of them would be stealthier than using one of the Humvees.

"What's the plan?" Chloe asked.

"We watch. If there's any way to tell if Matt's in trouble, we go in. Worse case, we'll be a hell of a lot closer if he does call for help."

NEAR FORT MEADE, MARYLAND
10:34 PM EST

"SO?" TAMARA ASKED.

"Another second. I've almost got it," Bobby told her.

"FYI, not the first time you've said that."

"If you'd stop talking to me, maybe I could...there! I think that's it." He pulled out from the rack where his head and arms had been buried. "Let's give it a try. Get in front of the camera."

The camera was aimed so that the rows of workstations would be seen in the background. It wasn't as dramatic a backdrop as the White House, but Tamara felt it would do.

She moved into position. "All set."

Bobby typed a few commands into the computer he'd been using, and Tamara's image filled the giant wall screen.

"Are we going out?" she said surprised. "Is this it?"

"Not yet," he said. "Only an internal test. But it means it works."

300

"So we *can* do it?"

"Yeah. Whenever you want."

"Now," she said. "Let's do it now."

Grinning, Bobby turned back to the computer. "I'll point at you when you're live, but give it a couple of seconds before you start. You know, for everyone to realize that jerk isn't on the air anymore."

He input the string of commands he'd worked out earlier. In theory, they would override the Project Eden signal and replace it with their broadcast, but since this was the first time he was trying them out, he couldn't help but feel he should be crossing his fingers. As he typed in the last few characters, he muttered, "Please work," and punched the ENTER key.

His gaze shifted to the four small monitors he'd hooked up on the neighboring desk. Each had a piece of white tape stuck in the bottom corner, with letters written on them—NA for the North American feed, SA for the South American, E for the European, and A for the Asian. Until that moment, all four monitors had been playing the message from the faux secretary general of the UN.

Now, one by one, Tamara's image began replacing Di Sarsina's. When she appeared in the last monitor—the one for North America—Bobby pointed at her.

She waited a few beats, and then began.

"My name is Tamara Costello. Some of you might remember me as a reporter at PCN. This is not a PCN broadcast. They do not exist anymore. None of the networks do. My purpose for speaking to you is to expose a lie you have all been told. Gustavo Di Sarsina is not the secretary general of the United Nations. I am not sure Gustavo Di Sarsina is even his real name. I do know that the United Nations no longer exists, and therefore it could have not initiated a worldwide effort to save those of us who are still alive." She paused. "The survival stations Mr. Di Sarsina talked about have nothing to do with survival. Mr. Di Sarsina and the people who are running these stations are the very same people who are responsible for releasing the Sage Flu on the world. The only purpose of these stations is to finish the job. To be clear, what I mean is that if you go to one of these 'survival stations,' you will die. Do not trust these people. Do not go anywhere near them. Do not let them know where you are. If you are someplace where English is not spoken but you understand what I'm saying, please, I beg you, translate my words so others will know, too. We need to stay alive. We need to survive." She paused again. "My name is Tamara Costello. You might remember me as a reporter at PCN. This isn't a…"

NB219
8:42 PM MST

"WE EXPECT THINGS will pick up in the next few days," the regional director for southern Asia said.

"You're lagging, and that's a problem," Perez said. "A few days is a few days too many. It should be happening—"

The door to his office opened and Claudia hurried in. "I'm sorry to interrupt, sir, but we need to end this call right now."

"What's going on?" Perez asked.

"You need to see this."

The center screen went momentarily blank before another image appeared, of a woman standing in some kind of control room.

"This just started broadcasting," Claudia said.

"What do you mean, broadcasting? Where?"

"North America for sure, haven't heard about anywhere else yet. It's knocked our message off the air."

He stared at her. "What? How is that possible?"

"We don't know, sir." Claudia looked at the screen. "You should listen."

She touched a key and the woman's voice boomed from the speakers.

"…is his real name or not. But what I do know is that the United Nations doesn't exist anymore, so there's no way it could undertake a worldwide mission to save everyone. The survival stations you've heard about? Those are being run by the same people who set off the outbreak in the first place…"

"How long has this been playing?" he asked.

"I don't know, but I can tell it's not a loop. She's saying some of the things I first heard, but not quite in the same way. I think it must be live."

"Has the cyber division been notified?"

"They're the ones who told me."

"And they can't take her down?" he asked in disbelief.

"They're trying, but they're not sure if they can."

"What about her location? Where is she broadcasting from?"

"Unknown at this point, but we're working on that, too."

"Is she also on radio?"

"Last check, no. Only TV."

Perez looked at the woman on the screen again, his eyes narrowing. How much damage could she actually do? Would anyone listen to her? Was anyone even watching television anymore?

"Find out how widespread this is," he ordered Claudia. "And the moment we figure out where this is coming from, get someone there to shut her down."

"Yes, sir," she said. "What should we tell everyone? If they haven't seen it already, they soon will."

Many of the monitors throughout the facility had been tuned to the Di Sarsina message, so they would now be displaying the woman's broadcast. Claudia was right. It would have to be addressed.

"Patch me into the general comm."

"HEY, CLIFF. LOOK at this," McCabe said to his colleague.

Cliff Eames swiveled his chair so he could look at the other security officer's screen. On it was a camera feed from level three, specifically the area in front of the main elevator doors. Both sets of doors were currently shut. The display on the digital panel next to McCabe's screen indicated both cars were up at the warehouse level, where McCabe and Eames were stationed. Standing to the left of the elevators, facing away from the screen, was a man in a gray security jumpsuit.

"Who is that?" McCabe asked.

Eames studied the man, but it was hard to tell much from the guy's back. "I'm not sure. Jones?"

"That's not Jones. Jones's thinner."

"What's he doing?"

Both men watched the screen. From the movements of the man's back and shoulders, and the occasional elbow sticking out to the side, they could tell he was busy at something.

"Got me," McCabe said.

Eames knew there was probably a mundane answer to his question, but it was a quiet night—it was *always* a quiet night—and they didn't have much else to do. "Back it up," he said. "Let's at least get a look at his face."

McCabe pulled his keyboard out from under the monitor, accessed the menu, and reversed the feed to where the man walked into the picture. He pressed PLAY.

"I don't know who the hell that is," McCabe said.

"Me, either."

Eames pointed at the screen. "Is he opening that?"

The man was carrying a duffel bag. As he reached the spot where they had originally seen him, he turned his back to the camera and began to unzip the bag, which was now blocked from view by the guy's body.

"Go live," Eames said.

McCabe switched back to a live shoot. "Dammit."

The man was gone.

McCabe quickly reversed the video until they saw him leave.

"His bag looks lighter, doesn't it?" McCabe said.

It did look lighter, but nothing obvious was left behind.

Eames rolled back to his own desk. "Find out where he went," he said. He adjusted the microphone connected to his computer, and tapped into the security radio system. "Aldridge, this is Eames in monitoring. Proceed to level three, main elevators. Make it quick."

THE BLACK PRIUS drove north out of Las Cruces with Ash in the front passenger seat, Hiller behind the wheel, and Chloe and Lin in the back.

Ash was holding the sat phone to his ear.

Two rings. "Can I help you?" a man said.

"This is Ash. Is Rachel there?"

"She's right here, Captain. Hold on."

A brief pause, then Rachel's voice. "Ash, what's going on? Have you found him?"

"He went to the base."

"God, no."

"We're heading in that direction right now, but we don't know exactly where it is."

The line remained quiet.

"Rachel?"

"I'm sorry, what?" she said, clearly dazed.

"Rachel, we *need* your help. Where precisely is NB219?"

"NB219, um, right. Let me check."

He could hear her asking someone for the base's location.

When she came back on, she said, "We have a set of GPS coordinates. I'm not sure if they're right, but they should be close. Is your GPS still working?"

"Last I checked," he said. "Text the coordinates to me right now."

MATT HURRIED DOWN the corridors, wanting to get back to the safety of the empty office as soon as possible. The placement of the plastic explosives had taken him longer than he'd wanted it to. One of the screws holding in place the plumbing-access panel near the elevators had proved stubborn and needed extra effort to remove. Once it was out of the way, though, stuffing the explosives into the available space had been easy.

He was two minutes from his hiding place when the speakers in the hallway emitted a reverberating *bong...bong...bong.*

After the last tone faded, a voice said, "Ladies and gentlemen, this is Principal Director Perez. I'm sure some of you have noticed that our televised message has been replaced."

Matt unconsciously slowed his pace. *Replaced?*

"For those who have not, the new message is an attempt to warn people from traveling to one of our survival stations."

It had to be Tamara and Bobby, Matt realized. They'd done it. They'd actually done it.

"This message is too little, too late, and, I'm confident, will prove to be ineffectual. We are, however, in the process of returning our own message to the air, and dealing with those who are trying to stop us. I ask that you continue with the excellent hard work you've all been doing. Soon we will be moving into our recovery phase and..."

Matt picked up his pace again.

To hell with the eleven p.m. meeting. This was his cue to act.

"EAMES, THIS IS Aldridge. I'm at the elevators. What is it I'm supposed to be doing here?"

Eames could see the man on his screen. He keyed his mic. "To the left of car one as you face the doors, see if there's something on the ground or the wall there."

"Uh, say again?"

"On the left. You're looking for anything that looks unusual."

"Unusual like what?"

"I'm not sure. That's why I need you to look."

Aldridge walked over to area where the man with the duffel bag had been standing. After a few seconds, he said, "Nothing on the ground, and the wall looks...wait a minute." He paused and leaned closer. "I don't know if this is what you mean, but there's a scratch on the surface right next to one of the screws. Looks turned recently."

That had to be it, Eames thought.

"You have something you can open the panel with?" he asked.

"Yeah, I got something."

Aldridge pulled a Leatherman multi-tool out of his back pocket and set to work. As with when the other man had been there, Eames's view was blocked.

Less than thirty seconds later, Aldridge said, "Holy shit," and moved quickly back from the wall.

Eames could see the panel was off, exposing an area with pipes running through. There was also something oddly shaped stuffed on the side.

"What did you see?" he asked.

"Somebody put explosives in there," Aldridge said. "There's a detonator sticking out of it."

"You're sure?"

"I'm no bomb expert, but that's what it looks like to me."

"Close down that area! Don't let anyone without authorization anywhere near there. I'm sending someone to take a look at it!"

"Okay," Aldridge said, sounding like he'd very much like to get the hell out of there himself.

Eames looked over at McCabe. "Did you find him?"

"One second." McCabe stared at his screen, and smiled. "Got him. He's in an office. Section 23. Room, um, 3C. I'll send someone in."

"No," Eames said. Who knew what this guy might have with him in there? There were people at the base better equipped than the security staff to handle this kind of situation. Eames put a call through to the barracks.

"SIR, WE HAVE a situation."

Sims was standing in the common room, at the back of the small crowd that had been watching the broadcast the principal director had just told them about. Sims looked back to find Neal Duncan, one of his men, standing behind him. "What kind of situation?"

"Security's on the line," Duncan said. In his hand was

the wireless phone servicing the room. "They're reporting an intruder who has possibly placed some explosives near the main elevators."

Sims whipped around. "Give me that."

Duncan handed him the phone.

"Who is this?" Sims asked.

"Eames in security, sir."

"What's this about explosives?"

Eames gave him a quick rundown, ending with a request for assistance.

"Keep your people away from there," Sims said. "We'll take care of it." He hung up and looked at Duncan. "Get the men, now!"

PRINCIPAL DIRECTOR PEREZ looked up from his desk as the door opened, and was surprised to see Claudia returning so soon after having left.

"Have they found her?" he asked.

"Uh, no, sir," she said, her face gravely serious. "There's something else."

"What?"

MATT REMOVED THE final item from the duffel bag, pulled on the straps, but left the apparatus sitting on top of his head.

He removed the remote control and unlocked the screen.

WICKS HAD DISTRIBUTED nearly half the devices by the time the principal director made his announcement over the intercom. After Perez finished, Wicks—like Matt—knew everything had changed. All he wanted to do at that point was get rid of the remaining devices and get out of there, so he was considerably less cautious in his placements. As soon as the last one was gone from his briefcase, he headed for the elevator, but was stopped before he could get there by security.

"Sorry, this area's off limits at the moment," the guard said.

"What's going on?" Wicks asked.

"Security matter, sir."

Wicks knew it had something to do with Matt, but what? Had they caught him? If so, even more reason for Wicks to get out of there right away.

The only available exit now, though, was the emergency stairwell. He took a second to remember where the entrance was and then headed off, hoping he wasn't already too late.

SIMS SPLIT HIS team into two groups. The first went to determine the nature of the explosive and whether it could be easily defused. The second—the group he took personal charge of—headed to section 23 to apprehend the intruder.

When they reached the correct hallway, they proceeded until they were four doors down from Room 3C.

Sims signaled one of his men to approach the door of 3C to determine if the intruder was still inside. The man moved down the corridor in a crouch and knelt by the door. After a moment, he held up his thumb and nodded.

MATT HEARD A noise just outside the office. It was faint, nothing more than a brush of cloth, but he knew what it meant.

It was okay. He was ready.

SIMS AND THE third man with him joined the scout at the door. Sims motioned for the others to get ready, then he grabbed the knob and threw the door open.

"Down on the floor! Down on the floor!" he yelled as he and his men rushed in.

The intruder was there, but not on the floor. He was sitting on the desk, a gas mask covering his face.

In a distorted voice, he said, "Sorry to disappoint, but you're a little late."

Sims took another step forward. "On the fl—"

"SORRY TO DISAPPOINT," Matt said, "but you're a little late."

The one in charge took an angry step toward the desk. "On the fl—"

Matt pushed remote button number one.

The floor rocked as the explosives ripped apart the elevator shaft. The armed men staggered and looked back at the doorway as if they could see what had happened.

As they were turning back, Matt tossed the final plastic device on the floor at their feet, and pushed remote button number two.

There was no blast this time, no rocking floor, only the hiss of sarin gas releasing from the device. Throughout the facility, the other plastic boxes would be doing the same thing.

"On the floor, now!" the leader commanded.

Matt didn't move.

"I said...on...the floor."

All three men began to blink as the odorless gas reached them. One started coughing, and then another, and then the last. Guns were quickly forgotten as the men dropped to their knees.

Matt rose and stepped over to the leader.

"How does it feel? Dying?"

"Go to..." The man coughed. "Hell."

"Maybe. You never know. You all, on the other hand, I think your tickets are punched."

He waited until the leader fell all the way to the floor before searching the guy's pockets and finding his ID badge.

"Let's see, Mr...." He looked at the badge. "Sims, Special Operations. Very nice. I'll bet that gives you all kinds of interesting clearance."

Matt picked up the man's rifle and rose to his feet.

"Thank you, Mr. Sims. You've been a big help."

He headed for the door.

ASH TILTED THE sat phone so he could look at the displayed map without snow falling on the screen.

"Should be right in front of us about a quarter mile," he said.

If Project Eden's base was anything like the one he and Chloe had broken into in Oregon, there would be a large, warehouse-type building at ground level. But the only thing in front of them at the moment was flat farmland covered in a light layer of snow.

"She didn't guarantee it was accurate," Chloe reminded him.

He huffed out a cloud of vapor and frowned. "We'll drive on another mile or two. Maybe we can spot it."

As he turned toward the car, Chloe said, "Uh, Ash. You think that might be it?"

He looked back around. About a quarter mile past the coordinates' location, the red glow of flames illuminated the clouds.

"That wasn't there a moment ago," he said.

"It just shot up," she said.

"Matt."

"That's what I was thinking."

"Let's go," Ash said, already heading toward the car.

WICKS HAD JUST passed level two when the metal staircase began to shake so violently, he had to hang on with both arms to keep from falling off.

His friend had apparently decided there was no longer any time to wait.

As soon as the shaking decreased to a gentle tremor, Wicks started up again, worried that if there were a second blast, the stairs wouldn't hold. When he opened the door on the warehouse level, he was greeted by a wall of hot air radiating from a growing fire toward the center.

Toward the elevators.

Thank God he hadn't been able to take them. He likely would have been dead by now.

The warehouse supplies were feeding the blaze, creating a fire too big for the overhead sprinklers to tame.

The main exit was on the other side of the flames, so his only choice was to use the auxiliary exit again. He'd have to use his own card to open it this time, which meant that if the computer databases survived, there would be a record of him leaving the building long before anyone else had a chance to escape. His only alternative would be to stay. Not an attractive option.

He swiped his card in front of the reader and rushed into the tunnel.

31

THE EXPLOSION KNOCKED Principal Director Perez to the floor. Claudia was only able to maintain her feet because she fell into his desk and held on tight.

As soon as he could, Perez shoved himself up.

"Are you okay?" Claudia asked.

"I'm fine," he growled.

"Your head," she said, touching a spot on her own forehead. "It's bleeding."

He touched his head and felt the cut that was spilling out blood. "It's nothing. Get security. I want to know how the hell that happened! I thought someone was taking care of it."

Claudia picked up the phone, but instead of punching in a number, she looked at Perez. "It's dead."

"Dammit. Can we get them on video?"

"Let me try." She circled the desk to his computer. It still seemed to be working, but after several seconds, she shook her head. "They're not answering."

"Can we at least find out if there are any cameras out there still working so we can see how extensive the damage is?"

"Should be able to."

It took nearly a minute before the center screen came on. The feed was from a camera in one of the hallways. No obvious damage, but several people were lying on the ground.

"Is this close to the explosion?" Perez asked.

"I don't know. The system's only giving me camera numbers, not locations."

"Are there any others?"

"Hold on."

The next feed came up thirty seconds later, an empty conference room.

"That doesn't tell us anything."

"I'm sorry. I told you all the labels are missing. I think the blast did something to the system."

"Keep going."

A new camera showed a wider hallway, lit only by two emergency lights spread far apart. More bodies on the ground.

"I recognize this," Claudia said. "It's one of the hallways leading to the elevator."

The blast concussion must have been intense enough to knock everyone out.

"Is that someone?" he asked. Something was moving in the shadows at the far end.

"I can't tell. Could be a camera glitch."

She switched to the next feed.

"Oh, my God," she said.

The image was of a common area. Like the corridor they'd seen first, there was no damage but there were bodies. Lots of bodies.

"This is near the barracks," he said.

That was nowhere near the elevators, and he was sure the blast could not have done that to everyone. Were they being attacked by a whole squad?

"Is there an escape exit in here?" he asked.

While most of the Project Eden bases were the same, a few details changed from location to location—an escape exit in the director's suite being one of them. Perez had been so busy since he'd taken over as principal director, he hadn't had time to worry about such things.

"I don't know," she said. "The previous director didn't share that information with me."

Dammit.

"All right, you and I need to look for it. There's got to be one here."

She glanced at the monitor. "If we go out there, that'll happen to us, too, won't it?"

"Claudia! Help me find the exit!"

NOT EVERYONE MATT passed in the hallways was dead, but there was no question they soon would be. He felt no compassion for any of them, no guilt for what he'd done. Every last one of them had taken an active role in the deaths of billions. They deserved their fate. Just like he would eventually deserve his.

A fire was raging at the epicenter of the explosion, its heat prickling his skin. He idly wondered if the flames would consume all the air down here. If so, those who had survived his gas attack would live only to suffocate a few hours later. Again, the thought did not trouble him.

Not surprisingly, the door to the principal director's suite was closed. Matt waved in front of the reader the ID card he'd taken from Sims, but nothing happened, not even a beep denying him access. He pulled out the card Wicks had given him, and encountered the same result.

That was all right. He had a solution.

Switching the rifle to semiautomatic, he aimed at the area around the lock and shot an arc through the door.

THE GUNFIRE DIDN'T frighten Perez. It merely focused his anger.

Claudia, on the other hand, screamed.

"Keep looking," he ordered.

He ran his fingers under the countertop behind his desk. Three inches from the end farthest from the door, he found a switch. He pushed it, but nothing happened.

What the hell?

Out in the antechamber, the gunfire ceased.

He pushed it again, and this time heard a click under the cover. He dropped to his knees, sure he'd discovered the way out, but what he found instead was only the latch for the exit door. The escape exit itself had never been built.

He dove toward his desk, pulled open the bottom drawer,

and fished around for the Smith & Wesson 9mm pistol he kept there. As he freed the gun, the door to his office flew open. He aimed across the room, but no one was there.

"Principal Director Perez," a strange-sounding voice said from the other room. "It's good to meet you."

Perez aimed at the wall he thought the man was hiding behind, and pulled the trigger.

"Good thinking," the intruder said. "And not bad on the aim, either. But these bases were built to last. No flimsy walls around here. Trust me, I knew the guy in charge of putting them in."

Who the hell was this guy?

"What do you want?" Perez said.

"Already have what I want, thanks. You just aren't aware of it yet."

Perez moved to the other corner of his desk so that he'd have a more acute angle on the doorway He couldn't see anything yet, so, with gun held out in front, he carefully stepped out from cover.

Across the room, Claudia coughed.

"Ah, that got back there quicker than I expected," the voice said.

As Perez narrowed his eyes, unsure what the man meant, he had the sudden need to blink.

Another cough, but this one was his.

"Downward spiral from here, I'm afraid," the voice said.

Perez staggered back to his desk, his chest heaving. Between blinks, he saw something move into the doorway. He lifted his hand, raising the gun, only he wasn't holding it anymore. He looked around. It was on the ground where he'd started blinking. He took a step toward it but began coughing again.

"You won't need that anymore," the voice said, closer now.

The voice belonged to a man, that much Perez could tell, but what the guy looked like was hidden behind a full-face gas mask.

"How you feeling? Pretty crappy, huh?" The man looked

past Perez. "I think your friend over there's done for. Sorry about that." He turned back to Perez. "You know what? That's a lie. I'm not sorry."

Perez could feel his strength draining away, but he wasn't ready to collapse yet. "Who...are you?" he said.

"Me? I was a member of Project Eden, way before your time." The man looked around. "I helped build this place. Yeah, but then I realized what was really going on. Been trying to stop you guys ever since. The destruction of Bluebird? That was my people. The message you were telling everyone about tonight? Mine, too."

The gnat, Perez realized. This man was the gnat who had been bugging the Project for years.

"You aren't...going to stop...anything," Perez said, forcing each word out. "The Project's too big."

"I guess that's a wait-and-see thing, isn't it? Only you won't be around to see it. But trust me, it's going to happen."

Perez doubled over in a coughing fit.

"Bet that hurts," the man said. "You know, it's amazing what you can find when you hunt around a deserted military base. I guess I could have taken a nuke, but that would have been too heavy to carry in here. The gas is a nice touch, though, don't you think? From the poetic point of view, it would have been better if it was some kind of deadly disease you all weren't vaccinated against, but this will work faster."

Perez wasn't about to give the man the satisfaction of his death. With his last ounce of will, he pushed himself up, and said as forcibly as he could, "This isn't going to kill me."

"Perhaps not," the man told him. "Could be not enough of the gas got back here to kill both of you. That's a shame."

He raised his rifle and shot Perez in the thigh.

Screaming, Perez fell to the ground.

"Caught the artery on the first shot. Not bad," the man said. "Now you *are* going to die. You're going to bleed out right there on that nice carpet, in this nice office." The man plopped down on the desk. "And I'm sitting right here until you do."

Perez rolled onto his back, knowing the man was right.

I was so close. A few more weeks, maybe a month, and I would have truly ruled the world.

Through half-closed eyes, he looked at the man and whispered, "Fucking gnat."

MATT WAITED UNTIL he was sure Perez was dead before leaving the office.

The former principal director had said his death would not stop the Project, and that was true, but it was a big step in that direction.

He wondered if Wicks had been able to get out. He hoped so. His old friend had done a lot for the Resistance from the inside, and didn't deserve the death the others here had received.

Matt, on the other hand, wasn't so sure about himself. There was a part of him that wanted to pull off his gas mask, and face the punishment he felt he deserved. Maybe if Wicks hadn't come through with the information he'd passed along, Matt could have gone through with it, but now it wasn't an option.

There was a thud somewhere in the hall behind him. Thinking it was probably the echo of something collapsing closer to the explosion, he kept walking.

Someone yelled behind him, the voice so strained and raw he couldn't make out any words.

When he turned, he saw he was no longer the only one still breathing in the hallway. Down by the last corridor intersection, a woman was leaning against the wall. She was staring at him, her chest heaving. It wouldn't be long, he knew, before she joined her dead colleagues.

As she pushed from the wall and took a few staggering steps toward him, he realized he'd seen her before. She was the woman who had been in the office with Perez. Matt had seen her crumble to the floor and assumed she'd died.

Yelling again, she raised her hand as if to point at him, only it wasn't her finger she was aiming in his direction.

32

BELINDA RAMSEY'S SNOWMOBILE ride south has taken her just over the Illinois border when the motor begins to smoke. Another two miles on, the machine dies. With no other options, Belinda starts hiking toward the town of South Beloit, hoping she can find someplace warm to sleep. She tells herself she will look for a new snowmobile, but in the morning. She's too tired to do that now.

As she nears a neighborhood on the edge of town, she hears something in the distance. At first she thinks someone has left a music player on somewhere, perhaps looping through a playlist that will go on and on until the power finally goes out.

But it's not music, she soon realizes. It's words being spoken.

She skips the neighborhood and continues toward town, toward the sound, and it's not long before she can start making out what's being said.

"...help you. We will be in the parking lot of the high school on Prairie Hill Road in ten minutes. We will stay there for an additional thirty. This is the Untied Nations. We are here to help you. We will be in the parking lot of..."

Belinda starts to laugh in happiness. She's not going to need a snowmobile tomorrow. She's not going to ever need a snowmobile again. The UN is here. Her nightmare is over.

She searches for a road sign and finds she is actually *on* Prairie Hill Road. But she hasn't seen a high school yet, and has no idea how far away it is.

Though the snow is not as deep here as it was in

Madison, it's still too deep for her to run through, so she has to settle for walking fast. Even then, it's over twenty minutes before the high school comes into sight. She is both relieved that she doesn't have far to go, and scared to death that the UN will already be gone.

But a blue tourist bus with UN painted in white on the side is idling in the parking lot.

She weeps as a soldier meets her at the lot's entrance. She thanks him over and over as he gives her some food and guides her onto the bus.

Three of the seats are already taken. Their occupants, wrapped in blankets, stare at her. She smiles hesitantly, then notices not one of them is sitting near another.

Hiking her scarf over her face, she takes her own isolated spot.

As the bus begins to roll, she leans back and relaxes. Before sleep can take her, though, she remembers her journal and her promise to record her journey. She opens it, enters the time and date, and then writes a single word:

SAVED!

BEN BOWERMAN STANDS in the modest living room of the Cape Cod house in Santa Cruz where he found Iris the previous day. He has returned because it's the only place he knows that she might come back to. But she is not there.

He's now sure he will never see the picture his mother loved so much again, or retrieve the earrings he'd picked out for Martina. Tomorrow he will head south once more, this time in the car he found in Salinas. Tonight, he will find a hotel and sleep.

But he finds he can't leave the house just yet. He wants to know what happened here, what he got tangled up in. If there are answers in the house, he figures he will find them in the dead man's room.

Seeing Mr. Carlson on the bed for a third time is not nearly so disturbing as it was before. Ben can see now there's something under the man's hand, partly hidden by the covers. A piece of paper. Ben teases it free without having to touch body or blanket. There are words scribbled on it, but the writer's hand was so shaky Ben can only make out "Iris" and "door."

He searches the dresser but the closet is where he finds his answer. Tucked against one end is a filing cabinet, and every item inside pertains either directly or indirectly to Iris, Mr. Carlson's daughter.

The words on the documents say many things, but all paint the same picture. The girl does not see the world the same way others do, and never has. Drugs have been tried, hospital stays, intensive therapy. Some appear to have worked better than others, but none truly well.

Ben wants to still feel angry at Iris, but he doesn't.

What he feels instead is tired.

AT SOME POINT, Martina gives up looking for the girl and just drives. She goes into the hills above Ventura, back to the coast, and finally down Highway 1 through Oxnard toward Malibu.

She runs out of gas not long before the sun goes down, so she leaves the bike at the side of the road, wanders aimlessly onto the beach, and sits on the berm crest, facing the water.

If she's paying attention, she will see a beautiful sunset, but she's not. Her mind is both idle and racing.

She doesn't mean to, but she will sleep here tonight. And when she wakes in the morning, though she won't voice it, she will feel for the first time that she is completely alone.

THE ONE THING Sanjay did not take from the Pishon Chem compound was a box of syringes. While the others are resting as they wait for the sun to set, he and Kusum search local medical facilities until they collect enough syringes to give shots to everyone they have rescued.

Once darkness finally falls, Sanjay, Kusum, Jabala, and Prabal say good-bye to Arjun and Darshana, who will be staying in the city to try to stop others from going to the survival station. They then head out of Mumbai with the newly inoculated escapees, in a bus they find on a nearby street.

When they arrive at the boarding school, those they have rescued are given food and shown to empty dorms, while the boxes of vaccine are stored away.

"Why are you not sleeping?" Kusum asks Sanjay later as they lie in bed.

"Why are you not?" he counters.

"I am thinking about the vaccine."

It's what he's thinking about, too. "We cannot wait for people to come to us," he says. "We need to somehow let them know we can help them."

"I know," she says. "But how exactly are we supposed to do that without the people from Pishon Chem finding us?"

"I have no idea," he said. "*That* is why I cannot sleep."

THE RESTAURANT DINING room of the Isabella Island Resort seems a lot smaller after so many hours with everyone jammed into it. Or maybe it's knowing what they're hiding from that's making it feel like the walls are pushing in, Robert thinks.

The liquid that coated the windows after the plane flew over is now dry, but no one is foolish enough to think the danger has passed.

As the evening grows late, the satellite phone Pax has brought with him rings. When he finishes talking, he waves Robert over and says, "You're going to want to turn on the TV."

Robert does, and is surprised to find that Gustavo Di Sarsina has been replaced by a familiar face—Tamara Costello, a reporter he has seen on TV in the past.

No one sleeps for hours, as they all watch Tamara deliver her message over and over, never quite the same way twice.

When the TV is finally turned off, even Pax's most ardent critics are starting to believe he's been telling the truth.

Robert's eyelids grow heavy as he lies next to Estella later.

"Do you think they might come back?" she asks.

"Who?"

"These people. Project Eden. Do you think they will come back to make sure we are dead?"

Robert puts his arms around her and pulls her to him. After a moment, he whispers the only answer he can come up with. "I don't know."

BRANDON MAKES A deal with Davis. He points out there is no way Davis can stay awake twenty-four hours a day, so Brandon lobbies to help with night watch and takes the first shift, from eight p.m. to one in the morning.

He likes the feeling of responsibility it gives him, but it's still a poor substitute for going south with his father. He should have been on that trip instead of that idiot Rick. He understands why his father left him behind, but that doesn't mean he likes it.

He is stewing over this when Ginny walks into the living room of the house where they're staying.

"Sorry," she says. "I couldn't sleep."

"It's okay," he tells her.

She walks over and joins him on the couch that has been turned toward the window.

"I'm sure they'll be back soon," she says.

"Uh-huh." He doesn't want to talk about it.

"I wish your dad hadn't taken Rick."

"Uh-huh." He *really* doesn't want to talk about that.

She must sense his reluctance, because she says nothing for several minutes. When she finally talks again, she says, "It's never going to be the same again, is it?"

She could mean a million different things, and probably does. "No. Not like it used to be."

"So what *is* it going to be like?"

He shrugs. How the heck is he supposed to know that? But he realizes that's not what she needs to hear. "It'll be different, I guess. But someday it's going to be good. You'll be happy."

"I'm not sure I can ever be happy again."

He wants to promise she will be, but knows she will see right through him. So he focuses on the street, and says nothing.

When Ginny falls asleep fifteen minutes later, she slumps to the side, her head falling against Brandon's shoulder. He thinks maybe he should move it, but it feels good there, makes him feel like he's not the only person in the world.

Makes him feel like he's doing good.

ASH INSTRUCTS HILLER to drive the car to within a couple hundred yards of the warehouse. Though much of the structure is in flames, he can see the similarities between this building and the one in Oregon, and knows without question it belongs to Project Eden.

They grab their gear out of the back—weapons, rope, crowbars, wire cutters, and the like. Hiller pulls out a bag of gas masks and gives one to each of them.

"It could get smoky. These aren't perfect, but they're all we've got."

Ash dons the mask, and throws a coil of rope over his shoulder before heading as quickly as he can toward the building.

He is still a good distance away when a man, also wearing a gas mask, appears on the bank of an arroyo that runs near the building. Ash raises his gun, but then notices the limp and lowers his weapon.

"Matt?" he yells.

The man does not seem to hear him, so Ash pulls the mask off his face.

"Matt!"

The limping man stops, looks in Ash's direction, and

324

falls to his knees.

As Ash rushes over, Matt rolls onto his hip and lies back in the snow.

"Hey," Ash says. "You okay?"

He drops down next to Matt and pulls off his friend's mask. There is pain in the man's face, and his eyes are closed.

"Matt, can you hear me?"

The only reaction is a wince.

"Matt!"

It takes but a second for Ash to discover that Matt's shirt is soaked with blood. He rips it open, and in the flickering light of the fire sees a bullet hole in his friend's abdomen. He feels around the back, finds a hole where the bullet exited that's three times as large as the entry point.

Applying pressure to the wounds, he looks around until he spots Chloe. "Over here! Over here!" Once he's sure she's seen him, he focuses on Matt again. "You're going to be fine. Hang in there."

Matt's eyes flutter. "You..." he says.

"Quiet. Save your strength."

"No, you..."

Ash hears the sound of running feet approaching from behind him.

"What is it?" Chloe shouts. "Is that...Matt?"

"Get the first-aid kit!" he tells her. "And have Hiller or Lin call the others in. We need the doctor and Lily here now!"

Chloe runs back toward the car.

"Ash," Matt whispers.

"Don't try to talk."

Matt's eyelids part a fraction of an inch. "Augustine...green..sky." Each word hitches a ride on a different breath.

"What?"

"You...need to...know..."

"Augustine green sky?"

"Dream," Matt corrects him. "Dream sky."

"Augustine dream sky." As Ash says this, he sees some of the stress in Matt's face melt away.

"Yes," Matt whispers, his eyes closing again.

"What's it mean?"

Matt whispers again, but his voice is now too low to hear no matter how close Ash moves in.

"Don't worry about it," Ash says. "Don't worry about anything. It's going to be fine."

But he knows it's not going to be fine, and before Chloe can return with the first-aid kit, he watches helplessly as the man who founded the Resistance takes his last breath.

The Project Eden saga returns in 2014, with

Volume Six

DREAM SKY

Made in United States
North Haven, CT
21 December 2024